Breaking Wild

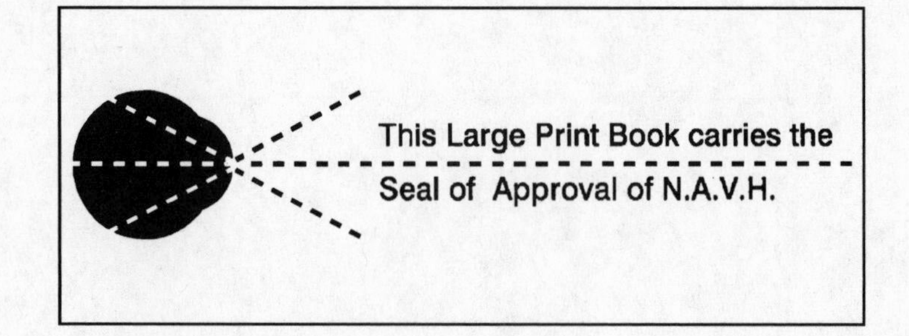
This Large Print Book carries the
Seal of Approval of N.A.V.H.

BREAKING WILD

DIANE LES BECQUETS

THORNDIKE PRESS
A part of Gale, Cengage Learning

Farmington Hills, Mich • San Francisco • New York • Waterville, Maine
Meriden, Conn • Mason, Ohio • Chicago

Thorndike Press, a part of Gale, Cengage Learning.

Thorndike Press® Large Print Basic.
The text of this Large Print edition is unabridged.
Other aspects of the book may vary from the original edition.
Set in 16 pt. Plantin.

LIBRARY OF CONGRESS CATALOGING-IN-PUBLICATION DATA

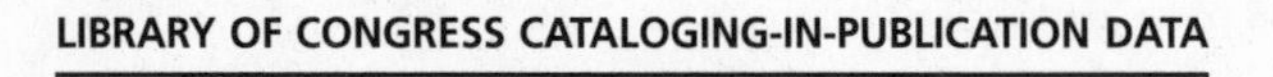

Names: Les Becquets, Diane, author.
Title: Breaking wild / by Diane Les Becquets.
Description: Large print edition. | Waterville, Maine : Thorndike Press, 2016. | © 2016 | Series: Thorndike Press large print basic
Identifiers: LCCN 2016006339 | ISBN 9781410490186 (hardcover) | ISBN 1410490181 (hardcover)
Subjects: LCSH: Missing persons—Fiction. | Wilderness areas—Fiction. | Large type books. | GSAFD: Suspense fiction.
Classification: LCC PS3612.E74 B74 2016b | DDC 813/.6—dc23
LC record available at http://lccn.loc.gov/2016006339

Published in 2016 by arrangement with The Berkley Publishing Group, an imprint of Penguin Publishing Group, a division of Penguin Random House LLC

Printed in the United States of America
1 2 3 4 5 6 7 20 19 18 17 16

For the town of Meeker, Colorado,
and
In memory of my big little sister,
Carol Houck Smith

ACKNOWLEDGMENTS

There are people who are kind and good and smart and loyal. And there are gifts we cannot name, the kind that take root and change who we become. The community and the land of northwestern Colorado where I lived for almost fourteen years will always be a deep reservoir within me from which I draw. And so it is to the people of that community that this book is dedicated and whom I wish to acknowledge with all the gratitude in the world.

This book is also dedicated in memory of Carol Houck Smith, mentor and publishing legend, a mighty force whose spirit clung to the land and open skies and the people of the West, and who worked with me on the earliest ideas and drafts of this novel. You are loved and you are missed.

I wish to thank the following people and institutions for their kindness and support:

Michelle Brower, agent extraordinaire,

who inspired and edited and saw the things I could not see. Sometimes a writer stops writing. When I met Michelle, I started writing again. You were the magic.

Kendra Harpster, my dream editor, always positive, always enthusiastic. You made this whole process effortless. A strong woman and such an astute editor. Some things are just meant to be.

To Leslie Gelbman, publisher of Berkley, and to her amazing team. I give thanks for you all every day.

My deep gratitude to those who assisted me with the research: Judy Eskelson, Susan Berthelson, Mike Washburn, Mike Joos, Dudley Gardner, Dale Atkins, Dee Lehman, Shannon Young, Ashton Robinson, Kris Hjelle, Nikki Stout, Mike Selle, Don Wade, Martin Lammers, Marvin Hansen, and Brad Merrill. And to Glade Hadden, the greatest archaeologist of man and story that I know. As both author and novel evolved, you've been a constant.

To Jim and Sue, for their friendship and lodging during my research trips.

To Deb and Bob, for offering me their hunting camp off the grid, where without electricity, plumbing, cell service, and Internet, I was able to stay until I finished the manuscript.

To all those who provided feedback, support, and editorial assistance: Bob Begiebing, Rick Carey, Dolly Viscardi, Alison Taylor-Brown, Nate Boesch, Julia Rohm-Ensing, Jordan Mazzola, Robin Barletta, Annie Hwang, Ann Hood, Suzanne Strempek-Shea, Clint McCown, Michael White, and Jack Scovil. I wouldn't be where I am today with anything less.

To the woman who provided everything and more and read countless drafts, my mom, Sandra Kyne.

To my colleagues at Southern New Hampshire University, my friends and students in the MFA program, and my dean, Karen Erickson.

I am also grateful for the support SNHU has provided me through summer grants, a sabbatical, and professional development.

For my late husband, Shaun Hathaway, lost and then found, you were my giant.

For all of my friends, and all of my family, especially my three sons, Nate, Seth (Joseph), and Jake, and for my best friend, partner, and husband, Gregg Mazzola.

We can never break free from the dark and degrading past. Let us see life again, nevertheless, in the words of Isaac Babel as a meadow over which women and horses wander.

— Maxine Kumin, "Women and Horses"

Bear

Amy Raye

It was snowing already, in early November, after days of hot, clear fall weather. The flakes landed on her tent like slow rain. She lay still, aware of every small, square inch around her, and in that stillness imagined changing her mind, sleeping almost warm for a few more hours, and after daybreak and coffee, packing up with the others and driving home.

Earlier that night, Kenny had asked her, "Do you still love him?" They'd been sitting by the fire. Aaron had already turned in.

She felt sorrow pass over her face when Kenny asked her this, and she knew Kenny had felt it, too, because he reached over to her chair, laid his hand on top of hers like something protective. He then moved his chair closer, lifted his arm, wrapped it around her shoulder, pulled her against him. It was an uncomfortable position, but she did not tell him that. He took his other arm, encircled her with it. He kissed the top of her head, pressed his face into her hair.

"You smell good," he said.

"I smell like elk piss and smoke," she said.

"No, I smell you."

"What do I smell like?"

"Like something tangy and salty and sweet, like something I've never smelled before."

And then her breathing and his became lost in the sound of the fire and the weight of moisture accumulating in the air. As brief as a moment, she felt a deep sense of the place, folding the days back to summer and wild rose columbine and life as pure as a mountain stream over a rocky bed.

"I'm going out in the morning," Amy Raye said. "I wasn't going to say anything. Yesterday I found a tree stand up on the mesa. It's a good spot. There's fresh sign."

"Do you want me to go with you? I want to go with you."

"No."

"You shouldn't go alone."

"Kenny." She said his name like she used to say that of her dog back home when Saddle was about to do something wrong. And then, "Don't tell Aaron," she said.

There were three of them — Kenny and

Aaron and Amy Raye. Kenny and Aaron hunted with rifles. Aaron had filled his tag on the first day, taking down a four-point bull elk they'd come upon at a watering hole. Kenny had filled his tag for a cow elk the next, from a small herd grazing in a meadow, making a clean shot at about two hundred yards. They'd quartered the carcasses and hung the quarters from a two-by-four that they'd nailed between two trees alongside the camp. But Amy Raye didn't hunt with a rifle. She hunted with a compound bow, which meant getting within twenty to thirty yards of an elk. Harvesting an elk with a bow during rifle season was legal but hardly heard of. Amy Raye knew if she was to have any chance, she'd have to head out by herself and find where the elk had scattered. Just the day before she'd broken off on her own, had hiked miles into the area, where she'd discovered excellent sign — elk urine, rubbings in the nearby trees, trails that crisscrossed, and fresh tracks. And in the grasses nearby she'd glassed smooth indentions of elk bedding. She'd come upon a tree stand tucked about fifteen feet high in a pinyon, with tree steps still in place. Hunters were supposed to remove their stands at the end of a season. The screw-in tree steps looked like they had been set for a while, a residue of dust and rain deposits coating the brown-tempered steel. Amy Raye had navigated a trail for herself away from the stand, and set several reflector tags on trees on her way out.

That evening before dinner, before she and Kenny had sat by the fire and Aaron had turned in, she'd walked through the woods to a shallow stream, barely three feet wide and six inches deep. She'd removed her clothes and squatted, her buttocks resting against her ankles, the water so cold it was painful. She'd rushed through the ritual, running a nylon brush over her skin. But she hadn't washed her hair. And now, lying in her tent, she wished she had, hoping her scent wouldn't keep the elk away.

She turned on her flashlight and reached for her phone to check the time. Three thirty. There was a text from her husband. Hey, are you having a good night? I'm getting stuff done. It's good. Miss you like skin. She wrote back, I am blessed to have you, but I am seriously going to try harder.

Still bundled in her sleeping bag, she shed her long underwear, then crawled out of the bag and unzipped the opening flap of the tent, the air not more than twenty degrees, she was sure. Snow was now falling in sporadic flakes, melting almost as soon as it hit the ground. Next to her tent was a plastic container where she'd packed a set of clothes for each day, each item having been washed clean of grocery store detergents and perfumes and her own perspiration. Moving quietly so as not to wake Kenny or Aaron, she pulled on a fresh layer of thermals, wool socks, camouflage pants, a camouflage fleece jacket, her green hiking boots, and her brown fleece hat. She switched out her flashlight for her headlamp, which she secured over her hat. Carrying a roll of toilet paper, she walked toward the woods behind the tent.

Less than five feet from the back wall of the tent was a divot in the ground carved out by the fresh claw marks of a bear, a mother, most likely, digging for bugs for her young. Amy Raye calculated the distance again. Less than two of her own strides. Tired, cold, and fully aware of just how close the bear had been to her while she'd slept, something like déjà vu grazed her heart, as if she had already stood here a half-dozen times, and if she had, some other living being had stood here within breathing room of her a half-dozen times, too.

Aaron's tent was across from hers, about fifty feet. If she stood still, she could hear his snores muffled beneath the covers. Kenny's tent was farther away, south of the fire pit and cookstove.

She walked about thirty yards north of the camp to Aaron's truck, lowered the tailgate for a table, and made coffee, every move calculated so that she wouldn't wake the others, so that they wouldn't insist on going with her. Aaron, whose breath smelled of cigarette smoke, and whose body labored when he walked, especially when climbing uphill. Or Kenny, sweet Kenny, who reminded her of a quarter horse stallion in the middle of summer, of Tennessee and hollers and hay trucks and alfalfa, and all those places she missed too often but knew she would never go back to.

The snow had stopped falling, but its moisture still coated the air. She drank a large cup of coffee, then poured another, more for the warmth than the caffeine. Silence hovered over her like a tarpaulin. The wilderness wasn't asleep. She knew it had awoken with her first stirring, was waiting for her next move, watching her. Its stillness was a sure sign. Sitting on the tailgate, her legs folded underneath her, she eased herself into the silence, becoming the same wilderness. The caffeine began to take effect and burned in her stomach with the anticipation she thrived from.

Amy Raye had hunted since she was a girl, going out with her grandfather. She didn't hunt elk then, nor did she hunt with a bow. Bow hunting came later. She hunted whitetail deer with a .243 Winchester rifle, and later a .280 Remington. While other girls turned sweet sixteen, she learned how to field-dress a deer.

Amy Raye's husband, Farrell, didn't hunt. He'd never even held a gun. It was after he and Amy Raye had met that she'd switched to bow hunting. Farrell didn't want guns in the house, especially with his daughter, Julia, who was four years old at the time and living with him. He was a man who hated violence of any kind, including harming the dreams of another. And it was that very nature of him that would have never let him stand in the way of his wife having the opportunity to make a trip like this. He would tell her that he loved the immensity of her and that this was part of that immensity.

Amy Raye finished her coffee and packed water bottles and food, enough for a full day. She sprayed herself with elk estrus as if it were perfume — her neck, under her arms, the soles of her boots. The warning labels on the bottle said not to spray the estrus on one's body or clothing. It was to be sprayed on the ground for the purpose of luring elk to a certain area, while the hunter hid away from the spot. Most hunters didn't adhere to those warning labels. The serious hunters didn't care if they smelled of elk urine; they became the female elk, mastered her call, a high-pitched mewing, much like the cry of a young cat. It wasn't just a bull elk that might mistake the hunter for a female. It was the mountain lion, as well.

Amy Raye stepped into the tree stand harness she'd stowed in her pack, pulled the harness straps over her shoulders, and tightened the leg and waist buckles. She set her bow, quiver, and packing frame in the extra cab of the truck, and then climbed into the driver's side. Aaron had left the keys on the floorboard, Amy Raye knew. She picked up the keys and closed the door, shifted the truck into neutral, and let it roll down the slow decline toward the road, her foot pressing intermittently on the brake, the wet earth and rock turning beneath her.

Pru

The morning Colm stopped by was no different from most others. I was sitting on the porch having my coffee, a quilt pulled snug around my shoulders. Kona lay curled in a tight circle at my feet, and just beyond was the river. I could hear it twisting over a bed of rocks, tiny caps crashing forward, a sign that a storm had settled in the mountains. The third rifle season for deer and elk had closed the day before. Hunters would be packing up camp and heading home; the grocery store aisles would be rid of orange vests and carts stocked with coffee, beer, cold cuts, and toilet paper; the hotels would empty out. Ever since the beginning of archery season in September, I'd been driving up and down four-wheel roads in my government Tahoe, checking hunters' licenses and scouting camps for illegal kill. Two weeks ago I'd been called to a scene where a man from Texas had nearly lost his left foot in an all-terrain accident, his Sorel boot only shreds.

I work for the Bureau of Land Management as an archaeological law enforcement ranger, with the only certified search-and-rescue dog in the county. Because I'm a ranger, I do a little bit of everything, especially during hunting season. My job falls under the Archaeological Resources Protection Act. I enforce the laws against archaeological looting. I survey for disturbance, walk sacred ground. I'm a guardian of sorts, a police for the past.

I've been a morning person for as long as I can remember, craving the solitude when I awake as much as a strong cup of coffee. Most mornings I will read. On days when I know I'll be in the office and not in the field, I'll take Kona on a run with me. That morning I watched the sky, listened to the river, thought about starting a load of laundry. I still had another hour or so before Joseph would be getting up for school. Joseph is a beautiful blue-eyed boy with hair the color of sun-bleached hay. "Pet me," he used to say, when he was competing for attention with the border collie we used to have. And so I would stroke his hair and kiss his cheeks, salty from play and the outdoors. "How much does Mama love you?" I'd say. "Big much," he'd say, holding his arms out wide. Then I would take him to me like a mother bear with her cub.

But these days Joseph is taller than I. He's been driving for over a month now. I try to tell myself his getting his license is a good thing, that he is growing up. But still there's something else. Something I can't put a name on. Something that happened so fast, I never saw it coming.

An icy breeze ribboned through the air. I slid my bare toes underneath Kona's belly and drank the rest of the coffee, the liquid having turned lukewarm. A dog barked in the distance. Kona raised his head, his ears alert. Then the crunching of large tires against loose stone. The truck's beams soon rounded the house and lit up a pathway across the tall grass toward the riverbank.

I knew it was Colm. Knew the sound of his vehicle and the way he slammed his door.

"Morning," I yelled through the screen.

Colm climbed the porch steps and lifted the screen door slightly to open it. The door needed new hinges, another item on my to-do list that I kept promising myself I'd get to.

Kona settled back down when he saw it was the sheriff.

"You're up awfully early," I said.

"No different than you."

"Want some coffee?" I started to get up.

"Stay put. I know my way to the kitchen."

I've known Colm since before my son was born. Colm would read the gas meter each month at a small rental house where I used to live. Like me, Colm isn't from Rio Mesa. He moved here as a young man, somewhere in his early twenties, taking on a job with White River Natural Gas. Then when the only television tower was shut off, when residents in the county who wished to watch TV were forced to buy into satellite, Colm began installing dishes and network boxes. His work brought him into people's homes, where he was offered coffee and beer and neighborly conversation, the kind of conversation that led to ideas. Colm became someone people got to know and like. He listened and had a way of letting people know he'd heard what they'd said, heard it and thought about it and thought about it some more. Maybe it was the way his green eyes would fasten intently on the eyes of another, or the way he'd nod contemplatively, or the way he'd wait calmly, his whole body still, for a person to finish speaking before he'd respond. I'm not sure who first introduced the notion that Colm should run for sheriff. But once the idea got around, it spread like a rumor in a small town, the kind of rumor people get accustomed to real quickly until it is simply the way things are, or in Colm's case, the way things would be.

Colm appeared with a mug in his hand. "How was your weekend?" he asked.

"Not bad. Yours?"

"Can't complain." Colm sat in the cedar-backed chair beside me, his big knees squared out in front of him. "I saw Joseph the other day. Over by the school. He seems to be getting along all right."

"Sometimes I worry about him," I said.

Colm blew on the coffee before he took a loud swallow. "Course you do. You're his mother."

I smiled a little. And then that part of me that had curled itself deep down in my chest started to stir. That part of me that wanted to say, *He's all I have,* but instead I said, "It's five o'clock in the morning. My coffee isn't that good to bring you out here."

Colm took another swallow, pulled back his lips, and exhaled slowly. "A call came in last night. Missing hunter."

"Where?"

"East Douglas. She came out here with a couple of guys from Evergreen. Took the truck out by herself sometime yesterday morning. The guys she'd traveled with called a little while ago. She still hasn't shown."

"Did she have her cell with her?"

"If she did, she's not answering. Or can't get a signal."

"Where's the camp?" I asked.

"A pull-off in Pintada Draw. One of her friends thought she might have headed east toward Big Ridge. Said he thought he heard a gun go off later that morning, but he wasn't sure. Except she was hunting with a bow," Colm said. "Her friends filled their tags with rifles a couple of days ago."

"Anyone out there yet?" I asked.

"Deputy in Rangely is on his way now. See if he spots the vehicle, a black Ford 350. I'm going to try to get a helicopter out there this afternoon."

Colm ran his fingers through his straight black hair flecked with gray. He paused just a second over the nape of his neck. "She probably huddled up somewhere for the night. Once it starts getting light she'll find her way back."

"Did she have any food or water with her?"

"Her friends thought so, but they weren't sure."

Colm was now looking at me dead on. I

knew he was concerned. He wouldn't have shown up at my house at five in the morning if he hadn't been. He was following protocol. Wait till first light. Sheriffs mounted anywhere from fifty-five to a hundred full-fledged searches in Colorado each year, and most of them were successful and short-lived. Only a handful of times would the search turn into the kind of harrowing saga every sheriff feared. Yet with each missing person, the potential presented itself.

"We're going to have to get a ground team on location," Colm said. "If Dean finds the vehicle and no hunter, be a good idea for you and Kona to team up with him before the place starts getting mixed up with too much scent."

"What's her name?" I asked.

"Amy Raye Latour. Thirty-two. Husband and two kids back home."

It had been cold during the night. So cold that I'd gotten up a little after two to add more logs to the stove. "East Douglas is a big area. May take Dean hours before he finds the vehicle."

"Where you planning to be today?"

"Piceance Creek. Wanted to check out a few camps that are clearing out."

Colm's head lulled into an easy nod. His

eyes stared off through the porch screen. He had a big heart. He would worry about this woman until he found her, and yet it wasn't just the weight of the missing hunter that was pulling him down. Colm's divorce had been final for six months. I knew he still didn't sleep much. I could hear it in that deep throaty voice of his, see it in the folds over his eyes and the way his broad shoulders hung forward.

"You holding up okay?" I asked.

He shot me a quick glance. "Yeah." Then his gaze roamed off again. "I know I look like shit, but it's actually better having her gone. I just have to get used to it all."

I waited for him to say something else. When he didn't, I reached for his mug. "Want a warm-up?"

"No, I should get going."

I started to stand. Colm was still sitting in the chair.

"She never loved me. It's hard to admit, but it's true. Figure that. Fourteen years and she never loved me."

Though we'd talked about some of the details of his divorce, his emotions weren't something we'd touched upon. Still, his vulnerability didn't surprise me. It's one of those things a woman picks up on. "Colm, you don't really believe that."

"Sure."

"Why'd she marry you, then?"

"She liked my dog." Colm laughed and shook his head. "Goddamn woman marries me for my dog."

Colm wasn't trying to be funny. He'd had a Labrador named Ruger, black and overweight with a sloppy mouth.

"That's not why she married you," I said. "People change."

"Maybe." Colm was now leaning forward with his arms on his knees. His jacket, a dark brown leather, was stretched snug across his shoulders.

Colm had lost his dog a year back to cancer, and now he'd lost his wife. He didn't have any kids. Maggie had never wanted any. Perhaps she knew all along she would leave, even if she'd waited fourteen years to do it.

I dug my toes deeper beneath Kona's fur. "Ever thought about getting another dog?" I said.

"Thought about it."

"Maybe that wouldn't be a bad idea."

Colm reached over and gave Kona a pat. "You're a good boy. You keep Pru company, you hear?" Then Colm stood to take his mug to the kitchen.

"Leave it." I climbed out of the lounge.

It was somewhere in the twenties, and with the windchill factor, more like the teens, especially in the mountains.

"It's cold out there," I said.

Colm knew what I was saying. "I'll call you."

He lifted the screen door about a half inch off the planked flooring, pulled it toward him, stepped down, and shut the door behind him.

I carried the two empty coffee cups into the kitchen and set them in the sink. I would take a shower, eat a quick breakfast, get Joseph up for school. Colm might be calling soon. If Amy Raye Latour was still missing, I'd want to start searching while the hunter's tracks were fresh.

I walked down the short hallway to the bathroom, turned on the water, and held my fingers underneath the tap while I waited for the water to become warm. Kona lay on the floor beside the tub. Together we had established a routine that I'd come to depend on. I knew Colm would have to do the same, create new patterns of behavior to close the god-awful spaces of loneliness from losing someone he'd loved.

Amy Raye

Amy Raye drove several miles from the campsite, winding her way up steep pitches until she found a level clearing where she could park the truck. She got out and opened the door of the extra cab. It was then that she noticed the small cooler, the one Aaron and Kenny brought along in the truck each day they headed out. They'd pack it with sandwiches and bars so they'd have something to eat as soon as they returned to the vehicle. The cooler had been on the table by the cookstove the night before. Amy Raye had watched Aaron clean out the wrappers and wipe out the crumbs.

Inside were a couple of peanut butter and jelly sandwiches, a plastic bag filled with beef jerky, a yogurt, and a candy bar. Kenny must have packed the cooler for her after she'd turned in. She ate one of the sandwiches and some of the jerky. She put the other sandwich and the rest of the jerky in her pack. Then she took a couple of bites of the candy bar, left the rest of it, and closed the cooler. As she stood beside the truck, the coldness and dampness of the early morning began to cut through her layers of clothing. She was ready to start hiking. She picked up her orange hat off the seat, but thought better of it. The three of them hadn't come across any other hunters that week or rangers who would be checking for orange. Getting a shot at an elk with a bow meant getting within close range of the animal; it meant not being seen.

She checked the broadheads on her arrows, made sure they were tight, and secured three arrows into her quiver, the one with the best flight into the first slot. Then she fastened the quiver around her waist and right leg, a certain rhythm to her actions. She secured her pack onto her back. She'd return for the packing frame should she get a shot. She hung her elk bugle and the cow call around her neck. With the headlamp switched to low beam and her bow in her left hand, she headed northward along the ridge about a hundred yards to the place she would veer off, marked by two pinyons that grew like Siamese twins.

As she walked, her thoughts spread toward home and the children and to an afternoon not so far back when reluctantly she had agreed to hike with her husband up Ypsilon Mountain in the Mummy Range of Rocky Mountain National Park. Reluctantly because of the distance that had spread between them, a space as thick as a room full of grief.

But that weekend the children were going to be spending time with Farrell's sister, and Farrell, an amateur photographer, wanted to capture some still shots in the mountains, wanted his wife to join him. "Come on, the time will be good for us," he'd said.

The weather had started out pleasant that day, in the midfifties, with a dull sun that made the air feel warmer. Amy Raye had walked behind Farrell, though the trail was wide enough in most places for them to walk side by side.

"Are you hungry? Do you want to stop for lunch?" he'd asked.

"Let's go a little farther," she said.

She had fallen in love with Farrell for his kindness, the same kind of nurturing she'd received from her mother. And she fell in love with him because when she first saw him, he was playing the guitar and singing Harry Chapin's "Mr. Tanner," and Amy Raye knew all the words, and she sang along, and when she sang, she felt like a young girl all over again.

They'd met in Idaho Springs, a small town just off Interstate 70. She'd given up on college by then. She'd given up on a lot of things, yet somehow she'd managed to get by, and when they'd met, she was getting by all right. She was selling advertisements for the county's newspaper, the *Clear Creek Courant,* and working evening shifts at Night Owl, a liquor store run out of a trailer between a Jiffy Mart and a United Methodist Church. She was still young, and street-smart, just twenty-three years old.

It had been almost nighttime, two weeks into January. She'd come close to selling a full-page ad to a chiropractor who had wanted to buy her dinner. Amy Raye didn't want dinner, or him, and so she'd walked home through the snowfall, and as the moisture turned to slush in her hair, a red heeler with a slight limp to his left back leg trotted up behind her and wagged his tail.

She was renting the upstairs of a three-unit apartment house four blocks behind the Methodist church. The house, painted purple and mauve and light green, was one of the fifty or so Victorians in the neighborhood. She climbed the stairs to her apartment, wooden steps that ran up the backside of the house. At the landing, she looked over her shoulder. The dog sat at the foot of the stairs, his eyes fastened to her like Velcro on flannel, his tail pushing the sloppy mess on the asphalt into inconsistent mounds. She nodded, slush slipping from her hair and falling onto her cowboy boots with the thick rubber soles. Then she turned to unlock the door, and when she opened it, he had climbed the stairs, and he followed her inside. She bathed him that night, untangled his mats with her hairbrush, called him Saddle because she loved horses and because his coat was the color of chestnut leather. They ate chicken broth and French bread, and after she had read ten pages of *Love, Groucho: Letters from Groucho Marx to His Daughter Miriam* and reached over to the lamp and turned it off, the dog jumped onto the bed and lay next to her, leaning his warm back against her side. She fell asleep right away but an hour later awoke, and he was still there.

Wearing sweatpants, a thermal nightshirt, and thick wool socks, she rose from bed and asked him if he needed to go out. She slipped on a down parka, pulled a fleece hat over her ears, and stepped into a pair of tall rubber boots that she usually saved for mud season in spring. Saddle followed her out the door and down the stairs. The snow had stopped falling. They'd walked two blocks heading east when they'd come to a house with lamps glowing from inside, and silhouettes of people in the windows, and the sounds of an acoustic guitar and singing. They stood there, the two of them, facing the house. She didn't flinch when a bearded man opened the front door, and with a Southern accent, asked her if she'd like to come in. And the dog, too, she thought he'd said. She went inside the house, slipped off her boots, and walked soft-footed into the room from where the music came. Someone offered her a chair, and so she sat and listened to another man, who looked like a boy, smile and sing and play the guitar, and nod when others sang, too.

She didn't know then how short the man who looked like a boy was, just over five foot seven, with strong legs the same length as his torso, or that he would always wear soft clothes, corduroy and aged flannel and cotton as smooth as a lamb's ear. She didn't know that when they made love his skin would smell of sage and milk thistle, and his hair, damp with sweat, would smell like moist bark deep in the woods. Or that she would marry him, and by the time she was thirty-two, bear a son with him and be the stepmother to his daughter.

That day on Ypsilon Mountain, the distance between Amy Raye and Farrell began to change, the kind of change that begins like a warm current in a cold stream. And the sky began to turn. Amy Raye hadn't noticed the sky at first. She'd first noticed the ground, shadows from the clouds. Then drops of rain as they made small depressions in the sandy earth, and her husband's footprints before her, the treads of his hiking boots forming perfectly shaped ridges in the moist soil.

"The weather has turned," he'd said.

"Do you want to head back?" she asked.

"Let's hike a little farther and see if it passes," he said.

But the storm didn't pass. And then, as though there had been a great rip in the sky, the clouds seemed to burst. The rain poured down in steady, biting streams, and the soil quickly turned into puddles of sloppy mud.

"There's a shelter up ahead. Let's make a run for it," Farrell said.

Amy Raye wondered how he had known about the shelter. She would ask him later. He must have hiked this trail before.

The shelter was a small cabin with a lean-to porch. The front door was unlocked.

Amy Raye and Farrell shook the rain from their clothes and smoothed back their wet hair before they entered. Inside the cabin was a cot, a small table with two chairs, and a wood stove. Beside the stove was dry wood, about a tenth of a cord's worth stacked neatly against one of the walls, and on top of the wood was kindling.

Farrell set his pack on the table. "Are you hungry?" he asked.

"I could eat," Amy Raye said.

He unzipped his pack and took out a thermos, a plastic container with meat and cheese, another container with dried fruit, a package of crackers. He brought out two metal cups as well.

"I'll make a fire," Amy Raye said.

"Let me do it," Farrell said.

But Amy Raye reached for his arm to stop him. "No. You get the food."

"Do you have a lighter?" he asked.

"Yes. It's in my pack."

And so Amy Raye filled the stove with kindling and wood and lit the fire. She knelt in front of the stove, watching as the small flames caught. She added more kindling, closed the door to the stove, rubbed her hands together until they warmed, and then joined her husband.

He had poured hot coffee into each of the

cups and had arranged the food on the table. He pulled out a chair for his wife.

Farrell had packed the food that morning. He'd gotten the children ready to go to his sister's as well. He'd told Amy Raye to sleep in, but Amy Raye never was one for sleeping in. Instead, she'd lain in bed listening to the movements of the children in the house, their footsteps going up and down the stairs, the exchanging of words between them and their father. She rose from bed, dressed, went down to join them, wrestled Julia and Trevor in her arms, made faces, even flirted with her husband. He was making peanut butter and jelly sandwiches, whether for Amy Raye and him, or Julia and Trevor, she didn't know. She dipped her finger in the peanut butter jar. "Hey," Farrell said, pushing her away with his shoulder. With a flirtatious spin, she dabbed the peanut butter on his nose, then on the noses of Julia and Trevor, then on her own, challenging each of them to touch their noses with their tongues, when she already knew Trevor was the only one who could. They all laughed at each other's efforts, and Farrell took Amy Raye in his arms and kissed her nose and licked the peanut butter off her face.

Only weeks before, Farrell had asked her, "Are you still in love with me?"

They'd been lying in bed. Amy Raye thought he'd been asleep, the two of them having turned in hours before. Her breath tightened when he'd asked her this, tightened itself deep down in her lungs like a heartache, because for a split second she wondered if he knew, if perhaps he'd known all along.

"I love you, but I don't know that I'm in love with you," Amy Raye said. When too much silence followed, she continued. "Everyone wants love to be this great, life-altering experience, their feelings to be so special, so unique, so dramatic, so beyond anything anyone else has. Is that even possible?"

She was trying for a moment of truth, and yet even as she spoke the words, she couldn't tell the difference between truth and what she'd created.

"You are my love. You are my all," Farrell said. "It's simple for me."

"Is love really that simple, Farrell? Tell me, Farrell, exactly what you think love is. I've been spending lots of thoughts on this, and all the answers make love seem so common, and if love is common, does that make it any less? Love should be common?"

Farrell was on his side, facing her. "I care for you, Amy. There are different levels to the way one cares for someone. The intensity varies. That's what makes it more or less common."

Amy Raye felt the weight of her back pressed hard against the mattress. "You can't expect one person to be everything. You can't expect one person to meet all your needs," she said.

Farrell's body retreated, though he did not leave the bed. "All I want to do is soar with you," he said. And then he became too quiet.

Until that night, perhaps Farrell had hoped that whatever the distance was that had prompted his question about her loving him was related to something outside them, like work or the global warming of the atmosphere, or something with the children. Without asking, he could have believed whatever he chose to believe. Without asking, there was hope. Amy Raye wondered if she would have asked the question had she been in his shoes. *Yes,* she thought. She would have demanded to know.

And now they were in this cabin, protected from the inclement weather. There was stillness about them despite the sounds of the rain slapping on the metal roof. Amy Raye sat next to her husband and held the mug close to her mouth, letting the steam warm her face. "Sing to me," she said.

He laid food on a paper towel in front of her. "What do you want me to sing?"

She sipped the coffee, then set the cup down and picked up the cracker that Farrell had prepared for her with cheese and meat. As she began to eat, she felt her husband's knee against hers, a light touch. For some reason, she looked at him, and at that moment, it dawned on her that she had not looked at him, really looked at him, for a long time. Something warmed in her stomach. Was it desire? She set the food down and looked away, but he seemed to know. His hand reached for her leg; his fingers gently pressed upon her. Amy Raye wanted to cry for all that they had lost, for all that she had taken from them, for all they might have been. His other hand reached for her face, touched her chin, stroked her jawline, moved toward the back of her neck, beneath her hair that hung below her hat. His fingers gently massaged her muscles. But she could not look at him, as if she were afraid she might discover just how much she still felt for him, and once again fail the only one she had ever loved.

His hands pulled away, and Amy Raye wanted to tell him everything. Wanted to tell him she was sorry. She turned to face him, but this time he wasn't looking at her. Instead his eyes stared straight ahead.

"Is it too late?" he asked.

Amy Raye remained silent.

Farrell scooted out his chair and stood, and as he did he extended his hand to his wife. Hesitantly, she clasped his fingers, let him lead her away from the table and over to the cot. He let go of her hand just long enough to remove his coat and lay it on the mattress. Then he sat on the edge of the small bed, unzipped his wife's jacket, wrapped his arms around her waist, pressed his head against her abdomen.

Instinctively, Amy Raye held his head in her hands. She removed his hat, let it drop onto the floor, ran her fingers through his thick, mossy hair, her breathing deepening into a longing for him she had not allowed herself for some time.

Biting into the fleece of her shirt, Farrell lifted it away and tucked his head against her skin. "I didn't come to take pictures of the mountains," he said, the warmth of his breath creating shivers along her flesh. "I came to the mountains to take pictures of you."

"People take pictures of those things they may not see again. They take pictures to remember."

"I know," Farrell said. His lips grazed her skin. His hands reached for the waistline of her jeans. Amy Raye did not resist. She let him unfasten her jeans, slide them down her legs.

Amy Raye removed her jacket, pulled her shirt over her head, stripped down till her entire body was exposed to the cool air and to the eyes of her husband, because she wanted at that moment to make things right, because she wanted to give her husband something for all the things she had taken away. Farrell then removed his clothes, stood before his wife, and Amy Raye became filled with grief and a terrifying confliction. Farrell stepped toward her, reached for her hips.

Pru

It was late in the morning, around ten, the ground covered in a fine layer of snow, the sky a deep, smooth blue. I had just finished writing up a ticket for a hunter out of Wyoming who'd failed to retain evidence of gender on the deer carcass he was carrying in the back of his Dodge pickup. His license tag was for a buck, except the head and genitalia were gone. I'd put in a call to the Division of Wildlife to have the carcass withheld, but there were no DOW game wardens in the area, which meant I'd have to haul the animal to town in the back of my Tahoe. It was times like these I wished the government had given me a pickup. The Tahoe was for Kona's sake. He generally rode in the back with the gear: GPS maps, first-aid kit, extra clothing, spotting scope, rope, come-along, a couple of tarps.

The hunter smelled of campfire and body odor. His soiled cap read *Cowboys do it better.*

"Fine, take the animal." The tailgate of his truck was down. He grabbed hold of the deer's legs and, with one hefty pull, yanked the animal out of the bed and onto the ground, staining the dusty layer of snow dark brown. "Go ahead," he said. He leaned his flat hips against the tailgate and spit a stream of tobacco juice just inches from my black hiking boots. He obviously didn't think I could lift the animal. He didn't know I had a come-along.

I spread the blue tarp over the cargo floor, draped its end over the Tahoe's bumper, laid out the come-along, and then tied it to the seat belt anchor with nylon rope. I hooked the payout line to the deer's left back gambrel and began pumping the come-along lever like a jackhammer, slowly hoisting the bloody carcass into my vehicle. The cowboy didn't budge an inch, though the smirk on his face seemed to loosen its cement grip. He spit a couple more times, slammed the tailgate of his truck shut with both hands, and walked around to the driver's side.

"Have a nice day!" I yelled toward him as he drove off, his tires kicking up a spray of mud and snow.

I was glad the animal had been gutted

properly. I unhooked the deer and disassembled the come-along. Kona didn't like to share his quarters. He trotted over to the passenger door. I grabbed hold of a hunk of his black fur and tugged it playfully. Then I opened the door. "Think you're going to ride up front with me, huh?" Kona leapt in, pawed a tight circle, and settled down.

I called the DOW to see if there were any wardens out my way but didn't have any luck. I'd have to drive the carcass to town. I was about to head back to Rio Mesa when my cell phone rang.

"Pru, it's Colm. Where are you?"

"The middle of Piceance Basin with a headless deer in the back of my Tahoe. Where are you?"

"Listen, Dean found the vehicle. No hunter, no body, just the truck. How long till you can get out there?"

"I'll need to drop the carcass off first."

"Call the DOW," Colm said.

"I did. There're no wardens out this way. Most of them are up in the forest. I'm supposed to drop it off at the station."

"What about the warden over in Rangely?"

"That'd be Wally Henderson." I'd already started the truck and was pulling out. Kona's neck was stretched over the console, his head tucked in the crook of my arm.

"Go ahead and give Wally a call," I told Colm, knowing I'd lose signal soon. "Have him meet me at the intersection of 64 and 139. Tell him we got another gift for the food bank. Have Dean meet me there, too. I'll follow Dean out to the vehicle. Maybe Kona can track something. Any snow out there?" I asked.

"As much as a foot in spots. Mostly fresh."

Kona was avalanche certified. Still, fresh accumulation made any search more difficult. "We'll give it our best shot," I said.

Piceance Basin is a rolling expanse of knolls and ravines. I stared out over the thickening snow as my truck climbed a steep knob spotted with sage and juniper.

I'd already listened to the weather. Twenty- to thirty-mile-per-hour winds, with gusts up to forty. Temperatures were expected to drop to the low teens by nightfall, the clear skies being a sure indicator. Northwestern Colorado was known for its strong winds, currents that swept out the canyons and gulches, twisting and shaping the vegetation.

"Will you be able to get a helicopter in there?" I asked.

"One of the reserve guards in Rangely has a chopper ready. As long as the weather holds out."

"What about a physical description of the woman?"

"Around five-six. A hundred and thirty pounds. Blond hair. And let's hope to God she was wearing orange."

I worried about the cold. Hypothermia would have already been a likely factor. And with the reduction in body temperature came erratic behavior. They'd have to find tracks. No telling where the woman might have wandered if she hadn't been thinking straight. A standard-issue lighter could save a person's life. It was amazing how few people in this country carried one. But then again maybe the woman had been able to build a fire.

The connection was breaking up. "I'm losing you," I said. "I'll check in with you later."

Colm was sheriff of Paisaje County. The town of Rangely, about sixty miles west of Rio Mesa in an expanse of high desert and sage, fell within his jurisdiction. I drove with my windows partway down to keep the carcass cool. The sun and wind burned my cheeks as my hair whipped across my face.

I removed the glove from my right hand, rubbed my palm over the smooth area above Kona's brow, his black hair warmed by the sun. Kona and I were a good fit, but it hadn't always been that way. He was an alpha, and I was determined to be one, so neither of us was eager to let go and give in.

"Get a dog," Angie at the movie store had told me just three months after Joseph and I had lost Molly, the border collie I'd had since before Joseph was born. Angie, with her thick German accent, who kept dog treats behind the movie rental store counter.

"Down the road," I said. "It's not the right time."

"Me, I always say a dog can get a person through anything. Get a dog," Angie said again.

At the time, I was on my third rental. This one was a blue modular about four miles west of town. The small rectangle sat on a parched mesa overlooking a field of sage. In the evenings, I'd listen to the yipping of coyotes, the baying of mule deer, the rattling of snakes. And the next day when I'd walk the property, I'd find the baby rattlers in patches of sand basking in the August sun.

On a warm evening that past May, I'd taken Molly hiking along the ridge that backed up to the south edge of town. The sky had turned to dusk, and the deer were coming out to feed. So were the coyotes. One of the coyotes jumped into our path and lured Molly on a chase. But as is often the case with coyotes, Molly was being baited and was led to a pack on the other side of the ridge. I'd heard her cries before I could get to her. I'd heard the coyotes. And as I scrambled over the crest of the butte, as I screamed and threw rocks and charged the pack, Molly was already dead.

Right, get a dog, I had thought, knowing my heart was too vulnerable to risk losing anything else.

Then Angie called. It was late, ten or eleven. I was in bed, a double mattress on the floor, and was reading through the cooking tips that came with my new Kenmore gas grill. Joseph was sleeping beside me.

"I got a dog for you," Angie said.

"I don't want a dog," I told her.

"He's black. I'd say he's about four months old. Looks like a German shepherd. Somebody got rid of him."

"What do you mean somebody got rid of him?"

"You know the Dumpster behind the movie store? He was in a box behind the Dumpster. There were two others with him."

"Where are the others?"

"I got one of them here with me. I don't think she's going to make it. The other one, another boy, was already dead. I buried him in my backyard. But this one, he's strong."

"Why would somebody do that?"

"The box was taped shut. I heard this one crying when I closed up and took the garbage out."

And so Joseph and I drove to Angie's that night.

"Where are we going?" he'd asked, his voice full of sleep.

"To get a dog."

"I thought you didn't want a dog."

"I never said that. I just said I didn't want a dog now."

"So why are we getting a dog?"

"Because he needs us."

"Okay," Joseph said. "I like dogs."

"Me, too," I said.

"Where will he sleep?"

"With us."

"Okay."

But Kona didn't sleep with Joseph and me that night. Kona kept jumping off the mattress and running to the door.

"I think he needs to go out," Joseph said.

"I just let him out."

"I think he needs to go again."

So I would let Kona out on a short leash, all the while listening for the snakes that had overbred on the mesa, listening for the coyotes that lived in the rocky clefts as close as sixty yards away.

Finally I put Kona back in a box, because I didn't have a crate. And Joseph and I listened to him cry and bark and yelp until we pitied him and went to retrieve him, where we found that he had shat all over himself. We bathed him and played with him until the sun rose.

I squeezed a hunk of fur around Kona's neck, patted his head. Wally was pulled over in the dirt just to the east of where the highways intersected. He rolled down his window when he saw me approach.

"What was it this time?" he asked.

"No sex, no head."

"Tag was for a buck?"

"Yep. Last day of the season. Guy got desperate."

Wally opened his truck door and stepped out. "Go ahead and back up to my tailgate. We'll slide the animal over."

I did as Wally said, leaving only enough space to open my back vertical doors.

Kona had leapt over the seat and was on all fours, his tail wagging and his head lifted toward Wally, encouraging a pat.

"Hey, Kona." Wally grabbed him on both sides of the head, tousling him around.

Then Wally and I each took hold of an edge of the tarp and pulled it toward the bed of his truck.

"Keep the tarp," I said when we were finished.

"I got a clean one in the cab. I'll swap you out," he said.

Wally set the folded tarp in the back of my Tahoe. Just as I closed the doors, Dean pulled up. He climbed out of his deputy Cherokee and rubbed a hand down each of his legs, as if trying to adjust the tight fit of his jeans.

"Any luck yet?" I asked.

"Nope. Maybe Kona will have a better go of it."

Wally said, "I'm going to head out. Nice work, Pru."

I waved to him as he drove off. Then I tucked my hands in the pockets of my black parka, my back against the truck. I looked at Dean. He was short and stocky like a middle school linebacker, and wore a cap over his mostly bald head.

"Any leads?" I asked.

"Just the vehicle. A couple of miles into East Dry Lake Canyon."

I knew the Douglas Creek area well, a coarse arrangement of pipelines, oil and natural gas wells, and a vast expanse of boulders and draws. I'd surveyed maybe thirty sites in that area, rock art and shelters once occupied by the Fremonts, predecessors to the Shoshonean tribes. East Douglas was also one of the wild horse management areas. The herd was nonviable and was in the process of being zeroed out. There just wasn't enough genetic diversity anymore. The band used to be part of the Hill Creek management area in Utah. The horses would travel across the border back and forth between Utah and Colorado, but with the development of towns and highways, the herd in East Douglas had become isolated. There were only about thirty horses left. In all my time working the area, I'd never seen the horses, and they were becoming more and more difficult to catch and auction off. A bigger concern was the level of inbreeding that was going on with the ones that might be caught.

"Colm says there's fresh snow up there," I told Dean.

"Probably six to eight inches. Maybe a foot in the higher elevations. It's windy as hell. There'll be some bald spots on the western slopes. Dry powder. Didn't stick to the back brush or sage."

"Search and rescue been called yet?"

"Dispatcher's gotten hold of about ten

volunteers. They're planning to stand by until I call. Colm wanted you out there first."

Dean and I climbed back into our vehicles. I followed him about sixteen miles south on Highway 139 to the East Douglas Creek turn-off and made a left into Rocky Point Draw. The road twisted through the gulch, an arterial spread of arroyos surrounded by sandstone bluffs. The wind had already cleared a lot of snow from the base.

He stopped just before the steep muddy pitch leading to the Weatherman Draw site, a Native American Fremont shelter that had been excavated over the past three summers by different field schools led by Glade, the BLM's area archaeologist. I had been part of the excavation efforts by maintaining the surveillance of the site. This entire area was part of my own jurisdiction.

About fifty yards to the right of Dean's Cherokee, amid knobs of silver-green sage and fallen rocks, was the black Ford.

"Hell of a place to get lost," I said as I got out of my truck.

I opened the back of my Tahoe. "Okay, Kona." He jumped down beside me, wagging his tail. I buckled his tracking harness over his neck and shoulders, then attached his leash to his choker collar and led him to the black pickup, where Dean had already opened the driver's side.

"Up!" I said.

Kona jumped into the truck, acquainting himself with the hunter's smells, a pair of women's-size mittens in the passenger seat, an atlas of Colorado, a half-empty bottle of cinnamon schnapps. I knew too well the effect of blood alcohol in the cold. "Is the Hot Damn hers?"

"I don't know. The truck belongs to one of the guys."

In the backseat of the extra cab were a plastic container of hollow-point bullets for a .357 Magnum, a black leather compass pouch, a blaze orange cap with earflaps, and a small cooler. Inside the cooler were an empty sandwich bag coated with crumbs, a container of yogurt, and a half-eaten Snickers bar.

"She had lunch," I said. "What about the hat?"

"Could be hers. Could be one of the guys'. Colm's on his way out to their camp now. Without their vehicle, they've been stranded."

Using my gloved hand, I picked up the mittens for a scent item and placed them in a plastic bag. Maybe the woman was wearing glove liners. Most likely she wasn't planning on staying out long. From the way things looked, she'd probably hunted from the vehicle. Gone out that morning, and come back to the truck for lunch. If that was the case, she wouldn't have packed much water, and more than likely hadn't carried in much food.

On the seat of the extra cab was a packing frame. A lot of hunters would leave the packing frame at the truck. Kona climbed over the console into the front seat, his tail wagging furiously. He looked at me and let out a yip. He was ready. I switched his leash to the tracking collar and backed out of the truck.

"Go find," I said.

Kona leapt onto the ground. I led him around the vehicle. At the tail of the truck he held his head between his shoulders and the ground. I knew he'd picked up a trail. He circled behind me. After about fifty feet, Kona raised his head.

"He's lost it," I said.

"I'm sure the rain they got out here yesterday isn't going to help anything," Dean said.

I led Kona back to the truck where he'd first started to work the trail. Then I guided him into the wind, which was blowing out of the north and stirring up a fine cloud of snow. Kona worked a few yards, but again stopped. Once more, I led him around the vehicle, hoping he might pick up another trail.

At the passenger side, Kona's tail began to wag as he lowered his head. He was on. He followed the trail up a fifty-yard climb, making switchbacks from time to time, and occasionally losing the trail over some of the rocks. As we reached the top of the ridge, Kona lost the scent. The drop down the other side of the ridge was rocky and steep, with smooth boulders perched just over the edge like monuments. My best bet was that Amy Raye had climbed up there to survey the area, and then descended in the same direction she'd come.

We headed back down to the truck. "Nothing," I said to Dean, who was waiting for me at his Cherokee. "She was definitely here, but every trail leads to a dead end. Might as well get hold of search and rescue and see what they can find."

Dean cupped his hands around his mouth. "Amy Raye!" he yelled, drawing the name out. Dean and I waited, motionless, but heard only the whine of the wind.

Dean got on the radio. He told the dispatcher to go ahead and send the search-and-rescue crew out. He'd meet them at the Kum & Go in Rangely.

"You want to ride back to town with me? Grab a sandwich?" he asked.

"No, thanks. I ate on the way. I think we'll keep working the area."

"You know what Colm would say."

"Colm's not here," I reminded him.

Searches involved teams. Solo work wasn't allowed, and a dog didn't count as a partner. The last thing a search-and-rescue team wanted was to be looking for one of its members in addition to the missing subject. Still, good daylight was like water between the fingers.

"Leave me with a radio," I said. "I'll check in with anything I find." I wasn't looking at Dean, but was scanning the edge of the surrounding ridges, checking for any patch of color or sign of movement. "We still got a good three hours before sundown."

"He'll chew my ass," Dean told me.

"You're a tough guy."

Dean walked back to his Cherokee. When he returned, he gave me a handset. "Be careful," he said.

Once again Kona and I followed the scent trail up to the top of the ridge. I crouched close to its edge and adjusted my binoculars to their maximum power. I glassed the area, looking eastward toward the cedar and pinyon woods, but spotted nothing. Several times I stopped to sound a whistle I wore around my neck, hoping to attract Amy Raye's attention should she merely be lost. That was a search-and-rescue team's first assumption with a missing hunter. But I wasn't searching in the high timber where the aspen and spruce create a thick mesh whichever way one looks. I was at around eight thousand feet elevation in the high desert. Though there were dense stretches of pinyon and juniper, there were plenty of open vistas and cliffs where a person could gauge his or her bearings.

I had camped in the high desert plenty of times. Had brought Joseph with me to show him some of the archaeological sites that had been excavated. The first time I'd brought him with me, Joseph was nine. We were setting up camp on a ridge overlooking Soldier Creek, about sixty yards from the truck, a red and silver '98 GMC that Joseph was now driving. I was pitching the tent. Kona, only a year and a half at the time, was tied to a tree. He was a stubborn dog who would wander off at the least distraction. It was that same stubbornness that drove me a year later to begin training him as a search dog. "He needs something to do," Angie at the movie store had told me. "He needs to work." It was Angie who had put me in touch with SARDOC, Search and Rescue Dogs of Colorado. I spent the next two years training Kona through the group before he was certified. Though I'd already completed my law enforcement training, it wasn't until Kona became certified as a search dog that I'd become interested in working search and rescue.

But that day on the ridge with my son, Kona was still a headstrong puppy, despite being over a year old. Joseph wanted me to go with him to the truck to get something. Maybe he was hungry; we hadn't brought all of the food with us to the site yet. Or maybe he'd wanted to go back and get his pellet gun.

"Take Kona with you," I'd said.

"No, he'll just pull me."

I'm not sure what I said next. Something about the truck not being far, about it being good for Joseph to go alone, that there was a clear path between me and the truck.

Reluctantly, he'd said okay, either because he didn't want to be afraid or because he wanted to please me. Perhaps he felt both of those things. But after about twenty minutes he hadn't returned. I stopped what I was doing to listen for him. I didn't hear his footfall approaching the camp, didn't even hear the snap of a twig. I yelled for him several times. He didn't answer. All around us was rocky ground and twisted roots. He could have fallen. He could have hit his head. He might have wandered off in the wrong direction. And we were on a high cliff. What if his footing had slipped?

"Stay," I ordered Kona, who was still tied to the tree and had already begun to whine. I sprinted for the truck, a cold film of sweat on my skin as I continued to yell for Joseph, all the while getting no answer, all the while mad at myself for not having gone to the truck with him. I hadn't thought his going to the truck alone was a big deal. I'd wanted to get the tent set up. Then I was going to prepare the fire pit and organize the food. We were going to cook hot dogs and tell stories and look up at the stars.

Joseph wasn't at the truck. I continued to yell his name. Kona had continued to whine from the campsite and had now set into barking, making it difficult for me to hear anything else. I branched off toward the west of the trail, screaming for Joseph and looking in the dirt for his footprints. How could he just disappear? He was right there. He'd wanted me to go with him.

And then, faintly, I heard his cry. "Mom!"

I cried back, "Joseph! Where are you?"

And again, "Mom!"

I was moving in the right direction. Joseph's voice was becoming louder. He was crying. He was frightened, and I had let him go to the truck alone.

Joseph and I continued to call for each other back and forth until I spotted him crouched on the top of a rock at the edge of the cliff, about fifty feet above me. He'd taken the wrong path from the truck. He must have followed a game trail that led him to the edge of a rocky ledge. He was a good half mile from the truck. He'd gotten scared and run faster, had kept running, trying to find me, until the trail had ended. There he had stopped and begun to call for me. How long he'd been calling, I didn't know. It was easy for a voice to be carried in a different direction by the wind, to get lost in the crevasses.

I climbed the fifty feet or so of rocks toward my son. I grabbed him in my arms. "I am so sorry," I said. "I am so sorry."

He tried not to cry. He tried to appear brave. "I couldn't find you," was all he said.

Yes, someone could get lost in these parts. And a person unfamiliar with the terrain might be no better at finding his or her way than a nine-year-old child.

Kona pulled at the leash, eager to get going again. I commanded him to sit, then removed his harness. The harness had let him know he was there to work. It would no longer be needed. Kona knew he was on a job. "Climb down," I ordered Kona, who had been sitting alert, watching me, waiting for my next command. I followed him to the other side of the ridge.

A small creek meandered through the gulch, its edges splotched with red twig dogwood and mountain mahogany. The ground around it, lying mostly in the shadows of rocks and trees, was soggy with mud and snow. I searched for footprints but saw only those made by big game. We crossed the creek and headed east toward Big Ridge, a thick forested range and a steep incline that led to a slick rock face. The ridge eventually turned into Cathedral Bluffs and cut through the entire East Douglas area. Having covered more than a mile of expanse and come up with nothing, no tracks, no prints, no evidence that anyone other than wildlife had been there, I directed Kona northward, moving along the base of the ridge.

We came upon one of the oil well disposal pits, about ten feet deep and fifty feet wide, with field wastes, a side effect of the oil drilling. The pit was fenced and covered with bird netting. There were probably a dozen of these in the East Douglas area. I continued to glass our surroundings, searching the high points as well, maybe because that was where I had found Joseph. I imagined the hunter crouched somewhere, holding her knees to her chest, as Joseph had done. But my search for Joseph hadn't lasted more than twenty minutes. And he'd only been missing for about as long before I'd gone looking for him. This woman had been out there all night, even longer. Death wasn't out of the question. I'd spotted a few magpies, one of Colorado's many garbage disposals, and hoped they weren't a sign. Ravens, crows, and turkey vultures would also stay around in the colder months, as long as they could find carrion food. Or the woman could be lying injured somewhere. Could have lost her footing and fallen into one of the many clefts, one of my first fears when looking for Joseph.

Kona and I continued along the base of the bluffs and slightly west toward Rocky Point Draw. I yelled the woman's name. I waited. From the ridge above us, rocks loosened, and a couple of larger rocks tumbled halfway down the incline. I yelled the woman's name again, searched the area with my binoculars. I saw movement, something brown. Kona and I climbed the ridge about sixty feet before it got too steep. To our left, I spotted a deer standing still beneath a juniper, watching us. We walked back down the ridge and followed one of the arroyos as it curved westward. The sun's descent sent glaring rays over the rocks and lighted up patches of snow like flakes of sapphire. Once more I glassed the area with my binoculars. It was then that I spotted the winter hawk, his feathers the color of smoldering ash, his eyes watching Kona and me from the branches of a dead juniper about forty yards to our north.

A whine started up in the back of Kona's throat. He'd spotted the hawk, too. The bird didn't wait for us to close in on him. He expanded his wings, slowly raised himself higher, as if stretching, and took off in flight. His talons bunched in fists and his beak widened with a screech as he soared over our heads. I had never seen a hawk that color before. I'd heard of them, knew that sometimes a young hawk's feathers could first come in as a downy gray, but this hawk wasn't young. He was a couple of feet in height and strong. The hawk disappeared over the ridge behind us. For a second, I wondered if we should follow him, if in some strange way he would point us in the direction of the missing hunter. But I didn't follow him. Instead I brushed off such thoughts and led Kona in yet another direction.

Kona and I were just cresting the upper ridge that opened up to where the black pickup was parked when static broke over the radio. "Command, Alpha One," came Colm's voice.

Alpha One had long been my radio call on search-and-rescue missions, as Kona and I were usually part of the first team out on a search.

I stopped hiking and pulled the radio off my belt clip. "Alpha One, go ahead, Command."

"Alpha One, where the hell are you?"

"I'm about fifty yards due east of the subject's vehicle."

"This is a team operation," Colm said.

"I hear you."

"I swear, Pru, I'll take you off the search."

"You can't do that. You need Kona."

"Goddamn it, Pru, I need you, too." Colm expelled a long breath, the air crackling over the radio. "We're setting up headquarters at the opening to the draw. There's an empty compressor station where you and Dean turned off to head up to the bluffs."

"I saw it," I said.

"Meet us there. We already got three other teams ready to head out. I'm assigning you with Jeff Livingston."

"What about the helicopter?" I asked.

"I've got my guys clearing a helipad now."

"It'll take me some time to get down," I said.

"Did you find any leads?"

"Kona picked up her scent a couple of times near the truck, but the snow's making it tricky."

"How long will it take you to get down to the station?" Colm asked.

"Maybe a half hour."

"Jeff should be here by then. He's on his way."

I had worked search and rescue with Jeff once before. We'd been looking for a missing backcountry skier on the outskirts of Powder-horn, just east of Grand Junction. After a full day of search operation, the twenty-one-year-old man turned up with a group of friends in Cedaredge, never having known he'd been reported missing. He'd lost his cell phone somewhere on the mountain.

I guessed Jeff to be in his late fifties. He was quiet, which I liked, not offering much about himself. I had learned from Colm that Jeff was Mormon, and that he'd had a granddaughter who'd died from falling off a horse. Jeff dealt with the tragedy by helping others with theirs. He was a cowboy in the truest sense, providing for his family from the cattle ranch he and his sons operated in Dinosaur, about twenty miles west of Rangely. He'd sip hot water instead of coffee and speak with a voice as sonorous as the guttural sigh of a working dog that had just retired at the end of a day.

As Kona and I began the decline toward the Ford truck, again he picked up the scent. I climbed into the backseat of the vehicle. Once more, I checked the ammunition case. There were enough bullets missing to load a six-round revolver. Then I picked up the compass pouch, about five by four inches. The compass wasn't there, but tucked inside a pocket in the pouch was a yellow piece of paper from a legal pad. I unfolded the paper and read a list of coordinates, as well as east declinations. The last coordinates listed matched a couple-mile-square area of the northwestern corner of East Douglas Creek, with a ten-degree east declination. I carried a small digital camera with me in the cargo pocket of my pants. I took pictures of the items, including the list of coordinates. If the compass belonged to the woman and these notes were hers, she was more than adept at using the instrument. Too often the hunters I came across knew only how to use a compass to point them in a general direction, if they even carried a compass at all. But these notes indicated that the woman not only was proficient, but also would have had the knowledge and skills to adjust the compass to the location's declination, aligning the magnetic field's north to true north. If indeed these items belonged to Amy Raye Latour, I could assume she had the instrument with her and possessed the competencies and skills of someone familiar with the wilderness, or at least someone who had planned ahead before venturing out on her own.

Amy Raye

No more than a half mile in, her headlamp burned out. She dislodged her pack and rummaged through its contents, only to find she'd left the extra batteries at camp. Memory would have to carry her until the sun rose. She stepped lightly, her body cutting through the blackness of the early morning and blending into the moist reed grass and saltbush. The air felt dense in her lungs, cold and wet. She was climbing in elevation with another mile to go to the tree stand, a platform barely two feet square, with a seat less than half that size, anchored fifteen feet from the ground in the boughs of a sprawling pinyon.

She'd placed a couple of reflector tags on trees the day before, but without her light, there was no way to identify them. The air grated in her lungs. Her saliva tasted metallic. She stopped a few times to slow her breathing and to avoid a sweat. She wondered if she might be lost, and for a moment she thought of Kenny. He knew this country better than she, had hunted it before, having grown up nearby. It might not have been a bad idea to have him along.

Kenny and she had not made love on this trip, though she was certain he'd thought they would. Things had changed between them, had changed for her. Kenny had it all wrong. Of course she still loved her husband. She always had.

These were her thoughts as the incline began to level off and feel familiar, with less deadfall and vegetation. Yes, she was sure of it. She found the tree. She tied her bow to the thin nylon rope that hung from the stand, then climbed to the platform, stepping and pulling her way up by the metal pegs set into the trunk, careful not to catch her pack on branches. When she reached the top, she secured extra webbing around the trunk of the tree and hooked it into the carabiner on the back of her harness. She hung her pack on a peg, then hoisted her bow. She checked her watch. Not yet six o'clock. The sky was still black, blotted by a plush layer of clouds. She felt a sense of invisibility in the tree, in the outline of its mass, as she waited for daylight, as a muscle across her shoulder relaxed and she thought of other places she had been, the tree stands and blinds she'd set over the years, the mornings like this one.

She was seventeen the first time she'd hunted alone. She'd headed out from her grandfather's farm to a blind he'd built especially for her. She'd spotted a small buck, held him in her cross hair, before passing up the shot. But now, what she remembered most was the time she spent blending into the trees and foliage, and the calm that came over her. She'd been shy as a child. When she was alone in the woods, she felt safe. Even after hunting season was over and the guns were cleaned and put away, she would walk to the blind and sit for hours. No one would come looking for her. And after a while, she'd walk back to the house in time to help her grandmother with supper. Her grandfather would be sitting in his recliner reading the newspaper. He'd lower the paper just enough to see Amy Raye, and she'd know he was smiling, could see it in the way the skin around his eyes creased slightly upward. He wouldn't say anything. He would just look at her, and then raise the paper and resume reading, and she'd know that he understood where she'd been, as if he recognized the light on her face, could smell the air on her skin.

Before she left Tennessee for the last time, she drove by her grandparents' farm. Their truck was gone, so she assumed they weren't home. She hiked through the meadow and into the woods. It was a spring day, and the hawthorns and wild chokecherries were in bloom. She decided to check on the pond. She'd helped her grandfather stock the pond just the month before. She walked quietly, her boots landing as gently as moccasins, and all around her were the trills of the Tennessee warbler, the high whistles of the tree frogs, and the calling of the cricket frogs, like two small pebbles being tapped together.

A little deeper into the woods she saw him sitting in an ordinary lawn chair. Her grandfather's hands, like two enormous bear paws, cupped his knees. His feet were planted out in front of him. His head was tilted back and his eyes were closed. She placed her palm flat against the rough bark of an oak tree, stood still, and watched him. She wondered what it was that, like her, called him to this place. And after a while, as quietly as she'd approached, she left the woods that day. She walked past the fields and the pasture, and back down to the barn where she had parked her truck. She climbed in and drove away.

Pru

By the time I made it down the mountain to the command station, the sky had turned a deep navy. Searching in the dark wasn't new to me, or to any of the search team members, for that matter. Rescue missions could operate all through the night if the weather cooperated. But the winds and the weather in these parts could turn as quickly as a car on slick pavement. Colm would be keeping a direct channel open with Weather Control out of both the Rangely airport and Grand Junction Regional Airport, the larger commercial airport in Grand Junction. If he got word that the wind or snow would be picking up, he'd radio in his teams and call it a night. Colm's first priority always was to protect his crew.

As I pulled up to the metal building, I counted three deputy vehicles and recognized the other four trucks as belonging to longtime search-and-rescue volunteers.

Across the road from the warehouse was the helipad, a flat clearing with a radius of about forty feet.

I left Kona in the Tahoe and entered the command station.

"I told you he wouldn't be happy," Dean said when he saw me.

"He'll get over it."

"How did Kona make out?"

"Nothing," I said.

Jeff approached me. "Good to see you, Pru."

"Not the best of circumstances," I said.

Jeff's head tilted forward in an affirming nod. He wore a cowboy hat. He'd worn a cowboy hat on the last search, and I wondered why his ears never got too cold.

Two thirds of the space inside the command station was devoted to search equipment including the dispatcher radio, maps, a couple of computers, and a large GPS unit — all of which were lined up on three long folding tables. Colm was standing behind one of the tables, his hands on its edge, his body leaning over a large map. "We're going to work a two-mile radius tonight," he was telling one of the teams. "We'll be lucky if we can even cover that much in this vertical country. We've got six hours at best before another storm is supposed to blow in."

I walked over to the table where Colm was giving a briefing to the volunteers. He'd divided the search area into quadrants that branched out from the site of the black Ford, determined as the point last seen. When Colm saw me, he pointed on the map to the quadrant in the northeast corner. "You and Jeff will cover this area," he said. "Go in as deep as you can, but be careful. And listen closely to your radio. The weather might turn. How did your Tahoe make it back in there?" Colm asked.

"No trouble," I said. My vehicle had been adjusted with a four-inch suspension lift, allowing me to get around as well as any of the pickup trucks, and sometimes better with the extra weight.

"The other teams are taking ATVs in. Dean's going to load you up with the stretcher and first-aid gear. Go ahead and drive your Tahoe in, but if the trails start freezing over, use your judgment."

"How many other teams are you sending out tonight?"

"I've got three out already. The chopper should be here soon. Dean and one of the volunteers will be heading out with the pilot, a guy by the name of Franklin. The other volunteers will be maintaining the containment search."

A containment search consisted of sirens and flashing lights from trucks driven up and down the pipeline roads, hoping to attract the subject's attention.

"It may be against protocol, but I wish we'd started searching last night," I said.

"Looks like her friends already did." Colm inclined his head toward the other end of the building, where a group of men were standing around a wood stove. "Course without their truck they couldn't get very far. They've been up all night. We're lucky we're not searching for them as well."

I gauged fairly quickly which of the men were from the hunting party and which were the volunteers. The two men from Evergreen were camp-dirty, wearing damp coveralls splattered with mud and something darker — most likely blood from one or both of their kills. Their faces were unshaven. Their shoulders slouched beneath their Carhartt coats. One of the men looked like he was in his thirties. Waves of thick red hair bunched up between the edge of his cap and the collar of his coat. The other man might have been a good fifteen years older. He was heavyset, several inches shorter than the first man, and had a black beard, streaked with gray.

"Go easy if you talk to them," Colm said.

"They've already beat the shit out of themselves."

"What about the family?" I asked.

"The husband's on his way. Should be here in a couple of hours."

I asked Colm about the compass pouch and the notes I'd found.

"Could be hers. I'll check with her friends."

I looked at Jeff. "You ready?"

He blinked slowly and ever so subtly tipped his head.

There was something about a search that was compelling and heady. The urgency, the meticulous use of the senses, and the desperate need to replace what was missing, to smooth out what had become so devastatingly out of sorts. Perhaps Jeff felt all of these things as well. In the quiet of his deliberate movements, I liked to think that he did.

While climbing in the Tahoe to leave, I saw the helicopter approach. It floated toward the rough patch of gravel and snow. Despite the helicopter's loud percussion, I was able to make out Colm's voice over the radio as he gave the pilot a summary of the search mission's operations, the hunter's point last seen, and GPS coordinates. Dean and one of the volunteers walked out of the headquarters and rounded the building, making their way across the road toward the helicopter, their bodies withdrawing into their parkas and hoods as they braced themselves against the cold air and biting wind.

I backed my Tahoe away from the command station and began my climb up the narrow road toward the ridge. Jeff and I spoke little on the way up. I filled him in on my earlier search, on the broken scent trails and dead ends. The rest of our conversation was small talk.

"How's your family?' I asked.

"Family's good," Jeff said.

And later, "Everything okay on the ranch?"

"Can't complain. What about you?" he asked. "How's that boy of yours?"

"He's good," I said. "Home game this weekend. Rio Mesa versus Hayden. Last game of the season."

"Those are good times," Jeff said.

"Yes, they are."

I wanted to hold on to every one of those good times, as if at any moment they might be taken away. I was forty-two with no plans of having another child. I hadn't planned on Joseph either, and every day I counted my blessings that he was in my life. And sometimes I wondered if Joseph was the child Brody and I would have had, if in some strange way Brody had played a hand in it all.

I didn't always live in Rio Mesa. I'd grown up in a suburb just west of Liberty, Missouri, where until a year after high school, I'd lived my whole life. Brody had lived his whole life there as well. My father owned a feed barn, Mercantile Co-Op. We lived in a farmhouse, owned chickens. My upstairs bedroom overlooked hayfields, several hundred acres that would later be sold and subdivided. But I didn't realize that at the time. I was young, and I had the fields to explore.

Brody's family grew corn and sorghum. The Lidells lived a couple of miles from me in a brick ranch they had built before Brody was born. The original homestead was situated about two hundred yards away from their house. The family rented the homestead to groups of out-of-state pheasant hunters from November through January.

Brody and I were both sixteen. His hair was golden brown and his eyes were sky blue. He looked like he could be president one day, like he would grow up and do something important like John F. Kennedy, wear a coat and tie, talk to important people. We didn't know sex yet. We were good kids, the kind who would do what was right for the rest of their lives. He was already six foot three, and would probably grow another inch or two before we were finished with high school.

It was fall of our sophomore year. I'd been a runner for what felt like my whole life. I ran through the fields behind the house, ran after the chickens, ran the two miles to Brody's house, ran on the cross-country team at school. Classes had ended for the day. Brody had gone home, was working on the farm, driving the combine. I had dressed for practice and had met my teammates outside. We were going to run trails that day. I could smell the soil and leaves. We hit the pavement first, down a street, across another. I watched the guys take off. The girls were farther behind. I ran with a girl named Julie. There was an opening in some trees between the two houses. We left the pavement. My legs felt lithe and strong. We could no longer hear the boys. And the other girls, about five of them, had dropped far behind. We were now running downhill. I decided to sprint. My left ankle turned out. My leg buckled beneath me.

Julie came up from behind. "I'll get help,"

she said. She ran ahead. I lay back on the ground, pulled my left knee to my chest.

I heard the other girls approaching. "Julie's gone to get help," I told them. They moved on.

Time passed. I heard Julie's voice. I heard Brody's. He knelt next to me, scooped me up, his T-shirt damp with sweat. How did she find him, I wanted to know.

"I can walk," I said.

"I'll carry you," he said.

I wanted to make it back for Joseph's game, but I knew that would be unlikely if the search was still going on. That morning, before Joseph had left for school, I'd told him about the missing hunter. Told him I'd probably be called on the search. I'd asked him if he could spend the night at Corey's if I wasn't back. "I hope she's okay," Joseph had said. He'd understand if I couldn't make the game.

Climbing the final stretch to where Amy Raye Latour had left the truck was tricky in the dark, and the surface of snow and rock was freezing together into a precarious conglomerate, causing the Tahoe's wheels to slide just enough for me to grip the wheel tightly and straighten them out.

I parked the Tahoe in the same area as the

other teams' ATVs and the black Ford. One of the deputies would be driving the Ford back to the sheriff's station that night and canvassing it for evidence before releasing it to its owner. I wondered how long the other hunters would stay on, and hoped to God they wouldn't be making the four-hour drive back to Evergreen without their friend.

I opened up the back of the Tahoe, letting Kona out. This time I left the tracking harness in the truck. He already knew he was there to work.

Jeff and I secured our headlamps and turned them onto high beam. We each carried a large flashlight and backpacks with basic first-aid gear, water, food, extra batteries for our radios, and pouches of air-activated warmers for our hands and feet. I opened up the plastic bag with the hunter's mittens and held it to Kona's nose. His tail wagged as eagerly as before. He yipped a couple of times. "Let's go find," I said. He took off through the woods that lined the elliptical edge of the draw, this time heading north along the ridge of the bluffs. I wondered how he had missed this scent earlier in the day, but then realized the wind had changed directions, and though we were heading north, we were now moving downwind. Jeff and I followed Kona's lead.

Even with our flashlights it was slow going in the dark. Deadfall and rocks lined our pathway, not to mention the slick snow covering. About eighty yards into the woods, we came upon a wall of boulders, steep yet passable. "Climb," I said to Kona. He jumped and made switchbacks, and jumped again until he was at the top. Jeff and I looked for handholds — roots of juniper, tightly wedged rock points, or cracks, in which case we removed our gloves and dug our fingers into the tight crevices for support. Most of the climbing was legwork. Once at the top, we spotted the helicopter and another team's set of lights.

"If she were conscious, she'd hear the chopper," I said.

"Maybe not," Jeff said. "Sounds can fool a person out here. Especially if you're in one of the canyons or ravines."

Something moved about fifty feet to our left. I turned. The light from my headlamp caught the glowing eyes and white horns of a buck. Then the small male, with no more than two points on each side of his rack, turned and ran in the opposite direction, his feet tapping against the frozen ground, his body sweeping through the branches and oak brush. Jeff and I moved on.

Our night continued much the same, with

occasional crackles over the radio and voices from other team members checking in with Colm.

"Search Two, Command," came a voice from one of the volunteers.

"Command, go ahead," Colm said.

"We're over a mile in. Negative on any prints or signs of the subject."

GPS coordinates were then given, which I knew Colm was marking on the station's master map.

Occasionally, Colm's voice broke the radio's silence. "Command, Air One. Anything?"

But the pilot's report remained the same as everyone else's.

The wind bit and stirred beneath my layers of clothing, running currents over my skin, despite the working of my muscles.

"The weather's changing," I told Jeff.

"I think you're right."

"Don't your ears get cold?" I asked.

"Frostbite got them years back. I don't feel a thing."

Though we reported in to Colm every half hour or so, we had no news other than the points of our location. Kona picked up no scent either.

"We're in the wrong place," I finally said. "Kona's not getting anything. Not even a trace from the wind."

"Despite these clear skies, some snow fell pretty hard last night," Jeff said. "Blue Mountain got hit with more than a foot."

Blue Mountain was just west and slightly north of Rangely.

"If she's covered in snow, then she's not alive." I hated the way those words sounded. And yet I felt something true in what I'd said. For the most part, Kona was an air-scent dog, but because of his cadaver training in avalanche certification, he was considered a trailing dog as well. Other than a few earlier traces near the subject's vehicle, so far Kona wasn't showing any sign of air scent associated with the subject. If a person was covered by snow — during sleep or unconsciousness or in a state of hypothermia — the person's body heat would melt some of the accumulation, which, as temperatures dropped, would freeze around the person, sealing off the body's scent. The subject might then just as well be trapped under frozen water. In those cases, Kona would be of no help. Because of the winds, the low humidity of the West, and the ground's topography, snow accumulation in a single mile radius could vary dramatically, from a couple of inches where it might have scattered like fine grains of flour, to large mounds or drifts piling up several feet in arroyos and rocky fractures.

Jeff and Kona and I covered more ground, and after about twenty minutes we came upon one of the oil well disposal pits.

"Don't suppose she fell into one of these," Jeff said.

"It would have to be a deliberate suicide attempt. And there are much better ways to commit suicide than that," I told him.

As we continued on, I felt something taking hold of me — something black and looming. Despite Jeff's and Kona's presence, this was pure aloneness. Maybe it was from the thought of someone falling into one of the disposal pits, or maybe it was triggered by the very fact that we were looking for someone missing, someone integral to a community of life. It was the same kind of loneliness I had felt after Brody was gone, a kind of companion, that in some ways I was still afraid to live without.

More than four hours had passed when Colm made the call. "Command, calling all search teams. We've got a large storm pattern due west of here. It's moving in quicker than we'd thought. Start making your way back to the command station."

Each group responded in turn to Colm's call — Alpha One, Team Two, Team Three, and so on.

"Colm's right," Jeff said. "You can taste the snow. Feel it blowing in."

I knew what Jeff was talking about. I tasted it, too, like a faint mineral deposit on the back of my tongue, a cold in my airways that burned metallic. We hiked the two miles to the vehicle and then drove back to the station.

Kona followed Jeff and me into the command headquarters. A group of people — mostly men, a couple of women — were talking to Colm around one of the tables. Colm motioned Jeff and me over to him. "I want you to meet someone," he said. "This is Farrell Latour. Amy Raye's husband."

When Farrell said hello, I was surprised by the timbre of his voice, much like a teenage boy's. He carried a down parka in the crook of his right arm and wore Sorel boots that laced up to his knees. He'd come to find his wife. I was certain the two men from the hunting party had wanted to search as well. I also knew their assistance wouldn't be allowed. These men weren't trained in search and rescue, and any fresh track they made would have to be looked at as a potential sign of our missing person.

The husband had brought pictures. Colm had laid them on the table.

"This one was taken over the summer," Farrell said as he pointed to a photo. The woman's hair was dark blond. She wore a Rockies cap, was holding a bottle of beer. She was smiling coyly, as if teasing the person behind the camera. Her eyes were brown.

I looked at another picture. The husband picked it up.

"This is our boy, Trevor. He's four." Farrell set the picture down and picked up another one. "This is Julia. She's twelve."

"You have a beautiful family," Jeff said.

Farrell laid the picture on the table, still holding on to the photo's edges.

"Where are the kids now?" I asked.

"With my sister," Farrell said.

I cupped my hand over his shoulder. I almost said, *We'll find her. Don't worry.* But I couldn't. What if we didn't?

I walked over to the stove, removed my gloves, and began to warm my hands. Jeff joined me. He would be heading home to Dinosaur to get some sleep before the next shift. The rest of the search members would be staying at a hotel in Rangely. I was used to these kinds of unexpected interruptions. They were part of the job. I kept a small duffel bag packed with my necessary toiletries and basic clothing, as well as food for

Kona, in the Tahoe.

"I'll be back in the morning," Jeff told me. "Maybe earlier if the storm lets up and Colm sends us out again."

"Drive safely," I said.

I was sure Jeff sensed my defeat, and I knew he felt it, too. "Hang in there," he told me.

I inhaled deeply, letting the warm air from the stove seep into my cold lungs. I hated to admit even to myself that I was tired. But I was. "At this point, that's all we can do," I said.

After Jeff left, I sat on one of the metal folding chairs. Kona sat in front of me. I wrapped my arms around him, buried my nose in his fur. I thought of Amy Raye and her husband before Amy Raye had left home. Imagined him hugging her good-bye, telling her to be safe.

Colm laid a hand on my head. I was still wearing my fleece hat. He offered me a cup of coffee. "It's decaf," he said. "You need your sleep."

"You heading to town soon?"

"Still waiting for two of the containment volunteers to check in." Colm pulled up a chair beside me and sat down. "I checked with the hunting party. The compass was hers," Colm said.

"Any other ideas of what she might have had with her?" I asked.

"They said she kept waterproof matches in her pack. A fire-starter kit. She would have had her map. They weren't sure what else."

"She wasn't new to this sort of thing," I said.

"No, apparently not. Of course, with this weather, I don't see how she could get a fire going. Not with the storm we got moving in." Colm leaned forward, his forearms on his knees, a cup of coffee in his right hand. "There's something else. A couple of the volunteers were checking out Coal Draw, just west of where you and Jeff were. A big tomcat was following them. One of them turned around and caught the cougar's eyes with his headlamp before the thing took off."

"How close was it?"

"Twenty yards."

"Damn."

"I'm just saying." Colm gulped down his coffee.

"Did you let the other volunteers know?"

"It's one of the reasons I called everyone in."

"That's not a lion's natural behavior to get that close," I said.

"Unless it's hungry. Snow's coming early this season. Hunters have already been through the area, firing their guns, scaring off the game."

"What are you thinking?"

Colm looked over his shoulder as if making sure the woman's husband wasn't anywhere in earshot. Then he stared forward again.

"He couldn't even picture the area," Colm said. "He's never been out here before. Do you find that odd?"

"The husband?"

"Yeah."

"That may not be so odd. Maybe he doesn't hunt. This could have been her thing. Mother's day out."

"Yeah? I thought moms went to the mall or to a day at the spa."

"Not every woman fits Maggie's description."

"Maggie was never a mom."

"Sounds like you're still getting over her," I said.

"I'm just trying to put this whole thing together."

"Maggie or Amy Raye?"

Colm didn't like what I'd said, and he let me know so by the way he looked at me.

I held up my hand. "Sorry."

I changed the subject. "Cattle wander off cliffs on nights like this," I said. "What's the weather report for tomorrow?"

"Doesn't look good. Supposed to get new snow. Little change in the wind. You turn around after five minutes and your tracks are already gone."

Frustration was getting to both of us. We'd already put in almost a full day of search without finding a single clue as to the woman's whereabouts. Not to mention we were almost into the third day since the woman's disappearance.

"I know this isn't avalanche country," I said. "But there are some windrows beneath a number of the overhangs in the higher elevation. Could she be buried in the snow?"

"Could be."

"You've thought of that."

"I've thought about it. It's not likely, but it's possible."

"Any ideas?" I asked.

"Mesa County has a new electronic detection device. It picks up energy off watches, cell phones, handheld radios. It can pick up a frequency as much as eighty meters away, as long as there is insulation."

"Meaning snow."

"Yeah."

Colm sipped his coffee. I held mine to my

face, tasted the steam.

"One of their deputies is bringing it out to us tomorrow," Colm said.

"You wouldn't think the snow was deep enough."

"It's not, but like you said, there's some drifts."

"You know what you're saying?"

Colm nodded. "We'd be looking for a body, not a live person."

"We'd be switching to search and recovery," I said.

"It's too early to call it that yet."

Farrell approached us, stood next to Colm. "Can I ask you something? How long can she stay out there? Realistically, how long could she make it?"

Colm looked to me before answering. This was turning into the first multiday search we'd had in Paisaje County in five years, and the last had ended successfully with a backcountry skier finding a vacant cabin after spending only one night outside. People usually turned up within the first twenty-four hours. Men were the worst. They grossly underestimated distance and their ability. Women typically stayed put. Colm could tell Farrell we were at an advantage. We were looking for a woman.

"Maybe a few days. Maybe a week. We just

don't know," Colm said.

That night as I lay on the double bed in the small hotel room, drafts of cold from the window blew in. I thought of Amy Raye Latour out there in the cold. And I thought of her husband, in a part of the state he'd most likely never been before, by himself in another one of these rooms. I wanted to tell him I understood. But the truth was, no one can really understand what another person is going through. I didn't know what it felt like for him to hold his wife, to sleep by her side, what it felt like to bring a child into the world with her.

Kona, who had been lying beside me, stretched his torso and plopped his head on my chest. I stroked the short, silky hair on his ears. His mouth made a slight smacking sound.

I tried to calculate how far Amy Raye might have traveled from the truck. Typically when hunting for big game a person stayed within one, at most two miles of the vehicle. Packing an animal out any more than that could be an enormous feat. Perhaps she'd traveled farther from her truck than our search group had first anticipated, especially if she'd been bugling back and forth with a male.

I'd suggest to Colm that we expand our search. If the woman had been pursuing an elk, it would have been easy for her to become lost even with a compass. People rarely checked their maps when in the heat of a chase, and once someone was lost, panic could drive a person farther in the wrong direction. By the time she checked with her compass, she wouldn't have known where she was on the map, so there was a chance her directional device would have done her little good. This inhospitable country looked much the same, whichever way one looked.

There was another possibility. She might have gotten a shot, and if she hadn't made a clean shot, she could have tracked the animal for miles, possibly never finding him.

I'd talk to Colm. We'd have to expand our search. Maybe he was awake.

The wind rattled the windowpanes. The storm was moving in. I climbed out of bed, walked over to the large window, and pulled the curtain aside. My room was on the second floor, with an exterior door to a concrete walkway. The sky looked black and thick, like soot, despite the handful of parking lamps below. I opened the door, leaned my torso out. The temperature felt warmer than when I'd first turned in, maybe by ten degrees, the air more humid. In these parts, a warm trend nearly always preceded a snowstorm. Colm's room was three doors from mine. I stepped onto the cement and looked to my right. His light was off. Then I looked toward the lights in the parking lot to see if there was any snow coming down; the darkness and the overhang had made it difficult for me to tell. I thought I detected the beginnings of flurries, or else the wind was picking up flakes off the trucks. I stood there like that for a few minutes more, letting the cold and damp awaken my skin, stood there staring out over the vehicles, recognizing most of them as belonging to volunteers on the search. The whole thing was peaceful, as if I were the only living soul awake.

I closed the door and climbed back into bed. Kona was still lying at the foot of the covers. Despite my stirrings, he hadn't moved.

"Hey, boy," I said, nudging him with my foot.

I lay on my back, pulled the covers up to my chin. Kona moaned, a long sigh that rumbled in the back of his throat.

When I awoke I checked my watch on the nightstand. Four o'clock. I made coffee in the four-cup carafe in the bathroom. I took a shower. As I finished dressing, there was a knock on the door.

"Saw your light on," Colm said. A dusting of snow covered the shoulders of his jacket.

"I see the snow's coming down." I shut the door behind him.

"Four inches so far, and we're in the valley."

"Want some coffee?"

"I was going to ask you the same."

I walked back to the bathroom and filled two cups. When I returned, Colm was sitting on the foot of the bed next to Kona. I handed Colm a coffee and sat on top of the desk, facing him.

"We need to go out farther, expand our probability of area," I said.

"I was thinking a couple more miles."

My face settled into a slow smile of acknowledgment. "You didn't sleep much either."

"No."

"Your light was out."

"So was yours."

"So, what are your thoughts?"

Colm didn't waste any time. "We found the truck. We know she is there. We should have a hundred percent probability of area. So, one, she couldn't find her way back to the truck, panicked, and wandered off in the wrong direction. Two, she spotted an elk, maybe got a shot, traveled too far away from her base and wound up lost. Except if she was an experienced hunter and she was on a blood trail, she would have left marking tape. So she probably didn't get a shot, or else we haven't spotted the tape. Three, she got cold."

"But she had matches."

"Doesn't mean she was able to get a fire going. If she got caught up in that rain yesterday, she would have been soaked down to the bone. And that kind of cold can make a person stop thinking straight. People should learn from the animals," Colm said. "Find a warm spot and hunker down for the night."

"Maybe she did. Maybe we just didn't look in the right places."

"Maybe."

"Did you give any more thought to the lion?"

"Thought about it," he said.

"And?"

"That's another reason I want to expand the search. If a lion got her, Kona should still be able to pick up her scent."

Colm held his right hand over the top of the cup and was tapping the rim lightly, a gesture I'd seen him do before when he was thinking about something. "I put in a call to Glade," Colm said. Glade Caswell had spent the summer before surveying the canyon for cliff dwellings. "I wanted to know if he'd seen any old cache sites in the area," Colm said.

"What'd he say?"

"Said he found a cache northeast of Coal Draw on the top of the bluff, though he thinks it's pretty old. Found some cattle bones in there. A cow probably wandered off on open range. He wouldn't be surprised if there were other cache sites. He gave me some coordinates of some other areas to check out."

"Jeff and I were just up there."

"I know you were."

"What are you thinking?" I asked.

"Suppose our missing hunter isn't lost. Suppose we got a cougar out there who got to her. I'm thinking we ought to be looking for areas where there might be a cache."

"Jeff and I can do that," I said.

"If there's anything up there, it's going to be hidden in some pretty steep terrain."

I moved over to the foot of the bed and sat down, with Kona stretched out between Colm and me. "I'm not one of the volunteers. This is what I do. And Jeff knows this country and has hunted lion on his ranch for years. He's better than any of the deputies you have."

Colm's heavy hand braced my knee for just a second. "I want you to be careful," he said. "And I want you both to have guns with you. If there's a fresh cache up there, that cougar's not going to like you coming around."

I kept a .40-caliber Sig Sauer pistol in my glove compartment. I also had a Ruger Mini-14 patrol rifle and a 12-gauge Remington shotgun in the backseat of my vehicle, and I knew Jeff had a rifle in his truck.

"We'll bring our guns," I said.

Amy Raye

Twenty long minutes passed. Daylight could seem like an eternity away, especially in the cold. Amy Raye's body began to stiffen. She had to go to the bathroom. She shouldn't have drunk so much coffee. The morning would probably be long, another four hours in the tree stand if she didn't get a shot. This was the part she hated. Men had it easy. She slung her bow over a branch, took an empty water bottle with a wide opening from her pack, and lowered her pants to her knees. Supported by the harness, she leaned away from the trunk. She'd done this enough times, and for the most part was good at it, catching the urine in the bottle so as not to mark her spot. She shivered from the cold against her bare skin and the dampness of her clothes. The warm liquid ran onto her hand. She stopped midstream, not wanting to drip onto the stand, all the while cursing her mishap, mouthing the words silently. She screwed the lid onto the bottle, buried it in her pack, and sopped and lathered her hands in elk estrus, the pungent, sweet scent burning her nostrils and lingering in her throat like the residue of a bad taste.

She strapped her release onto her right hand and settled into her seat. With her bow on her lap, she fitted her best arrow into the nock point, wrapped her left index finger over the arrow shaft to steady it on the rest, and waited.

Hunting with a bow during rifle season was a mix of science and fate. It would be difficult to bugle an elk in close enough for a shot. They weren't as trusting once rifle season had started. For the most part, she would have to stalk the elk, knowing his feeding patterns, where he bedded down for the night. Do her homework. The day before when she'd first come upon the stand, she'd seen the signs of elk: the warm hollows in the timber where they'd slept, the rubbings on the juniper and pinyon, the pools of water saturated with prints and smudges from where they had wallowed, the scat, the urine. She'd been careful to remain upwind of the area. Yes, she was in a good spot.

Light rose from behind her like a blood-orange tide, slowly spilling its color through the clouds and between the branches of the timber. She circumnavigated the area with her eyes, identifying various landmarks for points of yardage. Running parallel about fifteen yards in front of her was a wall of four mature pinyon, the first two locking their branches together in an arc, creating an oblong ellipse through which Amy Raye could view the grassy clearing beyond.

With the light of dawn, the woods were no longer silent, a good sign. Amy Raye's presence had gone unnoticed. Camp robbers flushed through trees, the swish of air against their wings like the heavy breathing and snorting of a bull elk. Squirrels ran up trunks, leapt from one branch to another, simulating the hooves of an elk breaking ground, snapping twigs and deadfall in its path. Amy Raye's nerves felt like live wire conducting each sound. Keeping her head and body still, she swept her eyes back and forth over her surroundings.

Then a sudden slap in her lungs, that shortening of breath as she spotted him through the opening in the trees in front of her. Quickly, she did a range check, pinned her eyes on a landmark thirty yards to her left, and drew an imaginary border around the area's circumference as if she were the compass point. The elk was directly in line, standing broadside, an exact thirty yards, she was sure. She gauged his brow tine at roughly ten to twelve inches and counted four points from each side of his rack. With the forty-five pounds she was pulling, he was within reach of a clean shot. She raised her bow. The thirty-yard pin on her scope locked on the branches in front of her. She calculated the arc of the arrow. It should rise the fifteen yards and clear the opening. She drew her bow, steadied her left arm. She wondered if her breath would skew her aim. She held the air tight in her lungs. The elk turned his head, his eyes frozen at a direct point with her own. Seconds moved between them like rainwater through mud. She flexed her shoulders, creating enough back tension to discharge the release. The arrow sailed, cleared the trees, and made contact with the animal, its impact like a sharp clap against plywood. The elk pivoted and sprang in one broad leap back into the wall of timber from which he had emerged, his body crashing through the woods, snapping and breaking limbs.

The noise pulled away from her, the distance and trees and soil absorbing it like a vacuum. Eventually, all that remained was time and silence. The rule was to wait it out a half hour at least before tracking an animal. An hour was better. To move too quickly, to track him now, would kick in the fight-and-flight. When an elk knew he was being chased, his adrenaline would push him farther than he would go on his own, and the stress before his death could have a negative impact on the meat.

Amy Raye looked for landmarks, anything to pinpoint where the elk had stood. She knew it would look different once she was on the ground, and to track him successfully would mean knowing at exactly which place to begin the search. She spotted a large rock and made a mental note of it, as well as the profile of trees into which the elk had disappeared. So she would wait. And she would pray, because that was what she had always done when she'd taken down an elk or a deer. She would say the Lord's Prayer. "Say it like you mean it," her grandfather had taught her. "Then when it's time, climb down from your perch and find the damn thing."

And so she began to pray: "Our Father, who art in heaven, hallowed be thy name. . . ." She prayed for the animal. She prayed for her children — Julia, whom she loved as her own, and Trevor. And she prayed for Farrell. "Bless him, Lord. Push his day along with a happy grace. Keep him safe."

Farrell, as kind as anyone had ever been to her. At that moment, she wanted nothing more than to be wrapped in his arms and against his warm skin. She missed him with a terrible ache. Wished she could take him to all the places she had known, take him back in time to something pure, to summer and horses, and the farm she used to love. To the sheep and meadows and milk thistle, and her grandfather reading war novels to her when she couldn't sleep.

"Dear Lord, I don't deserve him. Look after him, I pray."

Pru

I followed Colm to the command post. Jeff was standing outside when we got there.

"Mornin'," he said, with a slight tip of the head.

"Morning," I said. "Sleep all right?"

"Not too bad. You?"

"I managed a few hours."

"I don't think the husband did."

"Is he here?" I asked.

"Pretty sure he never left."

Inside the metal housing, I saw Farrell sitting in a chair by the stove talking on a cell phone. He was wearing the same clothes he'd had on the night before.

About six of the team volunteers had already arrived and were waiting to get started. Colm motioned them to the command table where he would be making his assignments. I went over to check on the husband. He was now holding his phone down to his side.

"Can I get you anything?" I asked.

"No, I'm fine." He glanced my way briefly before looking once again through a frost-covered window. His eyes were a soft blue like his daughter's.

"I was thinking about this story Amy Raye would tell the kids, about a young Cherokee woman. She escaped from the Trail of Tears. Instead of moving to Oklahoma, she made her way across the Tennessee plateau and into the mountains. Amy Raye would tell the children stories of the woman living off the woods, making traps with her bare hands. She said Amadahy means Forest Water. That was the woman's name. 'Tell us another Forest Water story,' Julia would say. And so Amy Raye would make up another adventure."

Farrell was silent for a solid minute, and then he said, "Amadahy walked clear to the other side of the mountains, so the legend goes. She settled in North Carolina."

I reached out and squeezed Farrell's arm gently. "We're not giving up," I told him.

At the briefing, Colm assigned each team extended rays of operation from the truck's location, or the subject's point last seen. The members were to mark their tracks and radio back at measured points. Three volunteers would be arriving shortly from Mesa County with the electronic detection device. Colm had prepared area maps indicating snowdrift and high accumulation sites.

One of the reporters from the *Sentinel* stopped me on my way out. She asked me about Kona, how long had he been a search dog, was he avalanche certified as well. She wanted to know what my thoughts were on why we weren't finding any more marking tape, and did I think the woman had gotten lost early in her hunt.

"The snow was coming down heavily," I reminded her. "You get out in that kind of weather, you can't see three feet in front of you. There was a lot of wind up here yesterday. Maybe she tied more markers and we're just not seeing them," I said.

By daybreak the snow had come to a stop and the winds had settled down to twenty miles per hour. If the visibility and change in wind speed continued to improve, Colm would be able to get a helicopter back on search. No one was prepared to scale back. If anything, we would push harder, prepared for twenty-hour shifts if the storm held back. This was all we had. Third day. Chances of Amy Raye's survival were running out, as was Kona's ability to pick up a trail. No one wanted to think of another day without any leads. The search team's demeanor was all business.

I parked the truck at the base of the hill climb. Jeff loaded his .30-06 automatic. I strapped on my holster with my handgun and loaded my target rifle.

With the break in the storm, I'd told Colm I wanted to spend the first morning light glassing in a grid, the same strategy I'd used with Glade when canvassing an area for cultural sites. Had we missed any marking tape or some sort of flag of clothing? I might also be able to catch sight of the lion. It would be a long day, with us covering as much as seven miles by nightfall. We needed to make every step count.

I unlocked a box in the back of the Tahoe where I kept a high-powered spotting scope, two tripods, and oversized binoculars, 15×60mm. The higher-power lens would increase the magnification by fifteen times, and the sixty-millimeter lens diameter would adjust for the lower field of view. I fitted the optics, along with water and food, inside my pack. Jeff offered to carry the tripods. I used extra webbing to strap them onto the sides of his pack.

I had spent the previous day glassing the area with 10×40mm binoculars. Other than some initial scent leads near the location of the vehicle and the northern ridge of the trail, I, along with everyone else, had come up with nothing except a couple of strips of faded marking tape left over from a previous season, which the volunteers had removed. And now, finding tracks beneath so much new snowfall was less than promising. Even dogs trained for avalanche search and rescue would have a difficult time finding a scent with these kinds of winds. Each layer of ground cover had been too disturbed, resembling eddies on the surface of a stream, with few, if any, depressions.

With Kona leading a few feet in front of us, we hiked up the steep hill, easing back into the terrain we'd searched extensively the day before. Once at the top, I unpacked the optics and set up the spotting scope and the high-powered binoculars on the tripods Jeff had carried.

"Why don't you use the spotting scope," I told Jeff. "Mark off grids in your mind. Then pan back and forth till you've covered each grid," I said.

Jeff stood next to me, his torso slightly bent, while he looked through the scope. Using the high-powered binoculars, I glassed the skyline, then adjusted the glasses just enough to the right so that the left-hand edge of my field of view slightly overlapped with the far right-hand edge. Kona sat beside me, each movement of his head and eyes appearing as calculated as my own. For a moment I thought I'd identified one of the other search teams but then realized the team would have been in the wrong location. I readjusted the binoculars.

"Looks like we have a couple of new folks on the search." I was still squinting behind the binoculars. "The two guys from Evergreen."

"Can you blame them?"

"Did they get their truck back?" I asked.

"Supposed to get it back today. Been getting a ride in with one of the volunteers."

Static broke across Jeff's and my radios, and an occasional correspondence between Colm and the different teams, but nothing was said that would warrant our attention. I continued to glass the horizon. Not seeing anything out of the ordinary, I adjusted the binos again, just enough to lower my field of view, and searched areas of brush and shade where Amy Raye might have huddled for protection. I spotted a coyote and then a couple of deer grazing on some wheatgrass. I continued this process until I'd covered the entire terrain grid.

"Anything?" I asked Jeff.

"I'm not sure."

I moved away from my field glasses. "What is it?"

"Take a look." Jeff stepped back.

The scope allowed us to glass up to two miles away. As I viewed the area approximately a mile and a half to our left and northeast of the ridge, I spotted a sliver of orange in the branches of a juniper — marking tape, perhaps left over from a prior season, from a hunter other than Amy Raye, but we couldn't be sure.

"Think we should call it in?" I asked.

"Probably should."

I picked up my radio from my belt clip. "Command, Alpha One," I called.

After a couple of seconds, Colm's voice responded. "Alpha One, go ahead."

"We've spotted what looks like marking tape about a mile and a half northeast of our initial location. We're going to check it out."

"Go ahead and proceed," Colm said.

I made a mental picture of the tape's location, identifying geological land markings as points of yardage.

"Let's pack up the optics but leave the tripods here," I told Jeff.

Once again we secured our packs and our rifles on our shoulders. I'd kept Amy Raye's mittens in a bag in my coat pocket. I brought them out, allowing Kona to reacquaint himself with the scent. Then the three of us began the steep decline toward the marker, the land before us a mélange of fractures and boulders, the spot of orange too far away for us to see with our natural vision or the field glasses we carried on straps around our necks.

More static broke over our radios. I recognized the voice of the pilot. Colm had ordered him to cover the area south of the subject's vehicle. Jeff and I were in an area slightly north and east of the subject's truck.

Game trails corkscrewed down the ridge like runoff streams. Kona stayed just ahead of us, every so often stopping and looking over his shoulder, then trotting on again. After about a mile in, I stopped and looked through the binoculars to check for the markers I'd identified earlier.

"Heading in the right direction?" Jeff asked.

I lowered my field glasses. "Not too much farther."

Jeff said, "She was twenty-six when they married. But they've been together for eight years."

I hesitated. "Farrell and Amy Raye? How do you know?"

"I heard him talking to one of the other

guys this morning. They'll have been married seven years in a couple more months. The girl is her stepdaughter, but she lives with them," Jeff told me.

Jeff and I were now within twenty feet of the tree with the marking tape. Jeff's voice was soft, but also matter-of-fact. "It's hers."

I couldn't believe it. Even from where we stood we could see the bow and the quiver leaning against the trunk, almost hidden from the branches.

And then Jeff said, "He's onto something."

Kona was on the other side of the tree beneath a thick bough that was weighed down with snow, his tail wagging, his feet pacing frantically around a two-by-three-foot area as he sniffed the ground.

"What is it, boy?" I said.

Kona stopped pacing, his nose still to the ground. Air blew quickly in and out of his nostrils, sounding much like the occasional static on the radio.

I stepped to the other side of the tree, bent down, and ever so gently lifted the bough to get a better look.

Around the base of the tree was a small shelter, where only a light layer of snow had blown in, barely covering the boot impressions that had been left behind.

Jeff stepped toward me and crouched

down. He pointed to an area about a couple of feet in front of the boot imprints, just as I caught sight of the same thing — two rounded indentations like small craters, no doubt made by Amy Raye's knees.

"Either she was sheltering herself from the weather, or she was using this spot as a blind," I said.

With the bough still lifted, I looked at the quiver. Only two arrows were fitted into the notches, and on the fletchings of those arrows, each was marked with a number two and then three. The first arrow was missing. Hunters numbered their arrows by preference of flight. With her first arrow missing, I knew Amy Raye had taken a shot, but whether she had made contact with that first shot, I wasn't sure.

I reached for my radio. "Command, Alpha One."

"Command. Go ahead, Alpha One."

"We've found a Hoyt compound bow and a camouflage quiver. There's an arrow missing. It could be that she got a shot and was tracking the elk. You may want to check with the other hunters to see if she'd taken a shot earlier in the week."

"They didn't mention it, but I'll check in with them again," Colm said. "And we've got the pilot on his way. He should be at your location shortly. One of the volunteers from Mesa County is with him. They'll be canvassing the whole area using the electronic device."

I went on to describe the impressions in the snow and gave Colm the site's GPS coordinates. "And, Colm, Kona's picking up something. We've got a trail."

"I'm going to send all other teams in your direction. Let Kona keep working the area. Report back if you see any other sign of the subject."

"We're on it," I said.

AMY RAYE

Cold danced up and down Amy Raye's skin. She sat on her hands, bounced her legs, wiggled her stiff toes. Then rain, light splatters at first, barely finding the ground through the trees. She felt certain it was still too early to track the elk, but she couldn't risk losing the blood trail. She lowered her bow with the nylon rope, fastened her pack over her shoulders, and climbed down. Then she stepped out of the tree stand harness, stored it, and repositioned her pack.

She walked to the exposed rock that she'd sighted, the air settling over her with the color of steel wool. She searched the tall, wet grass for traces of blood. Finding nothing, she extended her radius from the rock, her back bent over the ground, her fingers combing the long blades. Still nothing.

She replayed the sound in her head, the whack of the arrow. Had it indeed made impact? Could it have struck a tree? A limb?

Perhaps she hadn't cleared the opening in the branches. Maybe the arrow had ricocheted. She walked back to the tree stand, searched the pinyons and junipers that stood in front of it, looked through their branches for the red fletchings of her arrow, inspected the surrounding ground. She had to have made impact. But the longer she went without sighting any blood, the more baffled she became. She returned to the rock. The rain fell harder. Cold water leaked through her clothes, dripped from the edge of her hat. She'd left her rain gear back at the camp, so she moved on, extending her search eastward into the timber and across a shallow creek bed, cratered by fresh elk prints both coming and going. She followed the receding tracks.

The rain continued to fall, seeping through the trees. Amy Raye kept going. Farther from the creek, fresh croppings of Gambel oak had taken hold, sprouts of tiny leaves still holding their autumn color, dabs of red that resembled blood. She inspected each one, surveyed the area around her. She spotted red, wedged on a branch of a pinyon. As she approached it, she recognized the fletching. The arrow had collided with the tree and dislodged from the elk, as so often happened when an elk charged through the woods. The broadhead had made impact, was fully expanded. A good six inches or more of the arrow shaft was covered in pink, frothy blood. The arrow had punctured a lung. Maybe two. With only one lung punctured, an elk could run so far that he would be difficult or impossible to recover.

Only one time before had she not recovered the animal, a two-point buck. And sometimes even now she let herself wonder how her life might have worked itself out had she and her grandfather found the animal on that October afternoon and made the hike back down to the farm before supper, before darkness fell and bad things happened. She was just shy of thirteen.

Both her parents worked on the weekends — her mother as a librarian assistant, and her father as a state patrolman. Every Saturday he would drop Amy Raye off for the weekend at her grandparents' farm, about three miles south from the downtown of Lynchburg, Tennessee, where they lived. She would help with the chores, anything that needed getting done, from shoveling out the manure in the barn to pulling weeds in the driveway and gardens. She'd hike the game trails on the Highland Rim, swim in the pond. And on a lot of those weekends, her cousins Nan and Lionel would be there. Nan was a year older than Amy Raye. Lionel, Nan's brother, was two years older than Nan. These three had grown up together, working hard in the heat, skinny-dipping at the end of the day, riding bareback and laughing about the way it made them feel between the legs. Behind the barn was a basketball hoop. When the girls were too small to make a basket on their own, they'd take turns climbing onto Lionel's shoulders, and would see which one could make the most hoops. Lionel was always a foot taller than Nan. By the time Nan was fourteen, Lionel was well over six feet and playing varsity.

It was a Saturday afternoon. Amy Raye's grandfather had said he'd been watching a young buck feeding up on the plateau. "He's just the right size for you," her grandfather had told her. Amy Raye had been given a .243 Winchester that past Christmas, enough caliber for her to take down a small deer. With her rifle slung over her shoulder, she and her grandfather hiked up to the plateau to settle into their blind, a small shelter made with plywood and two-by-four posts and painted brown and green.

By four thirty, they'd spotted the buck,

and Amy Raye took the shot. But she'd gotten nervous and had jerked the rifle. She'd hit the buck at close range, about sixty yards, but he didn't fall. She'd missed his vitals. Instead of hauling the deer down the hill and hanging him in the barn to process, she and her grandfather tracked the animal well into the night with high-beam flashlights her grandfather had carried in. It was close to midnight by the time they got back to the farm.

"Is he going to die?" Amy Raye wanted to know. "Is he going to rot out there?"

"You learned a hard lesson," her grandfather said.

He was tired, ready to turn in. "Could be that he's crippled up, that's all. Take this stuff into the barn. Maybe we'll have another go of it in the morning."

He handed her his flashlight and his pack.

"I'm sorry," Amy Raye said.

Her grandfather nodded in that deliberate way of his, holding his chin down over his chest and looking at her for a second or two. "Get some sleep," he said.

He was a tall man, big-boned. He carried the weight of himself into the house. Amy Raye didn't move. She wanted him to make her feel better. She wanted to cry. She imagined her own fists pushing down the ache that was rising up in her throat. He left the kitchen light on for her. After a few more minutes, the light to the bathroom turned on. Amy Raye could see it from the small window to the left of the bathroom sink. Then the light turned out. Amy Raye was fully awake.

Amy Raye turned away from the house and began walking toward the barn. Heat still cloaked the air, heavy in her lungs and on her shoulders. The barn doors were open, as they always were. At the back of the barn were a tack room and a large stall where a handful of sheep stayed. To the right were bales of hay, stacked ten to twelve feet high. To the left were four stalls. Van Gogh and Princeton were in the first two stalls. In the third stall was a Clydesdale that Grandpa Tomlin was keeping for a neighbor. Amy Raye had thought of Van Gogh, a light brown paint with white ankles and markings on his torso, as hers. She was seven when her grandfather had bought him, and she'd been the first to ride him.

Amy Raye hung the pack on a peg just inside the barn and leaned the rifle along-side the wall. Van Gogh pushed against his stall door and whinnied. *He knows it's me,* she thought. "Hey, boy," she said, walking over to him. She wanted to cry into his mane, and tell him how sorry she was for shooting the buck. Van Gogh nuzzled her shoulder, whinnied again. She climbed the stall door and wrapped her arms around his neck, her face pressed into his warm hide, and that was when she saw them, in the fourth stall.

Though the barn was dark, she could make out their shadows, Lionel's long legs and broad torso, Nan's thick red hair that bunched in curls down her back. She gasped, and as she did, Nan giggled.

"Hey, cousin," Lionel said.

"What are you doing?" Amy Raye said. "You're naked."

But Amy Raye knew what they were doing, as if something deep in her belly that fluttered and burned sudden like hot bubbles scratching to get out recognized it before her mind understood. She'd seen them naked before, when the three of them would go swimming in the pond, even after Lionel's penis had grown fuller and longer, and dark hairs had sprouted around it, and Nan's breasts had budded into smooth, round mounds of flesh as large as softballs. They didn't pay each other any mind then. Their bodies had felt as natural as the cool water against their skin.

"Come here," Lionel said.

Pru

After reporting in to Colm, I took pictures of the prints and items. Then Jeff and I continued to work Kona on the trail. "In town you can hear a car a mile away," I told him. "Even at my house, which is outside of town, I can make out the sounds of trucks on the highway. But here, it's like we're in some big void. Amy Raye's not going to hear us unless we're fifty yards in front of her, maybe even less."

Jeff and I followed Kona away from the shelter, where the trail made a couple of switchbacks, eventually heading due south and continuing to descend in elevation. For the most part, Kona's head remained near the ground, except for an occasional lift to clear snowflakes from his snout, at which time he'd blow hard, shake his head, even sneeze.

We were stepping over small juniper saplings

and deadfall as we kept making our way downhill. Up ahead a thick patch of mature juniper appeared. It was there that Kona stopped and lifted his head for a few seconds, his ears alert, his tail still. He would do that sometimes when he'd lost a trail, raise his head as if trying to ride the wind and pick up a scent.

"What is it, boy?" I said.

He gave me only a second's notice before taking off and weaving his way in and out of the trees in front of us.

Jeff and I stepped into the timber. The ground looked much like that underneath the bough, with only a dusting of snow and a smattering of leaves from the sparse Gambel oak, which allowed us to identify prints that appeared to have been made by a woman. Colm had given the search team a description of Amy Raye's boots — Merrell, rectangular tread, size seven.

"She was definitely here," I said. My pace quickened behind Kona's, and my eyes remained alert for broken twigs and depressions.

Our downward descent was leading us to a clearing at the hem of the timber where ashen light filtered through the dark branches. Kona glanced over his shoulder at me, then moved forward, his steps even, his body appearing stiff like it would get when he was fixed on something.

"What is it?" I said, my voice not much more than a whisper.

Kona neared the edge of the timber. Then he stopped, his head alert, his tail slightly raised. Jeff and I caught up to him. The terrain opened to a creek about fifty yards down from us. On the other side of the creek were five cow elk and three calves leisurely feeding.

A snapping of branches sounded from the woods beyond the elk. A small four-point bull emerged from the green shadows and began grazing with the others.

"She's not here," I said, my voice still a whisper. "The elk would know. They'd smell her scent. They wouldn't be grazing so freely."

"We're here," Jeff reminded me, his voice not much louder than mine had been.

Jeff was right. I recognized that we were downwind from the elk. Perhaps Amy Raye was also. "Go find," I commanded Kona again, hoping he hadn't lost the trail.

Once more, Kona glanced at me over his shoulder. He looked back at the elk, trotted forward a few steps, and let out a yip. The elk raised their heads, hesitated a few seconds, then turned their broad shoulders and lunged into the trees on the far side of them.

"Kona, no," I commanded, knowing he was up for a good chase. I reached inside my coat for the bag containing Amy Raye's mittens. I held the mittens to Kona's nose.

"Go find," I said again.

Kona's playful distraction was over. He was back to work. He turned his head slowly as if he were trying to pick up an air scent.

His stance tightened. He was onto something. Kona backtracked a few yards and then, with his snout close to the ground, made a turn to the right, following the inside edge of the timber. I identified a footprint here and there that the wind had not disturbed.

"We should alert Colm," Jeff said.

I reached for my radio. "Command, Alpha One. Kona's definitely on. We're in the woods just south of the marker, maybe eighty yards. There are footprints. We're now moving southeast along the edge of the timber."

"Alpha One, this is Command. We've got teams heading there now. Keep reporting back to me. Proceed forward. Make noise. Let the subject know you're there."

I photographed the prints as well as the surrounding area and moved on.

"Amy Raye!" Jeff yelled, his hands cupped around his mouth. He kept yelling out Amy Raye's name as he and I followed Kona. I continued to identify the boot prints that had been mostly protected by tree growth, the toe of the prints pointing in the direction Kona was moving.

Kona left the edge of the timber and began trotting southward through an open meadow or gulch, with his snout still to the ground. Jeff and I were about fifty feet behind him, searching the area for more prints, but we didn't find any. The snow was too thick. Kona began barking and wagging his tail. He was just on the other side of a large boulder. He'd been trained to sit when he came upon a search object. He didn't always mind. This time his front paws were prancing in place.

Jeff and I ran toward him. The weight of our gear pounded heavily on our backs.

A brown patch of fabric lay partially exposed. Kona pawed at the fabric again. "Kona, no," I said.

I crouched in the snow and brushed away the accumulation. Kona had discovered a brown fleece hat. When I picked up the hat, I saw the bloodstains and the tear down the back.

"Dear, Lord," Jeff said.

I reached for my radio and took a deep breath. "Command, Alpha One." I went on to report what we had found.

"How much blood?" Colm asked.

"A couple of inches in diameter," I said.

"Give me the points of your location. I'll have another team move in to assist. I want you and Jeff to keep working the area."

Kona began to whine. He was now about six feet from us and had picked up another scent.

"Hold on," I said to Colm.

I stood and stepped toward Kona. Then Jeff uncovered something with the toe of his boot. He bent down and brushed the rest of the snow off with his gloved hands.

"Command, we just uncovered another item," I said. "Looks like a .357 revolver. And, Colm, it's hers. It's got scent all over it."

I picked up the gun and opened its chamber.

Jeff and I made eye contact and looked at each other for a couple of seconds without saying anything.

Static broke over the radio. "Alpha One, Command, come back."

"Command, Alpha One, there's a missing round in the chamber," I said. I reported the coordinates for the items.

"Keep working the area. See what else you can find," Colm said.

I bagged the items and placed them in my pack. The hat could have been torn when she fell, I tried to tell myself, or the tear might have been made by a predator after she'd fallen. Forensics would have a better idea. I thought of Amy Raye's children. I thought of Joseph. The implications were all around us, and yet I just couldn't imagine a mother taking her life.

"It doesn't look good, Jeff," I said.

"No, ma'am, it doesn't look good at all."

We moved out twenty feet, and then fifty feet, searching for prints and seeing if Kona might pick up anything else, but the only tracks we were able to identify were those made by coyote or deer. I also continued to take photographs of the terrain to record the area we had covered.

"Let's check out the other side of the gulch," I said. If Amy Raye had indeed taken her life, her body would have been dragged off or scattered by coyotes or lion. We crossed a shallow and rocky creek bed. On the other side the snow deepened, maybe by three or four inches. We were heading into a basin.

"We should have brought snowshoes," I said.

"If we get any more snowfall, we're going to have to."

Kona wasn't walking in any particular direction. He hadn't picked up a scent. "We've been heading downwind," I said. "That's why Kona's been able to pick up a trail. Before we found the hat, I was thinking maybe the tracks were fresh, but I don't think that's the case. If we're in a drainage area, the scent will stay," I said.

I radioed back to Colm. "We're not picking up anything," I said.

"Team Three is approaching the new PLS. We'll get all efforts in the area and see what we can find. Go ahead and continue to work Kona."

The new PLS was now Amy Raye's hat and the gun, even though no one had officially identified the items as hers yet.

Between the breaking sounds of the radio, I began to make out the faint *chug, chug, chug* of the chopper.

"According to the coordinates, how far are we from the subject's truck?" I asked Colm.

"Looks like about three miles. Maybe a little more."

"Damn," I said, my voice as quiet as the wind that had stalled out on us sometime earlier in the morning. I held the radio down to my side. Colm had been right to extend the search area.

"Long way for a woman alone," Jeff said. "You got your cell phone with you?" he asked. "Want to see if you're picking up a signal?"

I removed my glove, unbuttoned the cargo pocket on my pants, and reached for my phone. I saw that I had a missed call from Joseph. He had been staying at Corey's ever since the search began. The call must have come in before I'd left the command station.

"I'm not getting anything," I said.

"You work this area a lot," Jeff said. "You ever get a signal?"

"Sometimes up on the bluffs I'll get a bar or two. Usually I have to drive back to the road and start heading out of the canyons."

The sound of the helicopter was getting stronger, though as low as we were I still couldn't spot it.

"We should have checked the pocket on her quiver," I said. "Looked for her cell phone or a camera."

I was thinking that if a cell phone or camera hadn't been in the zipper pocket of the quiver, then there'd be a good chance she had one of the two on her body. Even if they were in her backpack, hopefully the pack was still strapped to her back. The new detection device Colm had mentioned the night before would only be able to identify the subject if she was under snow and if she had some kind of electronic equipment on her that used diodes. Most hunters didn't wear watches. Didn't want the unnecessary sound. The experienced hunters would judge the time of day by the angle of light.

"Command, Alpha One," I said, holding the radio close to my mouth. "Is there a cell phone or digital camera in the subject's quiver?"

I waited and listened as Colm radioed back and forth with Terry Peterson, the leader of Team Three.

"Negative on a cell phone," Terry said.

Team Four had been ordered to return the quiver and bow to the command station. Team Three would be proceeding in the direction of Jeff and me.

"You okay?" Jeff asked.

"Yeah."

"Maybe they'll find something in this clearing," he said.

"That's just it. I'm afraid we won't like what we find."

Jeff rolled his chapped lips together. His bushy mustache was flecked with ice. "Answers are better than nothing," he said.

I thought back to a warm day in early June, when a cool wind from the hills dipped into the valley, and the bed linens, white with patterns of purple lilac, snapped on a clothesline and swelled like a sail. I was eighteen years old. I was lying on the floor of the front porch, staring up at a spiderweb, listening to the sheets, listening to the breeze in the cottonwood trees, watching a struggling fly that was caught in the elegant weave of gossamer. Earlier that day my mother and father had taken off together to get the mail, to pick up grain at the co-op, to check out a parcel of land that was for sale.

A two-hundred-foot dirt driveway wound up to the house, gravel-patched and gullied on the sides. Usually the sound of a vehicle approaching our house was that of an engine gearing down mixed with the subtle crunch of gritty-packed earth and an occasional rock-ping. I smelled the stirred dust almost immediately as my father's truck sped toward the house. I jackknifed to a sitting position and shielded my eyes.

The truck came to a stop, the engine still running. Dad opened the driver's-side door, stepped down with his left leg. His right hand gripped the top of the steering wheel. "Prudence, honey, there's been an accident.

There's been a bad accident. You need to come quick."

I ran down the steps. I got into the truck, the vinyl seat hot and sticky beneath my palms. "Where's Mom?" I asked.

"She's there now. Sweetheart, it's bad. It's real bad."

"Dad, what is it?"

"It's Brody, sweetheart. Something's happened to Brody."

Amy Raye

Amy Raye spotted drops of blood on saplings within inches of where she had found the arrow. Careful not to step on any recent tracks, she moved forward in an eastward direction as if connecting the dots. Sometimes the blood ran in a thick rivulet down a blade of grass. Other times it filled tiny pools in the ground. The trail led Amy Raye to a steep decline. Elk typically ran downhill to die. Even so, this elk wasn't giving up.

Amy Raye continued to follow him. A half hour passed, then an hour, then two. The rain fell steadily. Up until that point the elk had stayed in the timber, its blood trail protected by the shelter of the evergreens. He was losing more blood, and he was slowing down, leaving larger pools as he rested. But the terrain had reached an opening where the trees stopped. And there, Amy Raye lost the trail. The elk might as well have vanished. Rain had fallen for hours, had completely drenched the exposed grassy clearing, and it wasn't letting up, nor showing any sign that it would. Amy Raye leaned her bow against a tree and removed her quiver. She pulled the bugle and cow call over her neck, took off her pack, and stored the tools inside. Then she lowered herself to the ground, crouched on the balls of her feet. The tree's branches sheltered her from the rain. She drank water, ate a couple of pieces of jerky. In that moment, she felt everything — life, death, the tangy sweet smell of pine, the freshness of the rain. It was the immensity of those feelings that drove her mad at times. These were the moments when she would wonder about it all.

Farrell had thought this time would be good for her. And yet it was her love for him that might drive her away. Leaving Farrell would be the most honest and decent thing she had ever done. But to leave him would mean leaving the children. Being a mother was the one thing in her life that she felt redeemed her. She would still have time with Trevor, but Julia was her stepdaughter, and she worried about the time she would lose with her.

Her love for Farrell had been a selfish one, she knew that, mixed-up and needy. How could she ever explain it to anyone, especially to her husband? Still crouched beneath the boughs, she watched the rain drizzle from the tips of the branches and thought about how her life had gone so wrong.

There were the games when she was young; at least to Lionel and Nan, that was all they were. "Open your mouth wider, don't use your teeth." But Nan was always chosen. Nan was the better one. And so Lionel would fuck Amy Raye instead, that was what he said. Her grandparents would have already turned in. And her father would continue to bring her to the farm on the weekends, and she began to crave the things that she was too young to understand were not good for her. That's how it was for three years, until Lionel left, went to college, and Nan stopped coming to the farm, and Amy Raye found someone else.

It was the middle of summer. She was home alone. The neighbors next door were having a deck added on to the back of their house. They'd hired a carpenter who worked alone. Amy Raye had watched him come and go — a good-looking man, tan and strong, at least ten years older than she. She imagined the taste of his skin, imagined him aroused, and her power over him.

She was wearing a pair of cutoff jean

shorts, a tank top, was barefoot. She poured a glass of ice water, left the house, and brought the water to the man. He was bent over a piece of wood that was supported on two sawhorses. His jeans hung low off his hips. He wasn't wearing a shirt. Sweat glistened on his back. He startled when Amy Raye said, "Hey."

She handed him the water. "I thought you might be thirsty."

"Thanks." He took the water, gulped it down.

They were standing behind the garage. No one could see. She ran the toes of her right foot up the backside of her left calf, pushed her hair out of her face. She watched the man drink the water. When he lowered the cup, she stepped closer, reached for his belt, and with all the deftness in the world undid his buckle, unzipped his pants.

There was another time she had stopped at an auto parts store in Fayetteville. One of her front high beams had burned out. She bought a replacement. She knew how to change the bulb herself, but there was vulnerability on the face of the man behind the counter, and she liked his subtle lisp. "Could you show me how to replace it?" she asked him.

He was glad to. She'd parked at the back

of the store, under the shade of a large elm tree. And as he stood in front of the car and began to lean over beneath the hood and try to place his hand on the old bulb, Amy Raye pressed against him from behind and reached around him. It was all so easy, and the power was all hers.

She was careful in whom she selected. She'd watch the men before she'd approach them. And only once had she gotten it wrong, had things gotten out of hand. Saddle had been with her that time. After the man had struck Saddle with a limb, and Saddle had lain unconscious, Amy Raye had sworn to herself that she'd had enough, that she would turn her life around. And she did, for a few months, until everything started up again. And one other time, but that one hurt her in a different way.

Before Farrell and Amy Raye married she would go through periods of emotional withdrawal. The first time was after they'd dated for three months. She'd run into some hard times and he'd wanted her to move in. But she didn't want to move in. She couldn't see herself settling into a relationship, if for no other reason than she knew she would fail him. And there was something else, the stench of conformity. Instead she left Farrell, moved away without a word.

"Not even a postcard," he'd said to her when she finally called after four months had passed.

"Where are you?" Amy Raye had asked, hearing the noise in the background.

"Buffalo's."

She heard him take a swallow of his drink, heard the ice cubes clink against the glass. "What are you drinking?"

He told her he was drinking scotch.

"I thought you preferred Jameson."

She wanted to tell him about the man she'd seen at the Center Store, and again at the Golden Saloon, the one who looked like Farrell. She wanted to tell him how much she'd missed him.

"I need you," she said. She was crying then. "Something bad has happened."

And Farrell took her back, like she knew he would. She told him he was her all, that he surrounded her, even in the corners, and nothing was like him, nothing.

Over time, she would withdraw again. At first it would show itself as a lack of warmth. And then the sarcasm, as if she were punishing him for the only wrong he had committed, which was loving her.

At times Farrell would push back, try to set boundaries. Once he left for a weekend. He told her he needed to get caught up on some projects from work. He would be staying at the home of a client who was going out of town. He assured Amy Raye that he still loved her.

She imagined him arriving at the client's home, a high-end, three-room condo in Golden, elaborately furnished. She pictured him setting his duffel bag on the bed in the master suite, unpacking his laptop and setting it on a table in the living room that faced a window overlooking the mountains. Maybe he'd open a bottle of an expensive white wine he had purchased, pour a glass, and sit down at his computer. His intention would have been to work. But Amy Raye knew Farrell too well, knew him in a way that she believed no one else ever could. He would have been hoping for a call or a message from her, would have been checking his phone and his email, anticipating her apologizing for her ways, begging him to come home.

And so she sent an email. She could feel Farrell's heart lighten as he saw a message from her in his inbox. But she knew how Farrell loved her, did not want to lose her, knew how important it was for him to hold the family together, and that was the power she had over him.

You say you need this time to get your work done. Where is your honesty? You stick your hand in a bee's wick trying to extract some honey . . . and you get stung . . . who would have ever thought? I didn't look for your hand to sting. It's just who I am. Nor do I wish to sting anyone's hand. I feel something man/woman missing between us. Most likely it's just me. When all else fails, I'm a good bucket to throw it into.

She got the children tucked into bed that night, did the evening chores, crawled into her and Farrell's bed, and began to read. Several pages in, she heard the door downstairs open and close, heard Farrell's gentle footfall as he climbed the stairs. She did not look at him as he entered the room, removed his clothes, and climbed in next to her. She set the book down and turned out the light.

At other times over the years he'd wanted them to talk to someone, but she had refused, telling him he was making too much of things and that if he wanted to leave her he could. But she would be gentler and kinder after those conversations. And though she had always worked hard, she would work harder, folding laundry at midnight, hosing down the floor in the garage, spending even more time with the children, playing War and Trouble with them late into the night, even though she'd have to get up early the next day for work. She would lift the covers for Farrell when he'd crawl into bed with her, and wrap her body around him and whisper to him that she loved him. She would prove to Farrell and the children, and herself, that everything was good. These were the times she would go the longest without acting out, when she would convince herself she could get a handle on things. She could see everything during these moments, see camping trips and graduations and grandchildren, see Farrell and her living out their full potential and just how glorious it all would be.

But after eight years, Amy Raye knew she had tired Farrell out, and he'd begun to wear his fatigue like a submission. Instead of telling her he was leaving for a weekend, he would put more time into his work. The lovemaking had waned until it was barely lovemaking at all. The thrill was gone.

The hurting of him had tired her out, too. She'd begun to think of leaving him, of doing the most decent and honorable thing she'd ever done. She'd agreed to go on this trip, not because of Kenny, but to give herself time. Kenny had simply been another option.

Then she and Farrell had taken a day to themselves, had hiked Ypsilon Mountain, and when she saw him, really saw him, an aching love for him stirred, as if it had awakened from a long slumber and was bringing her to a precipice. Nostalgia churned beneath her skin, and at that moment, she'd thought of Saddle, who'd come to her in the night and led her to this loving man. She thought of her faithful dog, who was at least four or five when she took him in, who knew her better than any person, and had loved her just the same. He'd developed arthritis as he'd gotten older, and eventually developed cancer in his hip. The day she had to put him down, a beautiful, clear-sky morning in May, the vet met her in a field. She'd held Saddle in her arms until his eyes glazed over into a cloudy shade of blue. She had not told Farrell she was taking Saddle that day, and when Farrell called and found out, he came home from work, stayed with her, and held her when she cried. And that night when she couldn't sleep and went outside to search for Saddle in the stars, Farrell woke and found her. He wrapped Saddle's blanket around her shoulders and stayed with her until sunrise. And while Farrell had held her, she'd wanted to tell him everything; she'd wanted to come clean. She wanted to believe that he, like Saddle, could love her unconditionally, might even help her find her way back to the person she should have been.

Pru

Colm had reassigned the search teams. They would now cover quadrants from the point of the hat and gun. The area was teeming with operations. In addition to the air search and the electronic frequency detector, another volunteer from Mesa County had brought an infrared scanner to the site. The scanner had proven critical in a search during the summer when a hiker went missing in the Black Canyon near Gunnison. The scanner, being used from a helicopter, had picked up the flicking of a lighter from about a hundred yards away. The hiker had fallen down a ragged incline, sprained his wrist, broken an ankle, and suffered minor scrapes and bruises. But he was alive.

"Alpha One, Command," Colm called over the radio.

"Command, go ahead," I said.

"It might be time you looked for a cache," Colm said.

I asked him to relay some of the coordinates that Glade had given him.

"Heading there now," I said.

If Amy Raye had shot herself, her body could very well have been dragged off by a lion and concealed. Jeff and I made our way back up to the top of the ridge and then began climbing north. Glade had said the old cache was about twenty yards from the edge of the butte. Within another hour we were in the area.

"You see any feline prints?" I asked Jeff.

"Negative," he said.

And then maybe a hundred feet from one of the suggested coordinates Glade had given us, we found a cache in a grove of pinyons that backed up to a rocky overhang. After a lion fed on his kill, he'd cover it in a secluded spot, where he could return to feed on the prey for several days.

The cache looked old, maybe a couple of years. The trees and the overhang had buffered the area from the snow.

Jeff knelt and began removing some of the branches and debris the lion had used to cover his kill. I commanded Kona to sit, and then Jeff and I began inspecting the bones. There were a number of large rib bones, a femur, part of a spine.

"They go for the head," Jeff said. "Or the

windpipe."

I walked around the edge of the cache, my eyes searching the timber every so often for any trace of movement. I knew with a cache this old the lion would have long since moved on to a different area in his home range, but I also knew lion were territorial. Once they'd established themselves as residents of an area, they'd fight other lion to death to protect it.

And then I stopped. "Jeff, over here," I said.

Jeff stood and walked toward me. "Well, I'll be damned," he said.

We were both looking at the leg of a horse, the hoof intact.

"We're a long way from any of the ranches," I told him.

"That's not a ranch horse," he said. "There's no iron on the hoof."

We were looking at the leg of one of the wild horses. "Maybe that's why I never see the band around here," I said. "Maybe they got spooked."

"If there's a lion around, there's another cache," Jeff said.

"Don't know that we're going to be able to find it in this weather. Hard to believe we found this one." And then, "Jeff, what do you think the odds are of a cougar attacking

Amy Raye? I don't know that I can ever recall a lion attacking a person anywhere near these parts," I said.

"They don't usually attack horses either," Jeff said.

I'd read the reports of lion attacks, but those attacks hadn't taken place in remote areas such as this where the lion had plenty of hunting ground. Lion were typically wary of people.

"She was wearing camouflage," Jeff said. "She'd probably taken great pains to get rid of her human scent, sprayed herself with some estrus. Maybe she knelt down to tie her boot. She could have been crouched low while she was following the elk. I've always heard lion don't see too good."

Jeff was right. Amy Raye could have been an easy target.

"Two more dogs trained in avalanche searches are being deployed tomorrow. They're heading up from Garfield County," I told him.

"There's more snow in the forecast."

"That's what I hear."

"Be like wading through heavy water," Jeff said.

After the gun and hat were found, Colm told reporters, "We are in the phase of realizing the worst." Eighteen inches of snow were expected to fall over the next two days with gusts up to forty miles per hour. With the new evidence and weather forecasts, the search had officially moved into recovery mode.

"It's too dangerous," Colm said to me. "We're going to end up losing one of our own. We caught a small break in the weather today. We're not going to be so lucky the rest of the week."

Giovanni's in Rangely had delivered pizzas for the search crew. I brought Colm a plate with two slices of cold pizza and sat down beside him. A reporter was sleeping on the floor next to the stove. The other reporters had gone.

"What is it? Two in the morning?" Colm asked.

"Something like that."

Colm took a bite of the pizza and then offered it to me.

"No, thanks."

"Did you eat?"

"I did."

"You heading back to town?" Colm asked.

"Yeah, in a few minutes."

Amy Raye's quiver and bow were on the table. In front of the quiver, laid out evenly, were its contents: an Allen wrench, a wrist-strap bow release, a bottle of Zephyr spray, an eight-by-eleven-inch topo map that had been creased and folded, and a Suunto directional compass.

"The husband identified the quiver and the bow. Nice work."

"And the compass?" A wave of defeat grabbed hold of me. "At least there isn't a suicide note."

"Not that we found. Dean's clearing out her camp now, gathering her things."

"What about the missing arrow?" I asked.

"We talked to her friends. They didn't know what to make of it. All they knew was that she didn't take the shot when she was with them."

"Are you thinking the arrow was part of a suicide plan?" I asked.

"I'm thinking it might be. She marked the spot where she left her quiver and bow. She knew someone would eventually come upon them. With the arrow missing, we could assume she was tracking an elk. Without her compass and map, we'd think she became lost, died of natural causes."

"Have you thought any more about the lion?"

"I'm not sure what to make of that, but I'm not ruling it out."

"Where is the husband now?" I asked.

"His sister's with him. She got in a couple of hours ago. Had someone else watch the kids."

Static broke over the radio. Another team was reporting in. Still negative on any more findings.

"Was the husband here when I made the call about the hat?"

"Sitting right where you are. You've seen the families before. I don't have to tell you what it did to him."

In all of my eight years working Kona as a search-and-rescue dog, I'd only been on four searches where the subject wasn't found alive, and each of those times, the subject's body was recovered. The last time was the previous winter when a young man had been snowmobiling with his father. The boy had gotten trapped in an avalanche. The father saw the whole thing happen. The boy was only seventeen. Kona was the one who discovered the body.

"So the gun was hers?" I asked.

"The husband said she didn't own a gun. They didn't allow guns in the house on account of the kids. He thought the gun belonged to one of the guys she was with. We got a confirmation from the two friends when they got back in. Said she had borrowed the gun from Kenny, the younger of the two. Forensics will be able to confirm with us whether the gun was fired."

"And the hat?"

"We'll look for traces of gunshot. But I don't think there's any question the blood is hers."

Colm finished the slice of pizza.

"How are you holding up?" I asked. "Can I get you anything?"

"I'm all right. Thanks." Then he pushed the plate away. "There's something else. I made a couple of calls tonight. Thought Amy Raye must have some family that should know what was going on."

"Wouldn't that be the husband's job?"

"You'd think so. He said she hadn't had contact with her family since she was young. Said he'd written to them once, to an address in Tennessee, but he hadn't gotten a response. I had some folks at the office do a little checking around. I gave them a call. Father said he didn't have a daughter. A half hour or so later, the wife calls me back. She wants to know if their daughter is all right."

"How long had it been since the mother had talked to her?"

"Fourteen years. The woman was scared and she was torn up. Scared about her husband finding out she'd called, and torn up as hell about her daughter."

"Fourteen years is a long time," I said.

There were people waiting to talk to Colm. I put my hand on his shoulder. "I'll catch up with you later," I said.

Jeff and I would be getting a few hours of sleep back at the hotel and then heading out again before the next storm picked up momentum. We decided to ride together and leave Jeff's truck at the station. The gun and the hat had already been sent to CBI for forensic testing. But Colm felt certain the items belonged to Amy Raye. There were strands of dark blond hair with blood on them inside the hat.

"What if she was tracking an elk? What if she did get lost?" I said to Jeff as we made our way back to Rangely.

"What would you make of the gun, then?"

I knew Jeff was right. "If only we'd found her body," I said.

Back at the hotel, Jeff checked in at the front desk. I went on up to my room with Kona. I sent Joseph a text, told him I'd call him in the morning, told him I loved him.

He should have been asleep. He texted back. Love you, too, Mom.

Amy Raye

Hidden beneath the boughs of the tree, the rain dripping from the branches around her, she heard a rustle in the timber to her right, a lumbering sound, and immediately she thought of the elk. She turned slowly and reached for her bow. At close range she could put another arrow through the elk. To go for her gun in her pack would create too much noise. These were her thoughts when the large animal appeared no more than thirty yards in front of her. A bear's sense of smell was seven times that of bloodhounds. He would have known she was there. And it was late in the season. Most of the bears had hibernated by now. At first Amy Raye startled. The animal was brown, and larger than most black bears, resembling a young grizzly, and if it was a young grizzly, there would be an angry mother somewhere close by. But Amy Raye knew there were no grizzlies in these parts. She was looking at a cinnamon bear, a color phase of the black bear. And though she'd never seen a cinnamon bear before, she'd heard of them and knew their habitat was in the drier climates of the western states, usually northeastern Utah and Wyoming. The animal lifted his head and looked at her, as if curious, and she wondered if he would come any closer. Instead he just stood there and watched her. She knew she should probably stand up and back away, make noise.

And yet she didn't stand up and back away. She remained calm and watched the bear. She thought of the time she'd seen the grizzly. She could have returned to her small bunkhouse, cooked her dinner, kept Saddle safe.

And as she thought these things, the cinnamon bear walked on, crossed the meadow, and disappeared into the copse of Gambel oak and potentilla to Amy Raye's left.

Almost six years had passed since that time she'd left Farrell. She remembered the people whom she'd met along the way, the cottonwoods that only grew along a riverbank, the hills dotted with ranches, the sandy ridges. She'd moved to Palisade that spring, on the Western Slope, where she'd found work on a peach orchard, and Saddle made friends with a border collie with a banged-up hip. She worked from sunup to early afternoon pruning trees, planting younger trees that had been grafted two years before, and operating the flail mower — mulching the smaller branches that had been pruned. And when she'd finish her work on the peach orchard, she'd drive her twelve-year-old white Chevy pickup to Delta, where she burned ditches with a cattle rancher named Lew who was too old to care if she was a woman or a man, but in the end, they'd both come to enjoy each other's company. She slept in her truck, and bathed from the spigot and garden hose behind his barn. And once a week he treated her to dinner because he said she'd gotten too thin. He told her she was as capable as any man he'd ever known, and that comment alone made her like him more than most. He didn't ask her too much about herself. He didn't talk about himself either. Instead he talked about cattle and life and politics and the economy. He'd served in World War II, he'd sold carpet, he'd sold real estate, he'd been married three times, his middle name was Elwood. She learned these things from one of the other hires.

Her body grew lean and strong that spring, and while she was planting peach trees or burning ditches, she imagined driving somewhere as remote as Deadhorse, Alaska, a place she'd only heard about from a man in passing who'd worked in the oil field there. So when the ditches were burned and the trees had all been planted, she gathered the rest of her pay, and she and Saddle packed up and headed north.

After more than three days of driving, and spending two days in Helena, Montana, to have a faulty fuel line on her truck repaired, she and Saddle made it to Tok, the first town in Alaska after leaving Yukon territory. She stopped for fuel and then parked at the Border City Café to get something to eat. It was the middle of May, and there was a migratory bird festival going on, she was told by the couple sitting at the table beside her. They looked to be in their midforties. The woman wore a brim cap that read *Birdwatching Chick.* A pair of camouflage earmuffs hung around her neck.

"Where are you headed?" the man asked Amy Raye.

Amy Raye's hands were red from the spring cold. She wrapped them around a ceramic coffee mug for warmth. "I'm heading up to Deadhorse," Amy Raye told them.

"Up at Prudhoe Bay," the woman said.

"That's right."

"You got work in the oil field?" the man asked.

"No."

The couple had mostly empty plates in front of them — a few French fries on one, a slice of tomato on another. Amy Raye had just ordered a cheeseburger and potato salad.

"That's a good two-day drive from here, and not a whole lot of anything between. You ever been up that way before?"

"No. Never been to Alaska before either."

"Well, there's a lot of places to see other than Prudhoe Bay. All the docks and roads up there are restricted to oil field workers," the man said.

"I didn't know that," Amy Raye told him.

"My name's Ian, by the way."

Amy Raye shook the man's hand and introduced herself.

"And I'm Gina," the woman said. "We've just come back from the Arctic Preserve. A group of us were up there watching the loons and Arctic terns. Are you interested in birds?" she asked.

"No," Amy Raye said.

The man and the woman exchanged glances. "Where are you from?" Gina asked.

"Colorado. While I was working down there I met a man who'd just spent the winter at Deadhorse."

"Was probably exploring drill sites," Ian said.

"I think so. He said it was the farthest place in the United States. I thought I'd like to know what it was like to be at the farthest place in the United States."

"I guess that all depends on how you look at it. Farthest from what? You see what I'm saying?"

"I think so," Amy Raye said.

"If you were working in Deadhorse, you might say Key West, Florida, was the farthest place in the United States," Ian went on.

Gina leaned over the table. She pushed her plate away and folded her arms in front of her. "Why not drive down a little ways to some place like McCarthy or Kennecott? If I was from Colorado, I might think one of those towns was the farthest place."

"Gina's got a point," Ian said. "We stayed in McCarthy a couple of years back. It's remote, hardly populated at all. And Kennecott's a ghost town. But you can at least get food and supplies. And you can buy yourself a drink."

"How far is McCarthy from here?" Amy Raye asked.

"Not nearly as far as Deadhorse," Gina said.

"It's probably about seven hours from here. Some of the driving will be on unpaved roads, but it shouldn't be too bad. Just make sure you have a spare tire," Ian said. Gina smiled when Ian said this, and the two of them chuckled lightly. Then Ian looked away as if remembering, and laughed a little more. Ian laid his hand on Gina's back and rubbed her shoulders, and when he did, Gina leaned her body toward his.

They went on to tell Amy Raye about McCarthy, how it was situated in the heart of the Wrangell Mountains. They told her the town was surrounded by the largest protected wilderness on earth.

And as they talked, as Amy Raye watched the easiness pass between them, she decided she'd check out McCarthy. The area was considered endangered. Amy Raye wanted to know what that meant. She wanted to experience it herself. She decided that being in the largest protected wilderness on earth was more alluring to her than being in the farthest place in the United States.

The couple lived in Fairbanks. They would be heading in a different direction. They walked Amy Raye to her truck, were delighted to see she had a dog. They even gave

Amy Raye hugs good-bye, and in those hugs, she missed Farrell. She thought about how he would have liked these people. She almost told them about him, but she and Farrell had gone their separate ways. She had not checked in with Farrell since she had left, and she wondered about that as she saw this couple who almost seemed cartoonish in their bliss. There was a simple sweetness to them that Amy Raye wanted to believe was real.

It was close to eight that night when she got to McCarthy. She parked at the footbridge and grabbed her small duffel bag, and she and Saddle walked across the bridge and the half mile to town. She stopped at Lancaster's Hotel and checked into the one vacancy, a small room with a twin bed and thin mattress, and a corridor bathroom shared by other guests. She was hungry, not having stopped to eat dinner, so she walked next door to the Golden Saloon, found a quiet corner among the revelry, ordered a beer and a steak. She did not own a cell phone, though most everyone did, so she was glad when she saw a pay phone beside the restrooms, because as she ate alone, she missed Farrell, and without thinking too long about it, she found the coin change in her jeans pocket and stood up to call him. But when she pulled out the handful of coins, she found the small piece of paper with Lew's telephone number, so she called him instead. Lew did not pick up, and she wondered if he was outside doing a chore or putting tools away, or perhaps he'd driven to town and wasn't back yet. Before leaving Delta, she'd pulled up beside Lew in the yard. With his arms folded, he'd leaned on the rolled-down window of her truck. He'd asked her what she was running away from, and she told him she wasn't, that she just liked to get out there and see different things. He asked her if she'd gotten traveler's checks because he didn't like to see a woman alone on the road with all that cash, and he knew she didn't own a credit card. She didn't want him to worry, so she told him she'd gotten traveler's checks earlier that day, though the truth was, almost all of her cash, about twenty-eight hundred dollars, was in a side pocket in her small duffel bag. She carried another two hundred dollars in her wallet.

"Well, all right, then," Lew said. And he walked away, and Amy Raye felt a lump knot up in her throat because she'd seen his eyes get a little misty, and she knew hers were getting misty also.

Amy Raye hung up the phone and walked back to her table, the mood to call Farrell having passed.

The next morning after taking care of Saddle, who'd slept in the room with her, she returned to the Golden Saloon for breakfast. The manager was there and talked with her for a while. He asked her if she was going to have enough money to get back home. She told him she'd already spent a good two thirds of her money getting to Alaska and fixing her truck, and that she was going to have to stay for a while and hoped to find work. He told her about a friend of his who was looking for seasonal help.

"What kind of help?" Amy Raye asked.

"He's got some cabins about a mile up the road past the footbridge. You would have passed them on your way in. He wants someone to do the housekeeping and help take care of the grounds."

"I could do that," Amy Raye said.

"Might have a bunk you could sleep on also."

"What about my dog?" Amy Raye asked.

"That won't be a problem."

He wrote down his friend's number. Told Amy Raye to give him a call.

The friend ended up hiring Amy Raye and

giving her a place to stay, a bunk in an eight-by-eight shed at the back of the property. The cabins had been newly built and had a full house of reservations for the summer — backpackers and fishing groups and families. "We've got to be able to turn the rooms over fast," the owner told Amy Raye.

After work each day, Amy Raye would pick up fresh groceries or cook something on a camper's stove in the shed. She kept her costs down and was able to save up most of what she made, which was a dollar more than minimum wage, plus the shed. She was trying to live sober, and she thought living in Alaska was giving her the space to do that. She hadn't been back to the Golden Saloon. Hadn't slept with a man since leaving Farrell. Instead, when she had a day off, or finished her work early, she'd hike with Saddle or find something to read. She liked her lean body, was eating well. She even thought about finding work for the winter and staying on. She was living cleaner, and imagined living that way for the rest of her life.

But then one afternoon she walked the mile and a half to the Center Store, as she did most every day. She was almost to the store, taking her time along the dirt road. A breeze tousled the branches of the birch, stirred the rich scent of the black and white spruce. And then she saw him, along the edge of the trees, his body halfway hidden by the tall grasses. She had never seen a grizzly before. And when she stopped, the bear lifted his head over his left shoulder and looked at her. He appeared deliberate and calm. He was magnificent really, his size larger than what she might have imagined, and hefty, as if he could move boulders. And for a moment she just stood there, mesmerized by that magnificence, until he moved, took a few steps toward her, his head and shoulders now facing her, and she tried to remember what she was supposed to do when she encountered a bear. She walked backward, looking at him straight on. "I'm going to the store now," she told him, her voice as steady as she could manage it. She thought about singing. She'd read stories of people who sang when they hiked, to keep bear away, and others who wore bells on their shoes. She continued to walk backward. She continued to talk to the bear until he lifted his head, let out a gruff sound, and turned away.

She walked the rest of the way to the store. She wanted to tell someone about the bear. She wanted to tell Farrell. She needed to make it real.

She had just picked up some hamburger and pasta to cook on her stove. When she paid for her purchase, she saw a man ahead of her. He carried a bottle of water in his left hand and a small pack over his right shoulder. Maybe it was because of the man's stocky build, or the color of his hair — sandy like Farrell's — or the glint in his blue eyes. Maybe it was because the man looked at her for a second as if he recognized her, because in that moment she felt the gnawing ache of a hunger so deep, she knew it in her bones. As she left the store, she saw the man walk down to the Golden Saloon, so she and Saddle followed him there.

She entered the Saloon, leaving Saddle outside on the porch. He was the kind of dog who would stay wherever she told him to and wait for her to return. She saw the man right away; he was sitting at the small bar with a woman and several men around him. Amy Raye approached the bar and stood a few feet to the right of the man. She ordered a beer, and while she waited for it, she observed the man and listened to the conversation he was having with two others. The man would be heading out in the morning on a five-day trek in the Wrangells. He began talking about different entry points and trails into the mountains, running his plans by the other two men who were also backpackers. "Did you run into any more bear?" asked the man who looked like Farrell, so much so that Amy Raye wouldn't have been surprised at all if he had reached behind the bar and picked up a guitar and started playing and singing something by Greg Brown or Neil Young.

Amy Raye paid for her beer and moved to a table. She set her shopping bag next to her feet. She wondered how long she could stay at the saloon before the meat went bad. She gave herself a few hours. She would have a couple of beers, maybe a bowl of soup or a salad, because she could not pull herself away from the man who looked like Farrell, who was sitting next to a woman who looked Spanish, with Russian skin. The woman had full lips, large almond-shaped eyes as black as a crow's, but her skin was milky and pink and smooth. The woman draped her arm over the man's shoulders, said something in his ear, and then stood and walked over to a microphone at the front of the room. Amy Raye's heart pounded loudly in her ears, and she felt that hunger that reminded her of too many times she'd fed herself from men on the streets, and in cars, and in alleys, and of other bars and other places.

Amy Raye ordered soup and crackers and another beer, listened to the woman whom other people in the saloon cheered for. The saloon had become packed with warm bodies clustered around the bar, around the tables, making it hard for Amy Raye to spot the man. The soup turned lukewarm and then cold. Amy Raye dunked the crackers, sipped the beer. The woman was now singing "Can't Let Go" by Lucinda Williams. The tempo was hard and fast, and the woman's voice raspy.

A man wanted to buy Amy Raye a drink, the waitress said. Amy Raye looked up at the group of men at the bar, but she could not find the man who looked like Farrell, and she began to panic.

"Would you like another beer?" the young, blond waitress asked.

"I'll have a whiskey. Maker's Mark or Jim Beam."

But it wasn't the waitress who returned with the whiskey. Instead a tall man with a long, grizzly beard and mysterious blue eyes slid the double whiskey in front of her. "Mind if I join you?" he said. The man pulled out a chair and sat beside her, set his beer on the table. "I've seen you before," he said.

"Where?"

"Around. Walking the road. You live around here?"

"For a while," Amy Raye told him.

She didn't take kindly to men approaching her. She preferred it the other way around.

She slid the drink in front of the man. "I don't take drinks from strangers," she said.

"Name's Malcolm," he said, extending his hand.

She didn't take his hand. "You're still a stranger," she said.

"Well, now, how do you suggest we change that?"

"You drink the whiskey. I'll continue to drink my beer."

"Where you from?" he asked. He picked up the whiskey and drank down at least half of it.

"Montana."

"What's a girl like you doing in Alaska?"

"I have an uncle who owns some cabins. I'm helping him out."

"How long are you staying for?"

"Just long enough for my brother to get here."

"You two driving back to Montana together?"

"We're going to do some hiking first, but

then, yeah, we'll head back together."

"You ever been to Alaska before?"

"First time."

"Do you like it?"

"I like it all right." Amy Raye finished her soup. Finished her beer.

"Can I buy you another one?" the man asked her.

"Like I said. I don't take drinks from strangers."

Amy Raye ordered another beer. The woman continued to play the guitar and sing. The man sitting next to Amy Raye finished the whiskey, and she noticed his hands, the large turquoise ring on the middle finger, the brown spots from the sun. He had to be in his late forties or fifties.

"You have a boyfriend?" he asked her.

"We just broke up," Amy Raye said.

"A boy from Montana?"

"He's going to school in Bozeman. I live in Helena."

The man looked surprised. "How old are you?"

"Nineteen."

"Your mom tell you not to take drinks from strangers?"

"No, my dad did. Do you live around here?" she asked.

"I've got a place a few miles from town I come up to in the summers. I live in Wasilla the rest of the year. You like the music?" he asked.

"I do." Amy Raye pretended to be a little shy all of a sudden.

"Would you like to dance?" he asked.

At least a dozen people were dancing. The music had livened up, moving into straight country. Amy Raye let the man lead her onto the dance floor. Again she searched the bar and the rest of the room for the man who looked like Farrell. He wasn't there. The other two backpackers were now sitting at a table.

"How did you get here?" the man asked her as they danced.

"I walked."

The man tilted his head back and laughed. "No, how did you get to McCarthy?"

"I flew into Anchorage. My uncle picked me up."

"What's your uncle's name?" The man spun Amy Raye around, positioned his hand on her lower back.

"Chase Miller," Amy Raye said.

"Can't say I know him."

As they continued to dance, the man took more chances. His hands grazed Amy Raye's hips. He pressed his long fingers against her back pockets. His breath was on her neck. "My friends call me Mac," he told her.

"Hi, Mac," Amy Raye said, smiling up at him like a bashful girl.

But when the slow dance started, she said she should be getting home. The man whose friends called him Mac said he'd walk her out.

She let him pay for her last beer, and having forgotten about her groceries, she left the saloon with the man. Saddle, who had been lying on the porch, was already standing and wagging his tail.

"I can give you a ride back to your uncle's, if you like," the man offered.

He and Amy Raye had already begun walking the half mile to the bridge, with Saddle trotting beside them.

"I don't mind walking," Amy Raye said.

"You're a beautiful girl," he said.

As they were nearing the bridge, Amy Raye said, "I want to show you something."

She told Saddle to stay, and then she reached for the man's hand.

"Where are you taking me?" he asked her.

They stepped through tall weeds and walked toward an abandoned cabin hidden in the evergreens along the river. She'd found the building while exploring the river's banks. Sometimes campers made use of it, but most of the campers set up their tents along the banks on the parking side of the bridge.

At the back of the cabin, Amy Raye turned to the man, playfully pressed herself against him. "You think I'm beautiful?" she asked.

He slid his hand around the nape of her neck, combed his fingers into her hair, some of her strands getting snagged on his ring. Amy Raye reached for his belt, loosened the buckle.

"You're not even going to kiss me first?" he asked. He'd been standing with his back to the dark brown siding of the cabin. He grabbed a fistful of Amy Raye's hair and pulled her around, pinned her against the wood siding. He kissed her, pushing his tongue into her mouth, while undoing the buckle on his jeans. Then he shoved her down to the ground so that she was on her knees in front of him.

But he didn't let her finish. He yanked her back up, grabbing more of her hair. Using his other hand, he tore at her jeans while she tried to push him away. "So that's how you like to play it," he said. He let go of her hair and pressed his arm over her collarbone, rammed her back against the cabin. She twisted her hips and tried to kick away his hand that was pulling at her jeans, undoing the button, then the zipper. But he was a tall man, with big bones, and used his size to hold her in place. He managed to get her jeans down to her knees, and, lifting her off the ground, he forced himself into her.

She burned and ached and cried, and he thrust himself harder until he groaned, and when he was finished, he shoved her to the ground, and as she fell, a jagged limb dug into her naked hip and tore her flesh.

Despite the rushing of the river, Saddle had heard her scream. He'd run through the woods and around the old cabin, and with teeth bared, he lunged at the man. The man was ready for him. He grabbed the limb that Amy Raye had fallen on and hit Saddle hard across the rib cage. Saddle yelped, and before he could get back on his feet, the man hit him again, this time across the head.

Amy Raye was screaming. She pulled her jeans up over the wound on her hip and charged into the man. She grabbed the limb just as the man was getting ready to strike Saddle again.

The man swung the limb hard, tossing Amy Raye onto the ground. He dropped the limb, buckled his jeans, and walked away. Saddle lay unconscious. Amy Raye scrambled over to him, wrapped her arms around his neck, laid her ear against him. He was still breathing.

She scooped him into her arms and stood. The wound on her hip bled through her jeans and down her leg. She didn't feel the pain, just Saddle in her arms.

There was no one in town who could help her. She would have to carry Saddle across the bridge and the mile of road back to the cabins.

She stepped out of the woods with Saddle cradled against her. The man, called Mac, was now on the bridge and walking toward the parked vehicles. She didn't see anyone else around. Saddle was still unconscious.

Pru

When Jeff and I reported in the next morning, I could tell Colm hadn't gotten any sleep. "It's going on four days since she's been out there," he said. "Got another three inches of snow during the night. Supposed to get a storm this afternoon. I got to tell you, Pru, I'm not sure how much longer we're going to be able to keep this up. It's slippery as hell out there. Had a near call a couple of hours ago."

"What happened?"

"One of the volunteers lost his footing. Slipped on one of the ridges. He's okay, but it gave us a scare. Another team ran into some problems getting back. I had trouble picking them up on the radio."

Next to Colm, on the table, was a solar charger and a cell phone. Colm picked up the phone. "Dean checked out the camp."

"The phone's hers, isn't it," I said.

"It is."

"Are there any messages?"

"Don't know. It's got a passcode on it."

Looking at Colm, I caught his profile, the age on his face, the shadows along his jawline and beneath his eyes where his skin was thickening. Though I'd always thought him good-looking, in the weak morning light through the windows and the fatigue that Colm felt, for just that minute I glimpsed him as an older man.

"Why wouldn't she have her phone on her?" I asked. "It doesn't make sense."

"Unless she didn't want to be found," Colm said.

He reached down the length of the table for a plastic evidence bag. Inside the bag was a yellow piece of paper from a legal pad, the same kind of paper I'd found in the compass pouch two days before.

Inside the plastic, the paper was laid out flat, but there were creases throughout it, as if Amy Raye might have intended to throw the piece of paper away.

<u>November 3</u>

One of the things I love about you most is your ability to understand, and if you don't, you keep digging until you come to a peace with it. I have lots to learn from you,

Farrell. I have resolved a lot internally. You are a huge component of that. You have been my rubbing post. Sadly I've been running an emotional obstacle course to you. You are way too kind to me, more than I deserve, but I don't think it's wise of you. I don't believe on any level you are emotionally safe with me. I am a mess, I am not going to lie. I am no good to you the way I am.

"It feels unfinished," I said. "Where did Dean find it?"

"Inside the stuff bag for her tent, along with a couple of pens and a bottle of Advil."

The note had been written two days before Amy Raye had gone missing. "Has the husband seen this?" I asked.

"I showed it to him before you got here," Colm said.

"What did he say?"

"Said she had a tendency toward introspection. Said she wouldn't have taken her life, and that she seemed fine before she left."

"Did he know what the note alluded to?"

"He wasn't sure. He asked if he could have it. I told him we needed to hold on to it for now."

"Did Dean find anything else?"

"Some personal belongings. Extra gloves and batteries. A couple of books. Pru, I don't have to tell you, it looks like we're going to be back out here this spring."

"I'll be out here before that."

"I know you will. But just do your job. Don't take this on, too."

By two o'clock that afternoon, the snow started up again, and within another hour we were experiencing forty-mile-per-hour gusts, causing temporary whiteouts in places. Jeff and I were working Kona along Big Ridge, adjacent to the clearing where the hat had been found, and just east and north of Cathedral Bluffs, when Colm called the teams in. The weather service was predicting more than a foot of accumulation in the Douglas Pass region and some of the outlying areas. It took Jeff and me two hours to make it back to the station. We were the last team to report in. Then Colm made his announcement.

"As incident commander, I've got to make a decision. I have to be cognizant that these people have limits. I have to weigh risk versus benefit. Plans continue, but at this point, search and recovery have been demobilized," he said.

"Do you have any idea when the search will resume?" a reporter asked.

"This is a tough landscape," Colm said. "Usually on a search we can get snowmobiles and snowshoers into an area. This isn't one of those places. I don't see the search resuming until sometime in the spring," he said.

Another reporter asked, "What about the reports of a possible suicide?"

"Without recovering the body, we can't be certain," Colm told him.

At this point Colm had not made the media aware of the letter that had been recovered, and he'd yet to call it a suicide note, though I knew in his mind he thought it was.

I looked around the makeshift headquarters for the husband and his sister. They were standing toward the back of the room with Dean and a couple of the other volunteers. Dean had his arm on the husband's shoulder. One of the volunteers was rubbing the back of the husband's sister. There weren't many dry eyes in the room. Colm was thanking the volunteers. He thanked everyone from outside the county who had assisted in the search, and he extended his thoughts and prayers to the family.

■ ■ ■ ■

Colm and I watched the volunteers, slow to leave despite their exhaustion.

"They're good people," Colm said. "They gave it their all."

Farrell and his sister were there, as well. They thanked each person who had been part of the search.

"Do you think I made the right decision?" Colm asked me.

"I do. As hard as it is, you did the right thing. Jeff said the same. We're dealing with snow on sheer rock faces," I told him.

Colm looked at his watch. "You should probably get going. If you leave now, you can still make the game."

"It's hard to keep track of what day it is," I said. "I can't believe it's Friday. You going to be okay?"

"I'll be fine," Colm said. "Tell Joseph to break a leg."

"Not really something to say before a football game." I tried to smile.

Colm shook his head. "Sorry. I wasn't thinking."

"I'll have my phone with me. Call me if you need anything."

Amy Raye

Amy Raye was now on her hands and knees. The rain slapped hard on her back as she moved slowly through the grass, inspecting each blade, each indention. About four yards from the tree, she found a drip of blood on the underside of a stick. She tied marking tape to the tip. A couple of yards north of it, she found another drip spilling down the veins of a leaf. From there she found nothing. She moved in every direction. Her knees sank into the soft soil. The smell of cow elk estrus lingered on her skin, her clothes, despite the rainfall.

More hours had passed. She wondered how much area she'd covered. She wished she could get word to Kenny and Aaron. Cell phones were useless in these parts, as there was no signal, and the rain could ruin the battery, and so she had left her cell phone back at her tent. If she did not find the elk soon, she would need to hike back to the truck and return to camp. She'd have to solicit Kenny and Aaron's help. Still on all fours, she raised her head and searched the trees that surrounded the meadow. Perhaps the elk was dying somewhere close by. Perhaps he was already dead. She stood, moved in an outward radius from the clearing, then back, then outward again, looking for some sign: tracks, blood, broken branches.

She heard him before she saw him. A struggle for breath, and that tightening feeling in her chest. She shouldn't have taken the shot. He was still alive. She had miscalculated. The arrow had not killed him.

She stood, walked about twenty yards to her left, and there she found him, lying behind a rock, eyes open, his breathing intermittent and raspy. She'd left her quiver and bow back at the tree. She'd have to retrieve her gun from her pack and put a blow to the elk's head. She stepped around to the other side of the rock, out of sight of the elk. She was familiar with the stories of men and women who had been jumped by an elk and gored to death.

She determined from the irregular rhythm of the elk's breathing that in another half hour or so he would be dead. "Our Father who art in heaven," she prayed again. "Hallowed be thy name."

How long can one say the Lord's Prayer with a child while the sex from a lover is still on one's skin? And always there was the fear that Farrell would find out. There were times when Farrell appeared home earlier than usual, became aroused by a song or the smell of dinner, or the way the slope of her T-shirt revealed her soft cleavage. She'd turn and he'd be there, his hand scooping up the hem of her shirt, his thumb stroking the smooth skin on her waist. And she'd give back to him, desire him with the same kind of urgency she'd felt with someone else earlier in the day at having Farrell gone.

The first time this happened in their relationship, she was afraid Farrell knew. They'd been seeing each other for five weeks, had fallen asleep together four times, made breakfast, and made love. Farrell had stopped by one night unexpectedly.

"I thought you were working," she'd said, her voice tight.

"I decided to take a break. I missed you."

The light left his eyes. It was subtle, but she saw it in that second before he tried too hard to correct it. "I won't stay," he said.

And then the tightness in her loosened itself like particles of dry sand. She grabbed his hand playfully. In that moment, making him feel okay was the only thing that mattered. She vowed in her mind that she would change her ways, that she would give herself to one man, and in this moment of truth, all the other lies could be washed away. And so their patterns of behavior began.

Farrell followed her deeper into her apartment, past the sofa and onto the bed.

"I'm glad you stopped by," she said. She took his hand. "Come here."

Her bedroom lights were dim. She lit a candle next to the bed, curled up into his arms, sheets and blankets tangled around their feet, kissed him without slowing down.

In the beginning of their relationship, Amy Raye thought Farrell was just easy, but now she knew otherwise. He loved her, deep down loved her. And that was the one thing she'd always wanted.

If Farrell had ever suspected her infidelities, he had never let on. No, she was certain he hadn't. He had remained too pure in his devotion to her.

When she was young, maybe eleven or twelve, her mother had read her a story about the legend of Bluebeard, a nobleman who'd had many wives who had disappeared. When he married his seventh wife, he devoted great attention to her and lavished her with affection. She was happier than she had ever been. He tested her obedience and devotion to him by giving her a key to all the rooms in his great castle. He told her she could enjoy all he had and go into any of the rooms, except for one, whose door she was forbidden to ever open. One day, while Bluebeard was away, her curiosity became too great and she opened the door, and with that one act came the end of their great love, for she discovered the bodies of her husband's previous wives.

But Farrell wasn't like the seventh wife. He would never risk what he and Amy Raye had. He would believe what he chose to believe.

One night early in their relationship, Farrell and she had returned to Amy Raye's apartment after having drinks and dinner at Beau Jo's. They were sitting on the sofa, their legs extended over the coffee table, when Farrell asked her, "What do you think love is?"

Saddle jumped on the sofa and tucked himself next to Amy Raye's side. She stroked his neck and rubbed his ears. After a couple of minutes, she said, "I think love is a reflection of how you feel about yourself."

Farrell was quiet at first. His right arm was extended over the back of the sofa. He gently laid his hand on her shoulder. After a few minutes, he tugged softly on the strands of her hair, rubbed them between his fingers. "I think love is a lot like faith," he told her. "It's believing in what you can't see."

With her pack on the ground, she unclasped it as quietly as she could and reached for Kenny's gun, a .357 revolver, which she'd stored in one of the inside pockets. She switched off the gun's safety and stepped around the rock. The elk lay about thirty feet in front of her. Though he was still alive, he did not flinch. With the gun held in front of her and aimed at the elk's head, she stepped closer to him so that she could be sure of making an accurate shot. Within ten feet of the elk, she fired the gun. The bullet struck just below the right eye. The elk's head and body jerked, and then he was still. Amy Raye slowly dropped the gun to her side. She retrieved her pack from behind the rock and rummaged inside it for her rope, hunting knife, and bone saw. She'd have to dress the elk and bag the quarters before going back for help. She was too far out from the vehicle. Even in forty-degree weather, the elk's own body temperature would spoil the meat, and she knew the animal's muscles could generate heat for a couple more hours.

The rain had continued to fall and was now turning to sleet. Amy Raye could not remember having ever been this wet and cold. And she could not tell how much time had passed or how late in the day it was. There were no more shadows, just a steel-gray sky and rain that was turning colder.

Her gloves, soaked through and muddy, had become a hindrance, so she removed them and placed them in her pack. Then she tied long sections of rope just above the hooves of each of the elk's legs. She took hold of the ropes that were knotted around the left-side legs and pulled until she was able to roll the animal onto his back. She tied the other end of each rope to nearby trees, to keep the elk's legs apart.

With her eight-inch hunting knife, she made a clean incision just above the anus and clear up to the elk's neck. Then she pulled the hide aside and inserted her knife below the sternum. She cut through hide and muscle down to the penis, careful not to puncture the gut. Next she cut around the penis, though she left the scrotum intact for when she would turn in her tag. Using her bone saw, she cut through the sternum, and when she was done, she set the saw aside. Soaked in the elk's warm blood and the freezing rain, Amy Raye knelt beside the large animal, and in that moment she was certain she could feel his spirit clinging to the air like the cold breath of dew.

With both hands and several attempts, she pried apart the elk's rib cage. The steam from the elk's organs warmed her hands, and she hesitated for almost a half minute to enjoy the relief. Again she picked up her knife. She cut around the diaphragm, cut the windpipe, and began pulling everything down, separating the organs from the wall of the cavity.

Despite her shivering, she was able to remove the organs without snagging or puncturing them. She tossed the steamy guts aside. If the weather hadn't been so bad and she'd had more time, she would have deboned the quarters to eliminate some of the weight. But she was losing light. She wondered if there was a square inch of dry clothing on her. Instead, she'd strap one of the elk's shoulders to the top of her pack and set the other quarters a good fifty yards away and in a depression where the cold air would pool and the meat scent would disperse. With the meat set aside, scavengers would more likely be drawn to the smell of the carcass and the offal. Once she returned to camp, she'd dress in dry clothes. She'd put new batteries in her headlamp. Kenny and Aaron would have their headlamps as well, and they'd each have their packing frames. This wouldn't be the first time they'd hauled an animal out at night. She thought about the heat running full blast in the cab of the truck, thought about the other sandwich Kenny had prepared and how good it would taste.

She cut out the elk's liver and heart and placed them in the gallon-size plastic bag she'd brought. She didn't care for the taste of these organs, but her grandfather had taught her not to let anything go to waste.

Water dripped down her face, and snowflakes began to melt on her hands. The snow surprised her, and for the first time she wondered how far she might be from the truck. She tried to remember how many times she had stopped to tie marking tape. She couldn't remember, and yet she felt certain of the path she had taken since setting down her quiver, and once she had retrieved her quiver, she could use her compass.

She snapped the rope from the elk's right hindquarter and began removing the hide from the meat. The snow picked up. Branches broke behind her, no doubt from the wind, or was there something in the grouping of pinyon just beyond her? Maybe a deer. And she realized how crazy she was to have made this hunt alone. She wasn't a young girl hunting deer behind her grandfather's property. The rack on this elk was four points on each side. The time it would take her to quarter the elk, bag the meat, and begin packing it out could take her into the night. The others had planned on heading home to the front range that day. They'd all been tired and ready to get back. As it was now, the three of them would be up all night getting the elk out of there. She'd been thinking only of herself. Wasn't that the hell of it. That was the thing. And as Amy Raye worked as quickly as she could, as her knife made clean slices between the hide and the meat, her arms and coat and pants covered in blood, she began to regret everything she had done.

After she had skinned the shoulders and hindquarters, she severed the cartilage and connective tissue of each of the joints. She placed each quarter in a game bag. Then she removed as much meat as she could from the neck and cut out the backstrap that ran down both sides of the elk's spine. She placed these in a fifth game bag. All the while, the sky grew darker, the temperatures dropped, and the snow continued to fall.

She would sever the head from the spine when she returned with Kenny and Aaron. For now, using the extra rope, she secured one of the front quarters, a good sixty pounds, onto the top of her pack. She used the remaining rope to drag each of the other quarters at least fifty yards to a divot in the ground beneath a mature juniper. She cut several boughs from another tree and covered the meat to help it stay dry. But after dragging these quarters, after lifting and pulling them over rocks and deadfall, her arms and legs quivered from the sheer fatigue of it all. And so she pushed herself harder. She needed to make time before dark and cursed the fact that she had not packed extra batteries for her headlamp. Even if she'd had her headlamp, going over this terrain would be tricky. As she returned to retrieve her pack, she hastened her steps, all the while watching the ground for deadfall and jutting rocks. And then came the impact to her head, a heavy jab from an overhanging branch. The force of it knocked her off balance so that she almost fell backward but instead rocked forward and landed on her hands and knees. This was not the first time that day that she'd hit her head on a jagged limb. The junipers, especially, were twisted and gnarly, their trunks like petrified wood.

She felt light-headed when she stood, and also a throbbing pain. She pressed her palm where the limb had made impact, and when she did, she felt the tear in the fleece, and soon after the warm blood against her hand. She removed her hat and, using her fingertips, inspected the wound. If she had been home, she would have cleaned the cut properly and would most likely have gotten stitches. She replaced her hat, pressed her right palm against the gash, and continued to apply pressure for a few minutes until the bleeding slowed.

A hundred more feet and she was standing beside the carcass. She lifted her pack, carried it to the rock, and, leaning against the rock, slid her arms beneath the shoulder straps. She secured the hip belt and sternum strap. Then she stood, transferring the weight of the pack onto her back. But with the exertion, she felt the cut open again, and the blood trickled from the crown of her head through her hair and down to her left ear. Once more she applied pressure, and continued to do so while she walked around the rock. The snow was accumulating quickly and prevented her from seeing her tracks. Just ahead was the meadow. On the other side she should be able to pick up her trail and make the steep climb to the ridge. She was still light-headed, and worried about the climb. She stopped and drank at least eight ounces of water from the hydration reservoir in her pack, and thought about the Advil she had back at her tent. She should eat something, but she did not want to remove her pack again or waste what little daylight was left, and so she moved on, hoping for some shelter from the snow once she was in the dense spread of trees. Maybe there she would be able to find her tracks.

Upon crossing the meadow, the wind whipped through her layers. Carrying the weight of her pack with the elk quarter would be good for her, as the exertion would warm her body. But her head felt tepid and wet, and when she reached to check the gash, certain it was still bleeding, her fingertips pressed against her damp hair. She was no longer wearing her hat, and she could not recall when it had come off. Perhaps when she'd entered the meadow the hat had gotten snagged on a branch. Again she applied pressure to the wound, but this time she kept moving. She could not turn back, and wished she had brought the blaze orange hat she'd left at the truck. She was still feeling light-headed, which would worsen if the bleeding continued. And without her hat, her head was already becoming soaked from the snow. She would lose too much body heat should she stop, and how much farther until she would be at the truck? She tried to pick up her pace.

She was now at the far edge of the clearing. She entered the timber and looked for her tracks but could find none, and she wondered if in part the snow and wind had erased her path. Then she thought of the rain and how hard it had fallen. There would be no tracks. The rain would have washed them away hours ago. And she had been on her hands and knees much of the time. She continued on, confident she was moving in the right direction. She thought of the deadfall she had crossed over earlier and the steep terrain. Everything looked familiar.

Though Amy Raye did not have a watch on, she had to have walked more than an hour. She should have come upon her quiver. The taste of panic coated her tongue. With each minute that passed, she was less sure of herself. Perhaps her quiver was nearby, but with the snowfall and these thick woods, she'd have a difficult time identifying the marker, and to circle back would only waste time, and dusk was quickly approaching. More than once she'd almost slipped and lost her footing. The terrain was rockier than she had remembered. She stopped occasionally to take a sip of water, to catch her breath. She was carrying up to eighty pounds, and every muscle in her body felt stiff and ached. She thought of shedding the elk quarter, but something else was taking hold of her, an awareness of her surroundings, and the cold, and the approaching nightfall. She'd relied on her adrenaline, had attacked these woods, trying to make good time, and now with each step, she knew just how lost she had become.

Cougar

Pru

As I drove away from the command station, I felt the letdown from the search, as well as the fatigue, and yet with each mile closer to Rio Mesa, something different began to take hold of me, something large and warm and comforting. I tried to call Joseph, though I knew he would be in the locker room getting ready for the game. When I got his voice mail, I left a message. "I'll be there," I said. "Rio Mesa against the number two team. I think I'll bet ten on five."

Joseph and I had always made bets on the games. He played cornerback. Whoever's bet was the closest to the number of tackles he made had to pay up. I paid by taking Joseph out to eat. Joseph paid by fixing dinner. If we tied, we ordered out. "Two dinners on four tackles," Joseph had said the week before. I had bet on six tackles, and by the end of the game, Joseph had brought seven of the opponent's offensive carriers down.

This would be a big game. Rio Mesa was supposed to make it to state this year. Joseph was one of only three sophomores who started.

When I turned onto the driveway, Kona, who was riding in the back, immediately stood up. His tail was wagging; the tags on his collar were clinking together.

There was a snow shovel leaning against the house. I cleared the steps to the porch. The town had gotten only four to six inches so far, but the snow was still coming down. On the porch, I removed my boots and hung up my jacket by the door next to a coal shovel that I used to knock icicles from the roof. I stepped inside, set the keys on the counter, and glanced at the clock on the stove. A little after six. If I hurried, I could get a shower and still make it in time for the kickoff.

The water burned hot against my skin, bringing my blood to the surface, warming my cold bones and muscles. I dried off quickly and dressed in a pair of jeans, a thick sweater, my down jacket, and gloves. I picked up my keys off the counter. "You have to stay," I told Kona. "You be a good boy."

As I drove to the school, I pictured Joseph, his slight bowlegged stance along the sidelines while the offensive team was in the game, the way he would glance back at the stands every so often to see if I was there. I'd be stepping onto the field with him at the halftime ceremony, when the players honored their parents.

When I got out of the truck, I heard the band playing and people cheering. I jogged across the plowed pavement.

"Has the game started?" I asked, when I got to the gate.

"Just getting ready to." And then, "You forgot your program."

But I was already making a good stride toward the field, brushing shoulders with a couple of the people I passed, dodging kids who were running around in jerseys and tossing anything they could catch, from foam footballs to wadded-up paper cups.

Cheers erupted around me. The teams were taking to the field for the kickoff. I climbed the bleacher steps and looked for an empty spot.

"Pru . . . hey," a cheery voice called. "Come up here. We can make room."

It was Ellen, the tech who worked at White River Animal Hospital, seated two rows higher. Her son was a freshman. He played junior varsity.

I climbed up to the higher bleacher.

"You want to share my blanket?" Ellen asked.

Ellen was wrapped in a large, checkered fleece blanket. Beside her was a thermos. She wore a Broncos knit cap, and her face was mostly covered in a thick black and gold scarf, Rio Mesa's school colors.

"No, I'm all right," I said, though already my knees were bouncing.

"Go Cowboys!" Ellen screamed as the defensive team ran onto the field.

Cowbells rang from the student section. "Go get 'em, Joseph!" I yelled over the other cheers.

The student section was to my right. I didn't recognize all of the kids. There were new families in town that had moved in when the pipeline workers came looking for jobs and the gas companies had started drilling fresh sites. I hugged myself tighter, smelling wool and mustard and coffee, and a slight whiff of booze from the crowd around me.

Then Ellen told me she'd heard about a hunter going missing near Rangely. Someone had come into the animal hospital and was talking about it, she said. "I heard it was a woman."

"Colm called off the search late this

afternoon." I went on to tell Ellen what I knew.

Ellen wanted to know about the husband. She asked about the kids. "That poor family," Ellen said.

More cowbells, and cheers, and drumrolls sounded. I watched my son running onto the field to take his position in the lineup. The quarterback now had the ball. He fell back to make a pass. Joseph was laid flat by an offensive lineman. The short pass was completed. First down.

Ellen grimaced. So did I.

"That had to hurt," Ellen said.

And as I watched my son play, I thought about Amy Raye. I thought about the note that had been found. *I have lots to learn from you,* Amy Raye had written. Her words gave me the sense that her journey with her husband wasn't over.

By the third play, Joseph made the tackle. "Number eleven, running back for Hayden, is taken down by the Cowboys' number twenty-four, Joseph Hathaway."

Ellen was clapping. Cowboy fans whooped and cheered.

"That's my boy!" I hollered. I was waving my fist in the air and screaming with the rest of the fans.

After the punt, Rio Mesa's offensive team

took to the field. Joseph jogged over to the sidelines and glanced up at the stands. He was built just like my brother, Greg, same height, same broad shoulders. Oftentimes when watching Joseph, I'd remember all the games I'd attended when Greg had played wide receiver. Greg was three years older than I, and no doubt, growing up with him had played a role in my being a tomboy most all my life. That, and our father's insistence that we love the outdoors as much as he did. Though my parents owned a small business and managed their parcel of farmland, each summer they'd leave the co-op in the hands of one of their employees for a couple of weeks; they'd pay a neighbor a little something to take care of the chickens and any other animals we had at a given time; and we'd take off for one of Dad's many adventures — the Sierra Nevadas, Sawtooth Mountain in Idaho, the Grand Tetons. Dad had me carrying a backpack and hiking trails before I'd even started school. He'd plan these trips for months and outfit us with army surplus packs, down sleeping bags, and bedrolls of thin foam. Greg and I shared our own tent away from our parents. He'd tell me stories late into the night, making up adventures of long-forgotten Indian warriors. I'd lie on my back, smell the wild sage, listen to the gurgle of the snow-fed streams. And each day as we hiked, we'd keep our eyes peeled for arrowheads or potsherds. We never did find an arrowhead, or a projectile point, as our dad would call them, but we did find flakes of chert that we'd store in our pockets.

On that June day that Brody was killed, Greg was spending his second summer as a seasonal worker for the Rocky Mountain National Park in Estes Park, Colorado. He was sharing a cabin with four other men and spending most of his days clearing trails. When he came home for Brody's service, Greg did his best to console me, and the rest of the summer he tried to get me to come visit him at the park, but I was too thick in my grief to be apart from anything that Brody and I had shared.

There was a shrine for Brody at the edge of the field where he had died, cards and letters and stuffed animals from friends of ours in high school. I didn't leave anything at the shrine. Instead I would walk out to the middle of the field where he had fallen. I'd lie back in the grass where some of the bloodstains still remained and I'd imagine him lying beside me.

I worked at my parents' store a few days a week, usually in the back where I unpacked merchandise, or I helped unload bags of feed and grain from the delivery trucks. And in the fall, though I still lived at home, I attended classes at the University of Missouri in Kansas City. I was supposed to major in life sciences. Brody and I had planned on getting married that following summer. I would have stayed in college until I'd finished my degree. He would have taken classes and continued to work on his family's farm. We would have lived in a sixteen-foot trailer on a piece of property he had bought, while we built our house. And maybe we would have had a son as beautiful as Joseph. Maybe we would have had a few more.

Greg was a senior in college that year, and majoring in secondary education at the University of Northern Colorado in Greeley. He'd already lined up a job teaching freshman English at a high school in Boulder that next fall. He'd come home for Christmas break. That was when he and my parents sat me down. They said they wanted to talk to me. They said the Lidells were stopping by, too.

The dishes from dinner had been put away. Mom and Dad and Greg, Mr. and Mrs. Lidell, and I were all sitting around the table. Mom had made coffee but none of us were drinking any.

Dad said they wanted to talk about me getting away for a while. They thought a change of scenery would do me good. I wasn't comfortable with the conversation. I thought I'd been doing all right. I'd gone to my classes. My grades had been fine.

Mr. Lidell reached across the table and took my hand. "We're real worried about you, Pru. And I know it'd tear Brody up to see you like this."

Then Greg talked about the contacts he'd made while working for the Park Service. He said he had friends in Colorado who'd also held seasonal jobs. One of those friends had recently taken a position as a full-time ranger for the Bureau of Land Management. The friend was working out of the Grand Junction field office. He'd told Greg that the BLM was looking for seasonal workers for the summer and that there were several openings on the Western Slope. "He can put in a good word for you," Greg said.

I felt intrigued by the job, and yet terrified of leaving Brody behind. I looked at my parents. Their faces were hopeful.

Mrs. Lidell said something about Brody wanting me to be happy. And I thought about how strong she was, how strong she and Mr. Lidell both were.

I finished out my semester. Then I packed my truck, a red Tacoma. I would be leaving the next morning. It was a hot day in early June and unusually humid for Missouri. I put on my running shoes and took off down our road, ran past the fields and pastures, and I might have kept going, all the way to the cemetery another three miles out of town, but as I came up on Brody's house, Mr. Lidell waved to me from the driveway. He was working on Brody's car, an old Camaro. I stopped running and walked up the driveway, and for a moment, I didn't think I could do it, didn't think I could get in my truck that next day and drive away.

Mr. Lidell invited me in. The house felt dark, the curtains having been drawn to block out the heat from the sun. I apologized as I sat on the sofa in the living room; my legs were still damp and sticky with sweat. Mr. Lidell talked of a new minister at the church. He told me of the minister's family, something about him having four kids. I said that was nice. We were working too hard at conversation, and I had this desire to curl up on the couch from the exertion of it all.

Dinner was ready, Brody's mom told us. I didn't want to stay, but I was already caught up in the moment as we moved to the kitchen and sat around a large oak table. We held hands as Brody's dad prayed and my legs stuck to the shellac on the chair. When we finished praying, I picked up my glass of ice water. My wrist and hand shook. Brody's parents spoke to me. There were long pauses in the conversation. I concentrated on keeping my hand steady. This was our good-bye, only we didn't know how to say it.

The next day, I drove nine hours before stopping in Boulder, where Greg had just moved into his new apartment. We spent a couple of days exploring the area together. We hiked Gregory Canyon because I'd gotten a kick out of the name, and walked the trails around the Boulder Reservoir and Coot Lake, where local dogs swam. I told Greg he needed to get a dog now that he was out of school and had a real job, and he said he would.

I cried when we said good-bye, when Greg pulled me in for a hug and told me to be strong because I was the strongest woman he'd ever known. He said he'd check in on me and that he knew I'd be great. In two more weeks Brody would have been gone for a year, and though I'd be alone on the anniversary of his death, I'd be seeing Greg again soon. He and I agreed to meet for the

Fourth of July if I had the day off. Then I climbed into my truck, and with the windows rolled down, I held out my arm and waved to him as I pulled away.

Joseph and I had carved out a nice life for ourselves. I smiled at the thought of that. Again he made a tackle. Again I cheered. I drank some of Ellen's coffee. Brian, who worked at the post office, and was sitting behind us, offered me a shot from his flask. The sweet burn of Jack Daniel's warmed my throat and chest. He asked me about the missing hunter. I filled him in on some of the details, most of which he had already heard. He shook his head. "I feel bad for the person who's going to stumble on her in the spring," Brian said. He took another drink from his flask and passed it back to me. Already I was thinking about Colm. I hoped he was getting some rest.

By halftime Rio Mesa and Hayden were tied 7–7. The band was lined up on the track, preparing for the halftime show. I wondered when the ceremony would begin, the one where the players would be announced and their parents would be asked to join them on the field. The ceremony where the boys presented their mothers with roses because that was how it was done.

This would be my first time to be a part of it. The year before, Joseph had played junior varsity. I waited while the band marched out onto the field, and Ellen talked and poured more coffee, and Brian talked to the man beside him about the Broncos' upcoming game against the Patriots, and students moved up and down the steps to my right.

"What about the ceremony?" I asked Ellen.

Ellen looked confused.

"The one where the parents go down to the field," I said.

"The ceremony took place before the game. Right before you got here. I thought you knew."

"I thought it was at halftime."

Maybe the look on my face told her how miserable I felt. Maybe she saw the ache crawling up my throat, because she reached out her gloved hand and rubbed my shoulder. "I'm sorry," she said. Then Ellen turned to talk to someone behind us. I stared at the field, listened to the band play a bad version of Queen's "We Are the Champions."

A hand pressed against my back. Cheryl Manning, another mom, was kneeling behind me. "We made these for the mothers of all the players," she said.

Cheryl handed me a button with Joseph's picture. He was wearing his jersey and giving the victory sign. Strips of gold and black ribbon hung from behind the button.

"I thought the ceremony was at halftime," I said again.

"Don't worry about it," Cheryl said. "Joseph's playing great."

And when no one was looking, I wiped my eyes. I continued to stare at the field. I waited for Joseph and the second half.

The rest of the game didn't go as well. Hayden scored again in the third and made the extra point. By the fourth quarter Rio Mesa was at its third down on the twenty-yard line. The quarterback tried for a pass to receiver Tyler Cook. The pass was incomplete. Mesa went for the field goal and scored another three points.

The final score was 14–10, Hayden. The stands cleared. Ellen left, her plump legs moving in a hurry down the bleacher steps, her blanket under one arm, her thermos under another. "I've got to get home. Russell's driving in from Paonia tonight. Tell Joseph he played a good game."

Other people talked among themselves about Hayden's quarterback, about the weather, about the new restaurant going in at the Rio Mesa Hotel. Someone behind me talked about the five-point buck he'd spotted at Yellow Jacket Pass. I thought of Amy Raye Latour, and checked my cell phone in case Colm had called. As I descended the bleachers, I saw a program on the concrete beneath one of the seats. I picked up the booklet, folded it, and tucked it in my coat pocket.

Inside the school building, along the painted cinder-block walls, were signs the students had made for the game. Groups of parents stood together talking. I walked down the long hallway that led to the lobby and then to the locker rooms. Displayed in the lobby were the trophy cases and the pictures of the school's graduating classes. The pictures dated back as far as 1917. I recognized many of the family names, even recognized some of the faces of the men and women who still lived in the area. I brought the folded program out of my pocket. There was a special insert for the evening's ceremony, with a picture and small blurb of each of the players. The photos were organized by the players' class rank, with the sophomores toward the end. There was Joseph, his neck long like mine. His light eyes looked like glass in the black-and-white photo. Neither his dad nor I had blue eyes. Sometimes I was sure Joseph looked like the son Brody and I would have had.

Joseph and his friend Corey walked toward me. I watched my son, his uneven gait, the way his body rocked, his feet slightly turned out. Groups of other players were making their way down the wide corridor as well, none of them looking too happy.

Joseph's left hand was shoved into the front pocket of his jeans. He was wearing his jersey and carrying a yellow rose in his right hand. His hair was still wet and hung over his broad forehead. "Thanks for coming to the game," he said. He handed me the rose.

I wrapped my arm around his shoulders. "Joseph, I'm sorry. I thought the ceremony was at halftime."

"Is the woman okay?" he asked.

"We haven't found her yet." And then, "Do I dare talk about the game?"

"Offense sucked," Corey said. "Three turnovers on the fourth down. They should have punted."

"Coach's call," I said. "You got plans tonight?"

"Maybe. I don't know yet," Joseph said.

"Want to walk me to my truck?"

Joseph and I stepped outside and walked across the parking lot. "You played well," I said. "We'll do dinner."

"Okay."

Another inch of snow had fallen while we'd been inside the school and was still coming down. I unlocked the truck and set the rose inside. "Be careful," I said. "The roads will be slick. Curfew is eleven thirty."

"I know."

He stepped toward me, and I gave him a hug.

"Did she have any kids?" he asked.

My head rocked forward. "A stepdaughter and a son. Say a prayer for them," I said.

"Okay, I will."

I drove toward town. My wheels spun occasionally over patches of compressed slush that was beginning to freeze. At the center of town, I parked in front of the post office, a small, nondescript brick building. My post office box was on the right-side wall inside the foyer. I opened the box and scooped out the large pile of mail. I stopped at a nearby counter to sort through the items and discard the advertisement flyers in a recycling bin. The post office felt as cold and empty as it was. I would go home and build a fire, wait for the house to get warm.

My phone rang. It was Colm.

"They lost," I said when I answered.

"I know. I heard the score on the radio."

"You should be asleep by now," I told him.

"So should you."

"Yeah, well, I'm on my way home now."

"I called Hank Ruckman. As soon as this snow lets up, he's going to meet me out there and have a look."

Hank was the district wildlife manager for the DOW.

"You're thinking more about the lion," I said.

"I guess I am. Even if she did take her life, I'd like to know what happened to her body."

"What did Hank say?"

"He said when a lion makes a kill, most of the bleeding is done on the inside. The rest of the blood can easily be absorbed on the clothes or the thickness of the brush. The lion may have dragged her a hundred yards to a steep ledge, behind a rock crevice, a canyon, somewhere in the timber, and covered her to keep her cool. He said the lion could have finished her off in a couple of days. By the time we found the hat and the gun, there might not have been much left."

"What about clothing or her backpack?"

"I'm not sure. But the lion's scent could have thrown off Kona, could have covered up the scent of the subject."

"So her committing suicide is questionable," I said.

"It's always been questionable," he said.

"If she was attacked by a lion, would she have had time to fire the gun?" I asked.

"She might have if she'd spotted the lion before it attacked."

I wasn't so sure. Lion attacked from behind.

Colm went on, repeating a lot of the things Jeff had said and what I already knew, about Amy Raye wearing camouflage and smelling like elk piss. "Even so, according to Ruckman, the lion's kills are arbitrary," Colm said. "If he'll take out a horse, he could just as arbitrarily take out a person. Hank's going to go ahead and call their trapper. See if he can meet us out there as well. If we can take down that lion, we can check its stomach contents for any trace of human remains."

"I don't like the way that sounds."

"We need answers," Colm said.

"The snow's supposed to let up sometime Sunday morning," I told him.

"You want to go with us? You'd be able to lead Hank and his trapper into the area better than I can."

"Yeah, I'll be there."

"I'll call you," Colm said.

Flakes of snow had gathered on my windshield. I turned on the wipers. The blades smeared the flakes like chips of glass. The rubber of the blades squeaked against the pane.

I was just getting ready to put the truck in reverse when I saw Joseph with that uneven gait of his, hands in his pockets, no coat, snow melting in his hair, and Corey, a couple of inches taller than Joseph, broad shouldered, still wearing his football jersey. They were walking toward the courthouse lawn, where a handful of other teenagers were hanging out. Like most of the kids in town, they'd known each other all their lives. Sometime around fifth grade they'd become best friends. I was glad they had each other. I knew growing up without a dad hadn't always been easy on Joseph. And Corey had his own loss to deal with, a sadness that had affected the whole town. Corey had lost a brother in Afghanistan. He was in eighth grade when it happened.

I wanted to bring both boys coats and tell them to put their hats on. Instead I drove the rest of the way home.

Amy Raye

A little farther up the incline and perhaps Amy Raye would be able to see enough to gather some sense of the direction she'd been heading. If nothing else, she might be able to find shelter. She'd have to build a fire and wait out the night. And so she climbed, her body bent forward, her knees weaker with each step, as if any moment they might buckle beneath her. Just a little farther. She was on an edge now. She leaned forward until she was able to hold on to the wet rocks of the incline with her bare hands and get an idea of her surroundings. Just below the rocky ledge, maybe twenty feet, was a shelter, she was sure of it, an overhang with enough of a rock wall to serve as a buffer from the wind. She could stay there for the night. And so she grabbed a root with her right hand and a handhold in the rock with her left. She stretched her left leg over the edge until she found a crack with the toe of her boot. She wedged her boot into the crack for support, and let go of the root with her right hand. She would climb down to the shelter. But the weight on her back was too great, and her left hand slipped, her boot still jammed in the crack, the weight of her body and the pack and elk quarter propelling her backward and over, and then pain and noise, her ankle snapping. Her foot dislodged. She hurtled downward. Her hip slammed against a rock, and a sickening jolt so sharp from her ankle and through her leg, so acute she could not breathe. She had landed on another ledge, a good fifteen feet or more from the top one, and above her she could see the shelter, maybe five feet from her at the most. And nausea as soupy thick as the pain, snow melting on her face and lashes, and the misshape of the bone just above her ankle, like the arc in her bow. She exhaled in a long cry, and when she did, her voice echoed back at her. Her pack was behind her, the elk leg protruding at an odd angle alongside her neck. She shifted her hip away from the rock, and nausea surged through her until she dry-heaved. She pushed the elk leg away from her neck, her hands still covered in the elk's blood, or was it hers? She did not know.

She struggled to sit up, to assess the damage. Again she heaved, bile coating her throat. Her left leg was useless, and her left hip badly bruised. She cried out again, her tears mixed with the blood on her face. Once more her echo answered her, like something wild. Her body shivered with cold and distress, or was she going into shock? And the night would grow colder. And how had she become so lost? How had she plunged so wildly ahead?

Already the sky had darkened, the shelter appearing no more than a shadow in the rock face. She would have to use her arms and shoulders. She would have to find a way to climb. If she stayed where she was, she would not make it through the night, and she had no idea how long it would take Kenny and Aaron to find her. She unfastened the pack. She slid her arms from beneath the straps. Her jaw clenched as she shifted her weight, as she tried to slow her rapid breathing. Then she unzipped the top opening of her pack and pulled out the rope she had used to drag the elk quarters only hours before. How much time did she have left? A half hour, maybe less, before the gray-glow of daylight would be gone. She threaded the rope beneath the shoulder straps of her pack and around the elk quarter, then knotted the rope and pulled it tight. She placed the other end in her mouth so that her hands would be free to climb. With her palms flat against the rocky surface of the ledge, she lifted her hips and tucked her right foot beneath her, and as she did her voice tore out of her in an angry moan. Her left leg remained extended in front of her. She placed one hand at a time on the edge of the rock face, grabbed handholds, pulled and shifted. Her teeth ground against the rope. Another handhold, and another, her right foot feeling for some leverage, her fingers so cold, the tips numb.

Her hands reached the ledge where she'd spotted the shelter. She folded each forearm over the edge, pulled the weight of her torso. Her left ankle knocked against a rock, nausea like an icy stream. Again she heaved herself forward, until her entire body was on the ledge, a flat area maybe twenty feet from the rock face, and littered with dead wood and pinyon saplings. And there in front of her was the shelter, not just an overhang, but a cave, the entrance a triangular crevice, about three feet wide at the bottom, and another three or four feet high. She adjusted herself to a sitting position, pressed her back against the rock face, removed the rope from her mouth, clasped the rope with both fists, and pulled. About halfway up, her pack became snagged, or was it the leg of the elk, the bone that protruded from the game bag that had gotten caught? She jimmied the pack free, and when she did, she heard something fall out of the pack and drop well beyond the ledge where she had fallen. She hoisted the pack the rest of the way and grabbed hold of the elk leg, and when the entire bundle was beside her, she shoved it into the cave's entrance. Then she rolled onto her stomach, dragged herself an inch and then another.

Her body shivered. Her blood pressure was dropping. Shock wasn't out of the question. She groaned loudly. Her elbows and forearms dug into the wet dirt, her right knee bent up to her hip for leverage. She continued to move her body this way until she lay on the floor of the small cave, but just how far back it went she could not tell. What little light was left in the day was nothing more than a shallow, metallic glow across the entrance, across the disfiguration of her left leg. And the shivering created movement in her broken leg, and pain as sharp as a fingernail being ripped from its quick. She'd have to get warm. She'd have to build a fire, and to build a fire she would need to drag her leg yet again in order to gather wood from outside the cave. She had the wild sensation to take her knife, open her skin down to the bone, as if in doing so she'd be able to release the pain.

She loosened the game bag, unzipped her pack, and shoved her hand inside. She removed her bone saw, shifted other items around, and as she did she realized it was her binoculars that must have fallen. She wrapped her fingers around the plastic container with waterproof matches that she'd packed. She'd also brought a piece of flint that she could use with her knife, but the matches would be quicker. On the ledge outside the cave were dead wood, sticks, and bark. Again she pushed herself to a sitting position, lifted and moved her broken leg, yelled out in anguish, yelled for Kenny and Aaron, hoped to God they would be looking for her. She adjusted her weight and pulled her body back onto the snowy ledge, the numbing cold from the shot of wind almost a relief. Moving on her belly, she gathered sticks, broke off larger pieces of wood from deadfall and debris, cut through other pieces with the bone saw, collected pieces of bark, and continued to do so until she was sure she had enough to get her through the night. Only moments before she'd planned on seeking shelter, eating the remaining jerky and perhaps cooking some of the elk, rationing her water so she'd have plenty for the next day. She'd anticipated finding her way out of this place in the morning. Anticipated the sun breaking through the clouds, and when it did, she would have been able to get her bearings. And Kenny and Aaron would be looking for her then. Maybe they were looking for her now. She'd build a fire. They'd see the smoke.

She crawled toward the middle of the cave and lit a handful of bark shavings and twigs. Then she added a couple of small branches from which she had brushed off the snow. Though some of the wood on the ledge would have been too wet to light, she'd been able to gather enough dry pieces from beneath the trees, and soon the musty scent of the cave filled with the sweet smell of cedar.

Her hands were still mostly covered with blood. It had now dried and was flaking off like old paint. In that moment, she didn't care about the game bag. She didn't care that the meat would spoil in the warm cave. She was in too much pain, the kind of pain that feels delirious, transporting even, as if she could imagine herself someplace else, imagine falling asleep beside this warm fire and waking up to a blue sky, imagine a life and an ankle and a marriage unbroken. But as delirious as she felt, she also knew she must eat and did not know how much time would pass before she was found. And so as the chill left her body, she gathered more strength and pushed the game bag outside the cave so that the meat would not spoil, rolled the elk quarter, and kept rolling it until it was a good eight feet to the right of the cave's entrance. There she covered the shoulder with boughs she'd cut from low-hanging limbs. And once the meat was covered, she returned to the shelter.

She added more wood to the fire. She removed the remaining beef jerky from her pack, removed the plastic bag that held the elk's liver and heart. She would cook the organs. They could sustain her for a couple of days. And she would eat the remaining beef jerky. But for now, her stomach was too nauseated, and her leg was swelling. She'd have to collect snow and pack it around the break to keep the swelling down. Numbing her leg would help with the pain as well. She still had the sandwich bag from earlier in the day, and the bag holding the elk's organs, and the bag of jerky. She transferred the jerky to her pockets. She then used her knife to shave down one of the longer branches and turn it into a skewer. She pierced the heart and liver and set them aside. She tucked the three empty bags beneath her arm and scooted back to the ledge. There, she scooped snow into each of the three zip-top bags. The pain was getting worse. She knew the bone must be bleeding, and she would need to immobilize her leg. Her body was shaky, and again she was aware that her blood pressure was dropping. She crawled back into the cave, stoked the fire once more. She packed the bags of snow around her broken ankle, then lay back against her pack, all the while listening to the wind, an eerie howl like something wild. She willed the warmth of the fire and her fatigue to lull her to sleep, to give her some relief.

And she must have slept, because when she awoke, the cave was dark, and the fire was only embers. She blew on the embers and stoked them until the flame reignited. Then she added more wood. She wondered how long the fire had been out, and she recognized how warm the cave had remained. She had found a good shelter. The snow in the bags had melted. She would need to get more. But she was so tired, and she was weak. She lay back again. This time she did not close her eyes. She watched the fire's glow dance across the four-foot-high ceiling above her, dance around the cave walls. She sat up and added a larger piece of wood to the flame so that it would burn brighter, so that she could see better. There was something on the walls. She inched her way the few feet toward the wall in front of her. Painted in white and some red were pictographs. Other people had been here before her, and she felt comfort in that. Across the wall were swooping curves that resembled white birds. Another picture looked to be of a bighorn sheep with an oversized rectangular body. On the back wall of the cave were four prints of small hands, as if made by children, and Amy Raye wondered if a family had occupied this site. The dirt floor was softer toward the back of the cave, and the walls were warm from the fire.

Though her legs remained outstretched because of her ankle, she curled her body into a fetal position and laid her head on the fine sand beneath her. She thought of her children, of Julia's hands and Trevor's. She pressed her palm against the small prints on the wall beside her, imagined crawling on the bed with her sweet boy, Trevor, wrapping her arms around him while he slept. Imagined smoothing his soft brown hair and kissing his forehead, damp with sweat and the Dove soap from his bath. She'd pick up Chomper, his stuffed tiger, whom Trevor would bring to bed each night and inevitably push away as he slept. She'd reposition the tiger beside him. Then she'd go to Julia's room, her lively, spirited stepdaughter, who slept on top of the covers, because even at twelve years old, she hated for anything to confine her. She'd be on her stomach, sprawled on top of the bed, arms spread out, her dark blond hair falling in waves over her shoulders and across her face. Amy Raye would kneel against Julia's bed, careful not to wake her, hold her small hand, kiss her fingers, the sparkly purple polish on her nails having chipped away at the ends, her oversized T-shirt from one of the concerts Julia had gone to with her dad pushed up above her knees. Amy Raye would close the book Julia would have been reading, would reach over and turn off the small clip-on light on the corner of Julia's headboard. She'd kiss her stepdaughter good night. She'd tell her she loved her. And she'd tell her to be brave. She'd tell her that when the right man comes along — someone as good and decent and caring as her father, the kind of man who would hold her when she called out in her sleep because she'd dreamed of dark places and dangerous people, who would look into her eyes when he said hello and tell her he loved her when he said good-bye, who would kiss her good morning and kiss her good night, and tell her she was brave when she felt weak — to have the courage to love that man, and to go on loving him for the rest of her life.

Pru

I met Colm and Hank Ruckman, and the government trapper Breton Davies, at the compressor station. It was a Sunday morning, two days after the search had been called off. The snow had stopped falling sometime in the early hours. The sun was out and the roads were clear. But the clear skies had also brought on colder temperatures with a windchill near zero. Colm left his vehicle at the compressor station and rode with me. Hank and Breton followed.

"CBI report came back," Colm told me. "The hat was hers, just as we figured. The hair and the blood matched. But the blood wasn't from a gunshot. There were tree fibers along the tear. She had to have hit her head. Could have been running from something. Could have fallen down."

"Any traces of saliva? Anything that could connect the hat to a lion?"

"Fortunately, no," Colm said.

"And the gun?" I asked.

"We're still waiting. Should have something in a day or two."

Because of the snow, we didn't get far. We stopped our vehicles a little over a mile into the canyon and hiked the rest of the way. We'd each brought snowshoes. We fastened them onto our boots and climbed the hill in front of us. But the terrain soon became too rocky, and we took off our snowshoes and strapped them to our packs. I'd worked up a good sweat. I knew the others had as well; Hank had said something about needing to get in better shape. At least two hours passed before we made it to the clearing where we'd found the gun, and over the course of those two hours, we'd all fallen several times; the snow was up to our waists in spots where the accumulation hadn't packed down. Breton found lion tracks and claw marks on the trees. From the size of the tracks, almost five inches wide, Breton said we were looking at a big tom, probably seven feet long, maybe one hundred fifty pounds. I'd brought Kona with us and had reacquainted him with Amy Raye's scent, again using the mittens, which Colm had brought with him. But Kona didn't pick up anything this time.

Then late that afternoon in a rocky outcropping, a good seventy feet or more from where we'd found the hat, Breton came across what he thought looked like a cache. "Over here," he said.

Hidden in the rocks were some loose branches mixed in with snow. Breton cleared away some of the debris and brushed away the snow, and as he did, he exposed an elk leg.

"Well, I'll be damned," Colm said.

Hank and Breton examined the bone. I removed my phone from the cargo pocket on my pants and took a couple of pictures. "How did we miss this?" I said.

"The same way *we* almost missed it," Breton said. "A cougar camouflages its cache well. And then there was all the snow you had to contend with."

But I also knew Kona hadn't been looking for elk or tracking lion scent. And when we'd first come upon the cache, it looked no different than a mound of snow. We'd needed Breton's trained eye to find this cache site.

There was no hard evidence to warrant tracking the lion, but without anything else to go on, we were leaning in that direction. Perhaps if we were looking at a female, we might have had more reservations. The vicinity we were searching fell within unit twenty-one of the state's hunting areas. Hank said that Colorado Parks and Wildlife had set the mountain lion harvest quota at thirteen for that area. Only four lion had been harvested from that unit the year before, and for the current year, no lion had been harvested to date. Colm and Hank had to make the call. The very fact that this lion had been spotted made them uneasy. Lion were rarely seen, especially with all the traffic we had during the search.

"We need answers," Colm said.

Breton said he would bring his dogs, three hounds, and set them loose at dawn the next day. Weather reports predicted clear skies until Wednesday. He said he also had a mule he would ride so that he could stay with the dogs and cover more territory.

And so we made the hike back to our vehicles, unstrapped our packs and our snowshoes. I opened the rear hatch for Kona to jump in. Then Colm and I climbed in up front. We were tired and ready to get home.

About a mile out, Colm said, "It's pretty up here."

"Yeah, it is," I said.

The afternoon sun beat through the windshield. I lowered my visor. Colm did the same.

He'd turned quiet. "What are you thinking?" I asked.

"Just thinking about how pretty it is." A few minutes passed, and then Colm said, "Look at the way the light shines through those pinyons up there. Makes everything look like gold."

"It is pretty," I said.

"You know that big acre lot across from my house? There's some sandstone and pinyon. A couple of box elder, too. Sometimes I'll sit out on my front stoop. I'll just sit there and stare out at the trees. It looks a lot like this on a clear day. But no matter what the light is, it's a pretty sight."

I let the quiet stretch out between us. The rhythmic rocking of the truck over the uneven terrain had a lulling effect. Then Colm said, "I was coming home the other day and there was a sign on that lot. They've put it up for sale. Suppose someone's going to be building on it before long."

"So that's what all this deep thinking is about. You're worried about someone building on that lot," I said.

"Worried I won't be able to see the trees anymore," Colm said.

"You could buy the lot. Who owns it, anyway?"

"Moyer. Had it in his family for years."

"How much is he asking for it?"

"Suppose I could find out. But me buying the lot, that would mean something."

"It would mean you didn't want anyone building across from you," I said.

"It would mean more than that. It would mean I was staying."

"Are you thinking about leaving?" I asked.

I knew Colm wasn't from Rio Mesa. And with the divorce and all, maybe he was thinking about moving.

"Not thinking about leaving, not thinking about staying, but if I buy that lot, I'm going to have to think about it," Colm said.

I'd never thought about Colm leaving. I'd just assumed he'd always be around, and so I told him so. "Don't know that I'd like you leaving," I said. "Where would you go?"

"I could move back to Kansas. I have a couple of brothers living there. My folks are getting up in their years."

I was quiet then, uneasy with the thought of Colm not being around.

"You ever think of moving back to Missouri?" he asked me. "Ever think of raising that boy closer to home?"

"I've been gone a long time," I said. "Guess I think of this as home now."

Amy Raye

Amy Raye awoke to complete darkness and pain shooting up through her leg, and an odd feeling of displacement. But soon enough it all came back to her — the fall, the break, the shelter she had found. Though she did not know what time it was, she felt certain it was close to sunrise. She would have been gone a full day by now. People would be looking for her. And then she thought of Farrell. She imagined him getting the call from Aaron or Kenny, or even one of the authorities, and her heart ached because she knew how much her husband loved her. With all of these thoughts came a surge of adrenaline. She had hope that she would be found. She'd keep the fire going so that someone would see the smoke. And she'd have to take care of her leg. She'd have to keep it packed with snow. She'd have to immobilize it. She sat up and edged herself along the wall of the cave until she found her pack. She retrieved her matches and put them inside her coat pocket. Then she spread out her hands, moved them over the floor until her right hand felt the charred cedar that was still warm. Beside the burned-out fire was the pile of bark shavings she had gathered. She lit a piece of juniper bark and was then able to see well enough to get another fire going. She ate the remaining beef jerky and drank some of the water from the bladder in her pack. She looked over the wood she had gathered the night before. One of the limbs was almost three feet long and would work well as a splint. She'd need to find another limb about the same length to make the splint work. And she'd have to gather more wood, which, given the snowfall, wouldn't be as easy as it had been the night before.

She carried her knife in a sheath on her belt, and her bone saw under her arm, and scooted out of the cave and onto the ledge. She would have to work fast. Over a foot of snow had accumulated, and it was still coming down. The flakes were small and sharp and smited her face. The cold and the snow worked their way into her pants and gloves, up the sleeves of her jacket. But the deadfall was everywhere, and she'd been right. She'd made it through the night. The sun was beginning to rise, a welcome glow that allowed her to assess her surroundings. The ledge was large. It wrapped around the rock face like an enormous step that had been carved into the bluff, and climbed upward into an expanse of rocky terrain fleshed with pinyon and juniper. Amy Raye gathered armfuls of wood and tossed them into the cave. With her bone saw, she also cut live boughs, knowing they would smoke better than the wood and could be used as signal torches. And she found a perfect-sized limb for a splint. And so she returned to the cave. She organized the wood and the boughs. Then she sat beside the fire and, using her knife, began paring down a side on each of the limbs. The splints would need to be smooth and flat against her leg or she would not be able to withstand the pressure.

When she was finished with the splints, she untied her left boot and removed the laces. She winced at the thought of taking off her boot, which was already too tight because of the swelling, though she felt certain the compression had been a good thing. As if jumping into a cold pool, she counted to three, and then worked the boot off from the heel, and when she did, she yelled out in pain, her breathing shallow, like the panting of a wary dog. She picked up her knife and made a cut through the hem of her pants and along the inseam up to her knee. She put down the knife and, using both hands, ripped the tear the rest of the way up her thigh. She pulled the fabric aside and, still wearing her long underwear, placed the splints on each side of her leg. And the sight of just how badly broken her ankle was, how misaligned it was with the two pieces of wood, caused a deep intake of air that she held in her lungs. She ran her hand over the area where her leg should have been straight, then realized she should be thankful that the bone had not penetrated the skin, otherwise placing her at risk of infection.

She winced at the thought of running the webbing around the bottom of her foot and securing it to the splints. The pain was too severe for her to manage any leverage, and yet she knew she had no choice. She held the webbing on both sides, looped it over the bottom of her foot, pulled the webbing as tightly as she could manage, yelling out as she did so and fighting the nausea that clung to her skin in a cold film of sweat. She wrapped the webbing securely around the splints. When she was finished, she pulled down her pant leg and tucked the loose fabric beneath the edges of the nylon strapping. She was breathing too rapidly. She knew she was hyperventilating. She lay back and imagined labor, tried to remember how she had gotten through it. Tried to remember the focus. She looked at the cave wall, stared at the perfectly drawn claw markings of a bear's paw, fixed her eyes and thoughts so intently on that paw print as if her mind was no longer a part of her body. And in that moment she was there, in the hot bathwater where the nurses had left her, her back pressed against the white tub, her toes pressed against the porcelain at the other end, her eyes penetrating the tiny crack in the tile above the spout, looking deeply into that crack. And somewhere there was Farrell, his voice saying things she could not comprehend, his breath smelling of onions and milk that had expired. And hadn't it all been worth it, when the nurses returned and one of them said Amy Raye was ready, and the two nurses and Farrell carried Amy Raye into the delivery room and laid her on a table and told her to push. And from there everything went quickly, because she pushed two more times and then she heard her son's cries, and Farrell was beside her, and his breath smelled of warm milk and honey. She kissed Farrell deeply. She kissed the soft spot on Trevor's head, and she cried from the sheer joy of it all because she believed she had been given a second chance.

Pru

Three days after taking Hank Ruckman and Breton to the lion cache, Colm called. Joseph and I had just finished dinner and were clearing the table.

"We got him," Colm said.

I set a plate down on the counter.

"What is it?" Joseph asked. But I shook my head as I waited for Colm to continue.

Breton had tracked the lion all day Monday. Late in the afternoon on Tuesday, the dogs treed the big tom in a pinyon about a mile from the old cache. Breton made a clean shot, strapped the lion onto his mule, and brought it in. The DOW had the animal. Colm said a technician with the department would be running tests on the lion's stomach contents.

The next morning, I met Colm at the DOW. The technician had found traces of elk and deer in the lion's stomach and intestinal tract.

"What about any human cells, or any clothing?" Colm asked.

"That's where it gets interesting." The technician wanted to show us something, and so we followed her to the lab, a large room behind some partitioned offices. She had Colm and me take turns looking through a microscope at a slide.

"Looks like threads of clothing," I said.

She removed the slide and inserted another. On the second slide, we weren't just looking at threads, but a small piece of fabric, the color of dark crimson.

"It's not human," the technician said. "The blood on the fabric matches the traces of blood from the elk matter." She went on to tell us that the fabric was synthetic. "It looks like cotton, but it's actually stronger and lighter than cotton."

"Could it be from a game bag?" I asked.

"I think so," the technician said. "I have to run some more tests to be sure."

I looked at Colm. "Kenny and Aaron packed all of their meat out of there," I said.

"How fresh are these samples?" Colm asked the woman.

"They're fresh. No more than five days."

"There could have been other hunting parties," Colm said to me, no doubt reading my mind.

"Not since the search," I reminded him. "We found her bow. We found her quiver. There was an arrow missing. What if she got a shot?"

"And bagged this thing alone? Goddamn elk weighs over eight hundred pounds."

"Wouldn't be the first time a woman quartered an elk by herself," I said.

"And how did she plan on hauling it out of there?"

I knew Colm was right. An elk quarter could weigh up to eighty pounds, and Amy Raye didn't have a horse or a mule to pack it out. And then that sinking feeling. In my eight years working search and rescue, this was the first time we hadn't found the missing person, or at least found the subject's remains within a week of the initial report.

Colm walked me out to my vehicle.

"It's weird, you know. I feel disappointed. That's wrong, Colm. It's like I'd rather have answers than the hope that she's alive."

"Let's grab some coffee," he said. "I've got something I want to show you."

I followed Colm to The Bakery. Enid was working behind the counter. She and I talked for a couple of minutes. Having been eager to find out the lab results, I hadn't eaten that morning, so I ordered breakfast. "You want anything, Colm?" I asked.

"No. Just coffee."

Colm and I sat at a table in the back corner. He was holding a manila file folder in front of him.

"What is it?"

"Got the results back on the gun." He handed me the folder.

I looked over the report. It detailed levels of lead, antimony, and barium found in the barrel.

"So the gun was fired. That's not a surprise," I said.

Enid brought Colm and me a cup of coffee. He drank his black. I drank mine with cream.

"Keep reading," Colm said.

The second page began a long analysis with images of prints found on the gun. All but one on the grip had been smudged and couldn't be lifted. The other was a partial print of a little finger. The technician couldn't tell whether the whorls were from the left or right hand. Several prints had been lifted from the cylinder.

"None of them match Latour's," Colm said. I knew Colm had obtained Amy Raye's prints from items in the camp.

"What are you saying?"

"What if Kenny was the last one to fire the gun?"

"Do the prints match his?"

"I don't know yet. But I'm going to find out." Colm picked up his coffee, blew on it a couple of times, and then took a loud swallow.

"Was the revolver completely loaded when he gave it to her?"

"He said it was."

"Which would explain his prints on the cylinder. Colm, Kenny said he was at the camp. Amy Raye had the truck. Both he and Aaron passed lie detectors."

"Lie detectors aren't foolproof."

"And there's no way to know when the gun had been fired?"

But I already knew the answer to that. It was practically impossible to determine how long gunfire residue had been left in any gun.

Enid carried a plate of biscuits and gravy to the table. I handed the folder back to Colm.

"You're forgetting something," I told him. "If she fired the gun, she was most likely wearing gloves. That would explain the smudging of the prints on the grip."

"Maybe. But we found her gloves back at the truck."

"But we didn't find any liners. And we don't know if she had another set of gloves in her pack. Come on, Colm, it was thirty-six degrees that day. She wouldn't have gone out there without gloves."

Maybe we should be considering these things about Kenny, but I wasn't so sure. If Kenny had fired the gun, we could be talking murder, and an accusation like that could destroy someone's life. If only we'd found the body.

I shoved a forkful of biscuits and gravy into my mouth. Then another.

"Somebody's got an appetite," Colm said.

I stopped eating. "We need to be sure. Be careful, Colm."

Then I thought of something. "She was left-handed," I said. I remembered the bow. It was a left-handed compound Hoyt. "What side of the grip was the print lifted from?"

"The left."

I finished my biscuits, hoping the delay would emphasize my point. "That's what I thought," I said. "No prints were found on the right grip panel. No prints were found on the hammer. And the prints found on the left side were smudged."

Colm knew what I was saying. If Amy Raye fired the gun, she would have held it in her left hand, and if she had been wearing gloves, she would have smudged any of

Kenny's prints from when he'd given it to her with his right hand. Because Kenny's hand would be larger than Amy Raye's, a print of his little finger showing up toward the bottom of the left grip panel would make sense.

But Colm wasn't convinced. "We've gotten our search warrants for the computer and the phone records. Dean's driving over to Evergreen today to pick up the computer. We should have the phone records by the end of the day tomorrow."

"You're still thinking foul play."

"Foul play. Suicide. I'm not sure what I think, but like I said, from that bloody tear on her hat, either she was running from something, or she fell down, and if she fell, she would have fallen backward. She could have been shot. She could have been pushed. I'm speculating, of course."

"Or she was walking through the woods and hit her head. I do it all the time."

That night, Joseph and I were sitting on the sofa with our legs stretched out over a wicker trunk that we used for a coffee table. We had a bowl of popcorn between us and were watching the Steelers play the Broncos.

Joseph's legs were long, and I felt certain he would grow a couple more inches before he was finished with high school. He might even grow to be as tall as his father.

Brody had been gone for almost five years before I met Todd, and though I'd become friends with a couple of guys during that time, I'd yet to date anyone. I worked for the BLM during the week, and at seasonal jobs on the weekends. That particular fall I was helping out at a small meatpacking plant. The plant catered to the out-of-town hunters, turned elk and venison into sausage and hamburger, teriyaki steaks and jerky. The company packed the meat in dry ice and shipped it all over the country. It was on one of those weekends that Todd introduced himself to me. He was a guide for an outfitter upriver and had brought in an elk kill with one of his clients, a man out of Oklahoma. The client was in the office talking to the owner of the plant. Todd had remained in the back next to the freezer block where I was working.

"You must be new," he said. "I'm Todd."

"I'd shake your hand, but under the circumstances —"

"What's a woman like you doing up to her elbows in this stuff?"

"Just trying to pay the bills."

I was wearing a bloody apron that hung down to my knees and was making clean slices through the backstrap of an elk that belonged to another client, turning the meat into nice-sized filets. The elk that had just been brought in by Todd was hanging on a meat hook in the freezer. I wouldn't be able to get to it until the next day.

"Have you been working here long?" he asked.

"A couple of months."

"How come I haven't seen you around?"

"You ask a lot of questions," I said.

"Only with a beautiful woman." He adjusted his cap by placing his palm over his head, and I noticed how large his hands were, perhaps as large as Brody's.

"Maybe I'll see you around sometime," he said. He turned and began walking away.

I made another slice and set the meat aside.

"You want to go out sometime?" Todd had turned back around.

He was tall, several inches over six feet. His brown hair hung down to his shoulders and was tucked behind his ears. He wore a green cap with a fly shop logo. He was heavy-boned, with deep-set brown eyes, an angular face that was in need of a good shave.

"How do you know I'm not married?"

"You're not wearing a ring."

"I've got gloves on."

"They're transparent."

"They're covered in blood," I said.

"So do you want to go out?"

And in that moment perhaps my motions faltered, a hesitation as I made another slice, as I remembered Brody all over again.

"There's something very sexy about a woman holding a knife," Todd said.

I pointed the knife at him. "Watch it," I said.

"So will you go out with me?"

I didn't agree to go out with Todd at first. But two weeks later when he stopped in, I drank a beer with him at his truck before I drove home from work. And the week after that I took a walk with him on top of Hay Flats. Slowly, I let Todd into my life, let myself once again feel the arms of a man. Then there was the night when I was cooking spaghetti and Todd was sitting in the living room. I looked at him through the doorway. He was watching TV. I felt nothing. I knew then I didn't love him. I knew I never would. Todd had moved on before I'd found out I was pregnant. Last I'd heard he was with an outfitter in Montana. I tried to locate him once. Thought he had a right to know he had a son. But he'd moved on again, and after a while, I gave up looking.

"What are you thinking about?" Joseph asked.

"Nothing really. Why?"

"Are you watching the game?"

"Yeah. Sorry," I said.

And while I watched the Broncos make a field goal, and Joseph cheered beside me, I wondered why I was thinking about Todd after all these years, remembering how my body had felt, and what it had been like to try to love someone again.

Amy Raye

Sometime in the morning the snow had stopped falling. Gray light shone directly into the cave, and Amy Raye wondered about that. How could she be facing east? The truck had been west of where she'd shot the elk and quartered him. She tried to recall the map she had stared at for days, as well as the direction in which she had tracked the animal. To be facing east would mean she had been heading away from the direction in which she'd set out. And she could not help but wonder, given the look of the terrain, if she was as far east as Big Ridge and Cathedral Bluffs, dense terrain full of rocky crevices. How had she veered so far off course, and how would anyone ever find her? At a good pace, she could hike almost three miles per hour. She tried to remember how long she had tracked the elk. Had he moved in a straightforward direction, or had his path been erratic? The only thing she could be certain of was that she had tracked him moving downhill, which would have accelerated her pace. If the elk had been moving in a straight path, she could very well have covered six to eight miles, despite her slowing down to follow the blood trail. If she had been moving east, she would be thick into the bluffs. Even if a search party was looking for her, she doubted anyone would venture that far into the area, and with the snow, she wasn't sure they'd be able to even if they tried. And then there was the trek she'd made after quartering the elk, after he'd gone downhill to die. By that point she'd lost her visibility because of the snow. Instead of moving northwest back to the truck, she could have hiked southward. Again, she tried to recall the map, but without knowing exactly at what point she'd come upon the elk, there was no way to be sure of her location, except to know she was miles and miles out of any reasonable search radius. And again the thought that she would not be found. She was alone, and she was lost. "Help! Someone help me!" But her voice echoed back at her as it had earlier in the night, and her breathing quickened with the sheer terror of what she knew.

Maybe her path had been erratic, or

circular. Maybe the path of the elk had been erratic as well. Maybe she was not as far away from the truck as she feared. She would keep the fire burning. She would continue to hope that someone would see the smoke.

Her appetite burned in her stomach. This was a good sign, as the nausea seemed to be subsiding. The fire was strong. She held the skewer with the elk liver and heart over the flame. Despite everything, Amy Raye considered how lucky she had been. She had shelter; she had this warm fire and plenty of wood. She had food to eat. Yes, her left leg was useless, and her left hip battered with bruises, but her body was strong; no other bones had been broken. These were her thoughts as she cooked her first meal in this place and the aroma filled the cave and filled her lungs.

The fire crackled, and the pitch from the soft wood popped, and a strange peace settled over her. It was beautiful, really, this place, an anesthetic of sorts. She ate the heart first, and as she did, she thought of the animal whose life she'd taken, and who was now giving her food to eat. She remembered the sound of his last breaths, imagined his spirit moving on, imagined him running in a place without hunters and tags and ammo.

Her thoughts were startled when she heard a snapping of wood outside the cave, a small animal perhaps. She became still, slowed her breathing. The sound grew louder. Something larger than one of the squirrels or rodents was out there. And instantly she remembered the rest of the elk meat, her only source of survival should she not be found right away. "No!" She crawled closer to the entrance, wrapped her hand around a rock, threw the rock and screamed. She did not see the animal, but she heard him, another branch snapping, footfall moving away. Daylight streamed through the clouds. She was now outside the cave. She checked the elk quarter. It was undisturbed. Then she saw the cougar prints. She had lured him to her. He had smelled the meal she had cooked. He was hungry, also. She would lure him to her again when she cooked her next meal. She had to be smarter.

She scrambled as best she could back to the cave. She felt pleased with the splint she had prepared, as she was able to move a degree more easily than the day before. She emptied her pack onto the cave floor and found the stainless-steel water bottle she had caught her urine in maybe twenty-six hours before. It was still full. Cougar in these parts were afraid of humans. She could not let the lion become aware of her weakened condition. She would stake out and mark her territory. She would create the boundaries. And so using the urine, she dribbled it around the periphery of the cave, and then around the elk meat she had stored away from her shelter. She would continue to do this, she decided, until she was found, or until she made her way out of this place. Her own estrus would keep the lion away.

She also knew she would need more water, and the stainless-steel bottle would be her only means for heating the water and purifying it. And so she filled the eighteen-ounce bottle with snow. She would set it in the embers of the fire until the water boiled. After it cooled, she would store the water in the one-and-a-half-liter bladder from her pack. She would have to alternate between peeing in the bottle and using the bottle to heat the snow. She would also continue to collect snow with the three plastic bags she had. And then she thought of the elk meat. A front shoulder, not considering the bone, weighed approximately sixty to seventy pounds. As long as she could keep the meat cool and protected, she could ration it out, and should she not be found, she could keep herself fed. If she remembered correctly, one pound of meat would provide approximately eight hundred calories. But elk meat was leaner than other meat and might only provide her with a little more than half that amount in calories. To maintain her strength, she would need to consume no less than a thousand calories a day. A healthy intake would be closer to fourteen hundred calories. If she was not found right away, with at least thirty-two thousand calories, she could give her leg over four weeks to heal. Even then, without her leg having been set and immobilized with a cast, walking would be painful, and she would need some kind of crutch for assistance. If only she could set the bone, but there was no doubt the break had been clear through. There was no way she was going to be able to straighten out the bone. And too much movement could be dangerous. Hadn't she read about that? Yes, she knew she had. In a novel by John Knowles. She recalled the character Finny, recalled him falling down marble stairs and breaking his leg a second time, and he had died from the break. When doctors had tried to set the bone, the marrow had spread through Finny's bloodstream and gone straight to his heart. The whole story had fascinated her, because she hadn't known someone could die from a broken leg.

Thankful for food and water and firewood within easy reach, she returned to the cave. She organized the belongings she had and took inventory: an eight-inch hunting knife, a bone saw, over two hundred feet of parachute cord, webbing that she was now using for her splint, a stainless-steel water bottle, one quart-size zip-top bag, one gallon-size zip-top bag, a sandwich bag, a burned-out headlamp with no extra batteries, four waterproof matches, an elk bugle, an elk cow call, a small block of flint, a one-and-a-half-liter bladder, and a forty-five-liter-capacity backpack. For clothing she had a lightweight Thinsulate jacket, pants, a long-sleeve thermal shirt, a layer of silk long underwear, cotton gloves, one pair of ragg wool socks, and her green hiking boots.

She finished eating the heart, ate the liver, and washed both down with the remaining water she'd carried in her pack. She boiled the snow in the bottle. After it cooled, she poured it into the bladder. Then she boiled the water from the snowmelt that she'd collected in the bags and used as ice packs. She elevated her leg on her pack and lay back to rest. The day would pass slowly, and each day after that. How many days would she be in here? She picked up a piece of charred wood, reached for the wall behind her, and wrote her full name. Beside her name, she wrote the prior day's date, and beneath the date, she made a mark. She would keep track of her days, and God forbid, should she not make it out of here alive, should someone come upon her bones one day, she could be identified. But she would be found. Aaron and Kenny would be looking for her. She need only keep herself fed and warm until then. Maybe another day or night. It wouldn't be long.

She curled up beside the fire, determined to keep it lit, determined for someone to see the smoke, and as she listened to the flames crackle, as she fought sleep, she heard other sounds, branches outside the cave from the juniper and pinyon that had grown through crevasses in the rock, limbs bending with the wind and snow, and small animals somewhere outside the cave that in the thin night air sounded like larger ones. She thought of the rats that might have been living in her shelter; she'd seen their droppings. And with all of these thoughts and each sound that amplified in her mind, her breathing shortened into small clutches of air. She tried to regain her calm. She exhaled more slowly. She focused on the flames.

Sometime in the night Amy Raye awoke to the chugging of an engine in the distance and arose in a panic. Though the fire had died down, it was still burning. She grabbed one of the boughs beside it and lit the needles that had begun to dry, and all the while she was yelling, "I'm here, I'm here!" Surely this was the search crew that had come looking for her, and already she wanted to say she was sorry for causing such a commotion, wanted to apologize for not having been more careful, but that would come later. "Yes, I'm here!" she screamed, and she scrambled out of the cave, dragged her broken leg behind her, waved the burning bough above her. "Help!" she shouted. The sound of an engine was indeed drawing closer. She sat in a foot of snow, waved the bough, waved her other arm, looked to the sky. And why had she refused to wear orange, why had she left the orange cap back at the truck, and if only they could see the smoke, and yes, there it was, a helicopter flying above her. "Over here! Over here!" The helicopter continued past her. Surely someone had seen her, seen the smoke, would recognize the smoke as a signal. Surely the helicopter was simply turning around. It would pass over her again. She continued to yell. She continued to wave the bough and her arms, and the sound drifted farther away. She waited. It did not return. "I'm here! I'm here! Come back!" Why hadn't they seen her? But she knew; the fire she'd built was hidden inside the cave. And whatever smoke might have been seen from the helicopter would have appeared as no more than a cloud of vapor. And she wasn't wearing orange. She blended seamlessly into the terrain. If she could go unnoticed by an elk grazing within thirty yards of her, why would she think someone in a helicopter that was flying more than a thousand feet above her would be able to spot her on the side of this bluff? Yet the helicopter would return. Surely it would return. She waited until she began to feel too cold. She reentered the cave but remained close to its entrance. She wrapped her arms around one of the rocks that lay just outside the cave's opening, pressed the side of her face against the rock's smooth wet surface. *Dear God, please let them find me.* She would wait for the helicopter to circle back. People were looking for her. That was a good sign. She would stay awake. She would be ready when the helicopter returned. She looked to the sky, noticed how clear it was. There were so many stars, and she thought about that, thought about just how many stars there were.

"We think we are seeing too many to count. But we could count them," she had told Farrell one night. "We could map out the stars and count each one."

They had gone camping in Red Rock Canyon. Julia and Trevor were already asleep in the tent. Amy Raye and Farrell had remained by the fire.

"I love that about you," Farrell had said. "I love how you know all these weird things that others rarely think about."

"Knowing about stars isn't weird," Amy Raye said.

"Knowing how many there are is kind of weird. Weird in a good way. I probably have your mom to thank for that," Farrell said.

Amy Raye had already told Farrell about her mother's job at the library, and how when Amy Raye was young, she'd wait for her mother there after school. And during the summer, if Amy Raye wasn't at the farm, she'd accompany her mother to work. It was there that Amy Raye had fallen in love with books. If she wasn't reading, she was finding answers to the questions her mom would ask her: How are the clouds formed? How cold is the top of Mount Everest? How many stars are in the sky? Amy Raye would get paid a quarter for each answer that she found.

Farrell pulled Amy Raye against him and lay down so that they were looking directly up at the sky. "Tell me about her," he said. "What was she like?"

Amy Raye lay quiet for a moment as Farrell's fingers rubbed circles over her shoulders and gently traced the strands of her hair.

"She was pretty," Amy Raye said. "She had light brown hair and these brilliant blue eyes. Kind of like people who wear colored contacts, only she never wore contacts or glasses."

"What else?" Farrell said.

"She could be funny. I thought she was funny. She made me laugh."

"How so?"

"I don't know. It was just her way. Sometimes she'd say she wanted to go for a drive. She'd want me to go with her. Said we were going for a ride in the country, which was kind of funny because we already lived in the country. Then we'd drive by all the fields we could find that had horses and we'd name the horses and see which one of us could come up with the best names. One day she stopped alongside a field and got out of the car. She climbed over the barbed-wire fence and walked right up to this Thoroughbred. I sat in the car and watched. The horse didn't even run from her. Then she walked back, climbed over the fence again, and got in the car. She said she'd thought the white spot on the horse's forehead had looked like an oak leaf and that she'd been going to name him Acorn, but when she'd gotten a closer look, she'd been wrong. She said the marking looked like the star of Bethlehem."

"So what did she name him?" Farrell asked.

"Bethlehem," Amy Raye said. "And from then on when we drove by the field and the horse was out, we'd roll down our windows, and we'd wave to him and call out his name."

Farrell hugged Amy Raye closer and laughed. "Sounds like something you would do."

But these had been the days before Amy Raye had found her mom crying and sitting naked on the bathroom floor, and perhaps there was blood on the floor, as well. Before the days her mother would call in sick to work and stay in bed all day in a dark room, when she no longer stopped by the farm to see her parents, and cried each time she took communion in church.

"I think I would have liked your mom," Farrell said.

But then Amy Raye turned quiet. "I don't know," she said. "People change."

As Amy Raye lay with her face upon the cold rock, as she looked to the sky and waited for the helicopter to return, the wind shifted and blew through her hair and down her back like a gentle stroke of her mother's hand. Amy Raye searched the stars. She found Ursa Major, or the Great Bear, as some of the Native American cultures called it. She thought upon all the stories her mother had read to her of the Great Bear, how it was the guardian of the western lands, the people's spirit protector. And she thought upon the day her mother climbed the fence and named the Thoroughbred that had been grazing in the McAllisters' pasture, and by remembering she felt the moment happening all over again. And maybe the fence wasn't barbed wire. Maybe it was only cedar. Maybe the horse trotted away from her mom at first. Amy Raye couldn't be sure. But none of that mattered. What mattered was the way the light shone on her mom's face as she stood in the field and looked upon the deep brown horse, as she brushed aside the mane from his forehead. What mattered was the way her mom smiled, and that beautiful aching moment of how the world could be.

Pru

Several weeks had passed since Amy Raye had gone missing. Thanksgiving had come and gone. Dean had picked up Amy Raye's laptop, and while Colm pored over her cell phone records, a specialist with the Garfield County agency worked on the computer.

"The husband's not going to like what we found," Colm told me. We were grabbing a beer together at the VFW one night after work. "Of course, I don't see how he couldn't have known."

"Does this have anything to do with Kenny?"

"It has to do with Kenny *and* Aaron. From what we can tell, she was involved with both of them at one time or another." Colm and I were sitting at the bar. He took a slow swallow from his beer. "That's not even the half of it," he said. "We found dating sites, chat rooms, illicit emails. I got text messages coming and going. We know of at least two men she'd been seeing within the month of her disappearance."

I shook my head and ordered another beer. I kept seeing Amy Raye's husband, the pictures of the children. No matter how I tried, I couldn't wrap my mind around what Colm was telling me.

"And I got to tell you," Colm went on. "This whole thing's got me thinking more about that gun. It seems pretty goddamn interesting that Kenny was the only one who knew about Latour going off to some tree stand we never found. Then, only after we find the gun does Kenny decide to tell us it's his, and by the way he loaned it to her, seeing as how it's got his prints all over it. And I find it goddamn interesting that neither he nor that friend of his thought to mention their involvement with Latour."

"Did the husband know anything? Could this be some kind of scam?"

Colm was getting ready to take another drink from his beer. He held the bottle in front of him for a second. "I think it's more like an addiction. It's sad when you think about it. She's got a beautiful family. We found emails between her and her husband. You'd never know she had something going on. And there must have been at least a hundred pictures of her with the kids. It's like our missing person is two people. Makes me wonder which one we've been looking for." Colm drank several long swallows of his beer. Pool balls clacked behind us, and the chatter in the room was getting louder.

Colm's thinking surprised me. He'd hit on something going on with my own thoughts. Amy Raye wasn't all one thing or another. She was the mother and she was the wife, and she was someone completely different from both of these things. I couldn't help but wonder, as did Colm, if it was the stranger whose life had been put at risk, the one Kenny and Aaron had reported missing, or the one with a husband and children back home. The truth was, we didn't know who this woman was. I was fairly certain the husband didn't either. And because of that, we couldn't make assumptions about her motivations.

Colm set the bottle down and began turning it around and around against the sticky wood-grain finish on the bar. "You know, you hear about this sort of thing. But when you get right down into the thick of it, it's hard to believe." He shook his head. "Goddamn mess." Then he said, "I keep thinking, what if the husband didn't have a clue?"

I leaned in closer so as not to lose what

Colm was saying. He tapped the empty beer bottle against the bar. "It doesn't matter," Colm said. "I'm still going to have to question him."

"What about Kenny and Aaron?"

"I'm going to have to question them, too, and the whole sorry lot of other guys she was involved with."

"You could be shaking up a lot of relationships out there."

"Wouldn't you want to know?"

"Yeah, I would." I drank more beer, found myself getting quiet.

"At least Maggie never did this," Colm said.

And I wanted to say, *How do you know?* But I didn't. I thought back to Brody's funeral. I thought about the girl who was crying a lot louder than she had any right to. She'd probably gone to school with us, but I didn't remember having seen her before. And for weeks after the funeral, whenever anyone would leave cards at Brody's grave site, I'd read those cards and wonder if any of them were from the girl who'd cried all those tears. Greg said Brody had touched lives in a lot of different ways and everyone handled their emotions differently. Maybe we could never know everything about another person. I felt sad for

Farrell Latour, because if he didn't know those things about his wife, he was going to be grieving the loss of her all over again, and this second loss was going to be a lot worse than the first.

Though my work often involved assisting with search-and-rescue efforts and responding to accidents on public lands, the primary scope of my job was protecting the Bureau of Land Management's cultural resources from vandalism and looters, or pothunters, as they were often referred to. My job fell under the Archaeological Resources Protection Act, which dealt with federal and Indian lands. The law made it illegal for anyone to remove or damage artifacts of human life if those artifacts were over one hundred years old. The only exception would be if a person had a valid permit to conduct professional archaeological research.

Looters typically focused on sites that were likely to yield artifacts with high market values. Visitors, as opposed to serious looters, tended to be less selective, collecting small sherds and waste flakes, which over time could result in a serious depletion. And though picking up arrowheads wasn't something a person would get charged with under ARPA, it could be considered a misdemeanor. Oftentimes when conducting my work, I'd think back to my brother and me when we'd looked for arrowheads and picked up flakes. Most people, like us, had no idea that kind of activity was illegal.

At eighteen years old, when I took the job as a seasonal worker, my duties involved anything from spraying ditches for noxious weeds, to repairing roads by filling in potholes, to assisting geologists with field surveying. I spent my days outdoors, sometimes walking six to ten miles in ninety-degree heat, hot dust beneath my feet, and skies so blue I was certain heaven had never felt as close. And when I was alone, I'd talk to Brody, I'd talk to God, I'd talk to myself. When I arrived in Colorado, my capacity for grief was like the Grand Canyon. Some people don't make it out of the Grand Canyon. The rapids and the terrain can be highly unpredictable. And yet there is something about exploring an area by oneself. When I took my grief to Colorado, I found the space I needed. I found the wind and the sky and the sun and the rocks and the high desert pinyon and sage to be the most effective balm of all. It was there that my grief became quiet and allowed me to hear the whispers of something much greater than myself, and I couldn't get enough of it. And sometimes when I was working alone on a road, shoveling dirt and hauling rocks, feeling the muscles in my arms and legs and back, I'd feel Brody all around me as well.

The BLM was low on housing that summer. The two bunkhouses were already full with seasonal firefighters. Three other seasonal workers were sharing an apartment in town. I was going to be on my own to arrange for my living quarters. I'd brought basic camping gear: a tent, sleeping bag, foam pad, cookstove. I picked up a bear canister at the hardware store and a couple of other items, including a folding chair and a large cooler. I had over a million acres to choose from for my summer home. I studied the maps and looked for natural springs. There is not a lot of water in the high desert, and many of the brooks dry up in the summer. That was when I met Ray. He'd been working as a geologist for the BLM for over thirty years. He told me about an area at the base of Danforth Hills, up Cabin Gulch, where there was a spring that would provide plenty of fresh water and a nice swimming hole. He said there were lion and some bear in the area, but he doubted they'd pay any attention to me. And so I set up camp on an embankment just above the spring, with an unbelievable amount of sky above me. I'd never really thought of a place as home before. I had simply been a child who'd been growing up in her parents' arms, and who'd been moving into the arms of another. But lying underneath that big sky, the grief that had been winding itself tight inside me started to loosen, and I found myself settling into the depths of that land and sky as if it were the place I'd been born to find. My days consisted of waking up before dawn, working hard all day, and then driving up the four-wheel road to my gold tent and chair. I would sit in that complete quiet and peace and comfort, and I'd feel something infinite going on inside me. I knew I was home, and there was no way I could walk out of there come summer's end. I didn't want to be inside college walls, or working in my parents' store. I wanted to live with this vast beauty around me. I wanted to feel the fatigue at the end of the day from my bones and muscles having worked hard. I wanted big stretches of space to talk out loud all the thoughts going on in my head. The solitude I found that summer became my greatest companion. I'd already lost Brody. I wasn't going to lose this companion, too.

The field office didn't have any full-time positions that I qualified for, but the more tasks I completed, the more work different folks in the office seemed to find for me to do. And there were some changes going on with the permanent staff that ended up working to my advantage. By summer's end, Glade had been hired to head up all of the archaeology efforts. The office team had never had a trained archaeologist before. Glade was pretty much a one-man show with more work than he could handle, which included surveying and mapping hundreds of sites within the White River jurisdiction. I'd already proven myself a quick study when it came to surveying, and I was willing to work for minimum wage. Glade's passion for his work became a new territory for me, full of all kinds of possibilities. I felt protective of the places we mapped. We didn't have all of the cameras for surveillance at that time. Instead, I would backpack into the areas and hike and camp for weeks, patrolling the sites by foot.

By my fifth year on the job, the BLM had decided to send me for an eight-week law enforcement training program in Nebraska. The program would take place during January and February, when fieldwork was slow.

I'd been renting a small apartment close to town by then, a seven-hundred-square-foot building that had been converted into living quarters, on the edge of some public grazing land and the Smith ranch. I'd been seeing Todd that fall. By December, I was ready to break things off, and he didn't seem too unagreeable when I told him, so we went our separate ways. I didn't know I was pregnant when I drove to Missouri to stay with my parents for Christmas. My dad had come down with a stomach bug, and I thought I'd been suffering from the same. Then I was so busy with the eight-week intensive training program that I didn't pay my menstrual cycle, or lack of one, any mind. When I returned to Colorado, I bought a pregnancy test. It was nighttime and dark outside, and I closed all the blinds as if trying to create a cave in which I could hide when I found out the results. I peed on the stick and then carried it into my small living area. I set the stick on a coffee table, lit a candle, and sat on the floor.

And in those couple of minutes that followed, I knew I wanted to be pregnant, and I was afraid to look at the white piece of plastic, because I was afraid I'd find out I wasn't. But I did look, and I was pregnant, and hope perched on my body, as if this new life forming inside me were all the affirmation I'd ever need, and I knew then, in this huge awakening sort of way, that it wasn't grief that had driven me to Colorado. It was love. The capacity for my grief was all the love I'd had for Brody. And my own capacity wasn't big enough. I needed a space just as wild and vast as that love to set it free.

I worked out of the White River Resource Area office in Rio Mesa, which was responsible for approximately one and a half million acres of land. And most of that land was rich in Paleo-Indian heritage, especially in the Douglas Creek territory, the same area where Amy Raye had disappeared.

Throughout the year, I patrolled the different sites and investigated them for any disturbance, such as holes in the ground, back-dirt piles, discarded fragmentary artifacts, or tools left in the area. I also kept record of and looked into footprints on an open site. I reported my findings to Glade, who would then try to determine what artifacts might have been at the ruin before the area was vandalized.

The previous summer, I'd worked with a field school team on a stratigraphic excavation where several living sites had been stacked one on top of another. The earth had eroded away in a deep gulch that ran one hundred feet long. The site was named Hanging Hearths Shelter because the hearths were hanging on the side of the cut bank of the cliff.

But the site was also a prime target for vandalism, so I patrolled the shelter several times a week. I had set up a surveillance camera as well. The camera, built into a synthetic rock, operated with a motion sensor. When the sensor was set off, the camera took pictures that would trip the radio back at the office with a code and deliver the pictures digitally to my computer. I strategically placed cameras at shelters like this to catch any looters — amateur archaeologists who would scavenge the ruins before all of the permits had been obtained and a field school could begin.

Such was the case with Hanging Hearths Shelter. Prior to the first field school, I'd noticed a number of footprints coming and going from the area. Then pictures began to show up on my computer. One morning the camera captured a man and his dog walking up to the shelter. The man was carrying a shovel. By the time Glade and I got out to the site, the man was gone, but in one of his freshly dug holes, he had left behind a cigarette butt with his DNA. Colm was able to come up with a couple of suspects from the photo, and with the DNA, he was able to make a perfect match.

Though my fieldwork slowed down in the winter months, I still checked on as many sites as I could, particularly those with rock art, which could be vandalized at any time of year. I'd also make sure whatever cameras we had in place were working and had not been knocked down by wind or covered with snow. At present, we had several surveillance cameras positioned in the Douglas Creek area, including one I had installed at the recently discovered Coos shelter, situated in the southeastern corner of East Douglas Creek Canyon. A two-week excavation of the site was scheduled for the upcoming summer, just enough time for all of the permits to be obtained.

After Joseph and I returned from Boulder, where we'd spent Thanksgiving with my brother and his wife, I decided to spend most of December canvassing some of the areas where a fairly high volume of hunting tags had been sold. This was routine following a hunting season. I'd check on some of the sites in those locations by assessing for damage that might have occurred as a result of foot traffic and off-road vehicles. That first week after Thanksgiving, I was checking out some hunting ground in the West Douglas Creek territory, where over the years the BLM had surveyed several prehistoric astronomical drill hole sites, as well as an ancient lookout tower. The West Douglas range was situated on the western side of Highway 139, an approximately fifty-mile expanse of dry, rocky terrain. Even though the land had less drainage and forests than where we'd searched for Amy Raye, there was still a healthy population of wild game, including antelope, mule deer, and some elk.

The weather was clear that day, and I was enjoying the time away from the office, when Kona and I came across an elk carcass that I guessed to be a couple of years old. The bones had been scattered and broken. I didn't think much of the whole thing at first. It wasn't unusual to find the remains of an animal that a hunter had shot and field-dressed. And if the head had been severed, I could be sure the animal had been a bull elk, and that his head was mounted on somebody's wall. Kona and I walked on a little farther, and about thirty or forty yards west of the carcass, Kona sniffed out a skull that had been dragged beneath the branches of a large serviceberry shrub. My first thought was that the elk had been a female. Cow elks weren't trophy worthy. But in recent years, a lot of hunters had been taking the heads to the DOW to be tested for chronic wasting disease, a form of mad cow syndrome, which led me to wonder if this carcass was a case of poaching. I knelt to look at the skull. It was definitely weathered enough to be a couple of years old, and CWD inspection wasn't mandatory these days. Just beneath the left eye socket was a bullet hole. And that was when I got to thinking about our missing hunter. Her number one arrow wasn't slotted in her quiver. Everything in me believed she had to have gotten a shot the morning she went missing, and if she got a shot, she had to have been tracking the elk when she set down her quiver and bow. Her gun had fired one round. It seemed likely that she'd found the elk she was tracking and put a bullet in him to put him down. I felt certain a carcass was up there, and if we could find the skull, we could match it with the bullet. None of this would bring Amy Raye back, but it would help in giving us a better picture of what might have happened to her. If she had indeed gotten a shot and successfully tracked an elk, she wouldn't have been able to pack the animal out on her own. She would have gone for help, and as thick into the woods as she was, she could easily have become disoriented and gotten lost. Then if I factored in the harsh weather and her not having her compass with her, I didn't see any way she could have found her way out of there. I also didn't see any way she would have made it through the night. And without any body heat, none of the search's thermal detection devices would have worked.

Before returning to the house, I stopped by the office. It was dark by the time I'd made the hour drive back to town, and most everyone at the BLM had already left for the day. I turned on my computer and opened up my file for the search. I'd made copies of my files and given them to Colm, and I couldn't be sure what I was looking for, but something was gnawing at me, as if I just needed to be certain I hadn't missed anything. Throughout the search I had taken pictures of the area as well as of the items and tracks we'd discovered. There were close to sixty photos. I knew I was going to open and zoom in on each one and that could take hours. I walked into the small kitchen, filled a bowl of water for Kona, and made a pot of coffee. Then I called Joseph.

"I think there's some lasagna in the

freezer," I told him. "I may be a while."

One by one, I pulled up photos from the search. I zoomed in closely on each image, looked for marking tape, a footprint, anything out of the ordinary. I was tired and both Kona and I were hungry. I'd gone through about twenty-five photos. The rest of the employees had long since left. Kona was lying on his bed by my desk. He raised his head and a moan started up in the back of his throat. Someone was at the front door.

I stood up. Kona followed me to the lobby. There was Joseph standing at the glass door with that grin of his and a plate wrapped in aluminum foil.

I unlocked the door and let him in.

"I thought you might want some dinner," he said.

I said something to him about how thoughtful he was, and that, yes, I was starving. He walked with me to my desk and pulled up a chair beside me. I showed him what I was working on. He scrolled through some of the photos while I ate. I asked him about his day.

"Good," he said.

I kept eating. Then, feeling bad for Kona, I fed him my last couple of bites.

Joseph was studying one of the pictures. "Did you see this?" he asked. His fingers tapped away at the keyboard. He copied a corner of the photo onto the desktop and enlarged the picture. “Is this anything?” He pointed at an image in the upper right corner of the monitor.

I leaned in to have a better look. “I’m not sure. Can you zoom in any closer?”

“This is as good as I can get it,” he said.

Joseph had been able to enlarge the photo enough to capture the upper half of a pinyon and zoom in on what looked like something man-made.

“What do you think?” I asked.

“Looks like something metal.”

“Could be a tree stand,” I said. “It’s hard to tell. Might be worth checking out.”

I went back to my notes on the photos and found the location for where the image had been taken, which was less than a mile from where we’d found the truck. “You could be onto something,” I told him.

Amy Raye

Sometimes as minutes turned to hours and hours turned to days, Amy Raye would think about how simple life could be. She found pleasure in her routines, in the gathering of wood, the collection of snow for her water supply, her daily trek to her cache for meat, and the slow cooking of the meat over the fire. And she found pleasure in the beauty of things, the slant of light at different times throughout the day, the mountain air, the sound of the wind and the sifting snow. Perhaps this was all a preparation for how she would die, up here in this place. There was something almost peaceful in that. Her body would become fodder for the animals. She thought especially of the lion whose tracks she had seen from time to time around the vicinity of the cave, and whose tufts of fur she'd once found snagged on branches when she'd ventured farther from the cave in search for wood and the scarce pinyon nuts and juniper berries.

But nighttime was a different animal. And the lines between death and life blurred, each second stretching out for what felt like eternity as she waited through the darkness for sunlight. And the realization that *they* had stopped looking for her, that she would never be found, settled into her like a slow encroaching death. And as she stared into the blackness, imagining a drop of water or the wind or a small animal into a family of rats or a lion, as she felt that she was being watched, or that she had seen something — yes, she'd feel certain she had — the stink of her fear and madness would be suffocating, and she'd want to scream and run out of the cave and into the night, but she was not mad enough to do so, and eventually morning would come.

Other times during the day Amy Raye was seized with distress. Though she could now stand and hobble around by relying on a limb that she'd fashioned into a crutch, certain movements or pressures on her left leg still overwhelmed her. Worse were the muscle spasms that had set in. Without any salt or minerals, her electrolytes had dropped fearfully low, and the cramping in her leg sent such intense waves of pain that she thought she would surely black out.

And her supply of food was diminishing. She had been living out of this cave now for six weeks. She had rationed the elk meat as best she could, consuming a little more than a pound each day. She'd found Mormon grass and made tea. She'd gathered small portions of pinyon nuts and had tried to tolerate the bitter juniper berries. But she was sorely feeling the nutritional deficits, and she was losing weight. Already she had tightened her belt a notch and would soon be tightening it another. Her wedding band had become too loose, and so she had switched it to her middle finger. Her left leg had atrophied. More and more she began to fear for her future. At different intervals throughout each day, she would sit at the opening of the cave and call out for help, already knowing there was no one to answer her. She had done the best she could with her misshapen leg, and despite not having enough variety in her diet, she was thankful for the protein the elk had provided her. She'd created her own form of physical therapy to strengthen her arms and her right leg. Using the wall of the cave for support, she would extend her left leg in front of her and perform leg squats. She'd strengthen her triceps by planting her hands behind her and lifting her hips.

And each night she made a mark on the cave wall, recording another day that had passed. She would clasp her hands together and find her wedding ring, a small gold band. She'd play with the ring, twisting it around and around, as if it were a rosary.

Christmas was less than a week away. Had Farrell and the children put up a tree? Had he bought them presents? But she knew her husband. He would do that much for the children. And then she realized, he would have already been grieving for her as if she were dead. Amy Raye imagined people bringing food to her home. Imagined the women who would be eyeing Farrell as someone who was available. How much time would pass before one of those women would reach out to him, touch the places where he was the most vulnerable, those places where he felt needed? Farrell's blue eyes were so open and kind, they made a person want to explain her whole life to him. But what about now? Would his eyes still carry that same kindness? How long would he grieve before he was in the arms of another?

With her hands still clasped, she continued to hold on to her ring. She let her thoughts carry her to an overcast day in June, to

Farrell and music and the smell of the barn, to the north pasture and clover where they'd fallen asleep drunk and naked on a blanket under the moon and stars and woken to sunlight and dew on their skin. They'd lain on their backs and held up their left hands to the sun, till its rays caught their gold bands and reflected gold light back upon them.

It was in the pasture behind Idaho McKenzie's barn, where Amy Raye and Farrell had said their vows. Idaho was one of Farrell's closest friends. He played the mandolin in a folk group called Folk Yeah! His girlfriend, Hallie, played the fiddle, and Howard, a retired plumber, played the guitar. Howard was also a justice of the peace, so he did the honors of officiating the wedding. Idaho was Farrell's best man. Amy Raye wanted Saddle to stand up with her, but when Howard laughed a little too loudly at her idea, she chose Farrell's daughter, Julia, instead. Maybe fifty people attended, and Amy Raye did not know the names of most of them, and Farrell did not know the names of others. But the people were in good spirits and had brought food and drink. Amy Raye wore a white gunnysack dress and her gold and brown cowboy boots, and Farrell wore a gray tuxedo with an American Eagle bolo tie, and his black Justins.

Before they said their vows, Farrell played his guitar for Amy Raye and sang Kate Wolf's "Give Yourself to Love." A cool drizzle began to fall. Howard pronounced the two husband and wife, and people cheered, and the rain fell harder. Farrell kissed each raindrop on Amy Raye's face, and she laughed and cried. Folk Yeah! set up in the barn and made music, and everyone gathered around them and danced and ate and drank. After the rain stopped and the moon came out and stars began to appear, Farrell tried to waltz with Amy Raye to "Magnolia Wind," and when they stumbled and fell and got back up, he gathered her in his arms and held her close as they danced to "I'll Lay Ye Doon, Love," which Idaho sang with a Scottish lilt.

Amy Raye awoke the next morning with a fresh sense of purpose. The sky was clear and the temperatures outside the cave relatively mild, maybe in the twenties or thirties. She retrieved the remainder of the elk quarter. Her arrow had hit the elk's right scapula, the same shoulder that she'd hauled out, and the broadhead had broken through the bone and penetrated up to six inches. A scapula shot usually resulted in little blood trail, as the blood would get trapped behind the bone. Amy Raye thought about the long hours she'd spent tracking the elk, the small collections of blood, the rain that day. She was lucky to have found the elk at all. She carved what little meat remained from the shoulder blade and from between the tendons of the leg and set the bones aside. She knew the names of all the bones on an elk, the same as those of a deer, and as she cooked the meat, she recited the names — scapula, ulna, radius, tarsus, carpal phalanges, tibia, metatarsus, metacarpal. And upon reciting the names, she thought of her grandfather and the farm. And she thought upon a time when she'd been ten years old, when she'd worked on a science project for school, and she'd chosen to put together a deer skeleton from the bones she'd found on her grandparents' property and the woods beyond, carcasses left over from hunters or coyote kill. She'd soaked the bones in bleach in steel tubs behind the barn and then laid them in the sun to dry. Her grandfather had helped her drill holes through the marrow of the bones, until he came to one of the tibias.

"We've got us a cougar out there," he said. "See the end here, how it's broken off?"

Amy Raye held the bone, rubbed her fingers over its jagged edges.

"A cougar's got some strong jaws. Breaks the bone clean in half and eats out the marrow." He showed her the hollowed-out space where the marrow had been.

Amy Raye ate a small portion of the cooked meat and, using the gallon-size plastic bag, packed up the rest, no more than a couple of pounds, to bring with her. Despite the sun, the snow was deep, and she was not sure how she would manage over the rocks, but she had to at least try. She picked up the scapula. The triangular bone was about a foot long and maybe nine inches at its widest point. Though it would add extra weight to her pack, it could be of use to her. She scraped the scapula clean. Then she removed the shoelaces from the boot she could no longer wear and picked up one of the longer sticks she'd collected for firewood. Using the laces, she tied the end of the scapula to one of the ends of the stick. The shovel was small enough to strap to the back of her pack. She had no idea what the forecast would be. She could only hobble around at best. It would be days, maybe a week before she could cover enough distance to reach a road or find help. And yet if she stayed in the cave, where she could keep warm as long as she could gather firewood, within two weeks, probably less, she would be dead. Building a fire once she left was not a guarantee, given the snow and the winds that could pick up. She wondered what it would be like to die from hypothermia. Maybe it wouldn't be so bad. Her body would go numb. She wouldn't feel anything. She imagined crawling into a fetal position in a soft drift and falling asleep. But she knew hypothermia wasn't that simple. She'd read enough accounts of the hallucinations of those suffering from a severe drop in body temperature, heard stories of people who had stripped out of their clothes because of an imagined fire and a false sense of heat. She also thought of how difficult it would be to manipulate her legs and feet over the ice-slicked rocks. And what if she were to experience another fall, another broken bone? Maybe leaving the cave was a mistake. But if she waited any longer, she would no longer have a choice, and she wanted that choice. She wanted her children to know she'd done everything she could to return to them. She had already packed her few belongings, had filled her hydration bladder. Even though the game bag had been soiled with the elk's blood, she'd folded the four-foot cloth and used its drawstrings to create a bootie for her injured foot.

She lay back on the boughs she used as a mattress. She looked up at the cross she had etched into the rock wall. She did not believe the cross would protect her. She was not superstitious in that sort of way, and yet she had found that it brought her comfort.

Amy Raye thought about that comfort and the ways a child is raised. She thought upon the white church where her grandfather had been an elder, and, for years, her father had been a deacon. And while her father had been a deacon he'd visit the sick, and sometimes Amy Raye would go with him. She'd carry the large Bible and her father would carry a cup of coffee and a box of donuts that he and Amy Raye would have picked up at the Donut Barn in Tullahoma. If there were any donuts left after they'd made their visits, he and Amy Raye would eat them in the front seat of his patrol car. And on a warm day, they'd ride with the windows down and sometimes she'd lean her head out the window and let the wind blow her hair.

The big, brown leather Bible belonged to the church. It had been given to the congregation by Governor Buford Ellington in

1967, the same year he signed a bill repealing the Butler Act of 1925 that had outlawed the teaching of evolution in public schools. That was also the year he'd appointed the state's first black cabinet member, Hosea T. Lockard. Some old-time members of the church hadn't been fans of Governor Ellington. The church was known for its biblical conservatism, so the church didn't mind that Clyde Surgarton took that particular Bible with him when he visited the sick. He told Amy Raye that the big book carried with it healing powers.

"How so?" Amy Raye had asked him.

"Because it was given to the church by a man capable of changing his ways."

Those were the most profound words Amy Raye would ever hear from her father. And for a long time, she let those afternoons with him and those words define him.

After a fitful sleep, after eating a small portion of meat and drinking some Mormon grass tea, she looked the cave over one last time before leaving. A few bones from the elk's leg, the firewood, the discarded boot from her left foot, the small handprints on the wall next to where she had slept, the trapezoid figures that she had called carrot people. She had no way of knowing the weather that lay ahead of her. But for now sunlight shimmered over the snow and the morning sky was a cerulean blue. How many days had she held the image of the map in her mind, tried to recall its vertical scale, tried to remember those low chasms where the map's contour lines were spaced farther apart. But those chasms lay to the west of the bluffs. The cave faced east, and all Amy Raye could see from the ridge were dense woods and steep terrain. She felt certain she was in the thick of the bluffs, and if that was the case, she was standing at over seven thousand feet in elevation. Should she move eastward, that elevation would climb to over eight thousand feet, which would mean an increase in the snow-pack. She might very well become more lost than she already was. No, she would have to get around this rocky bluff in which the cave had been carved and eroded so many years ago, and to do that, she would have to climb. To the left of the cave, the ledge came to a dead end, abutting the vertical rock face from where she had fallen. To the right of the cave, the ledge continued to widen into an expanded step into the bluff of almost fifty yards. It was from this area that she had stored the elk meat and gathered wood. Each day she had explored it further, seeing how far it would take her. The ledge eventually merged away from the rock wall, to a more gradual incline of about forty-five degrees. The incline was littered with rocks and deadfall. And without the heat from the afternoon sun, the slope had remained mostly covered in snow. But if she could just get to the top of this hill, she could gauge the direction in which she would need to go, which would involve climbing down in elevation and moving westward, where she might be lucky enough to come across one of the pipeline roads.

And so she began the climb. Before leaving, she had sharpened the end of her crutch so that she might use it as a trekking pole. She bore her weight on her right leg and planted her crutch uphill. She rotated the crutch back and forth as if screwing it in place. Then she transferred her weight onto the crutch. With her right hand, she found a hold in one of the rocks embedded in the hillside and was able to pull herself forward. When that step was completed, she began the process all over again. It would take her a couple of hours to make this one small climb, an ascent that would have taken her minutes in her healthier state. But she knew she would have to fight off those kinds of thoughts if she were to continue to make progress, if she were to have any hope of going home. And with that thought her body felt a surge of momentum and she moved more quickly. She prodded the snow with her crutch, screwed the crutch into the frozen ground, pulled herself forward, again and again. Her mouth touched snow, and icy rocks abraded the sides of her face, and in her mind she saw Farrell and Trevor and Julia. Her anticipation of seeing her family became both an ache and a thrill so strong in her chest that she literally felt her heart had swelled.

She stopped only a couple of times to catch her breath. Her body was shaking from the sheer fatigue of it all, and the sun felt warm, as if teasing her forward. Maybe two hours had passed. She couldn't be sure, but at last she'd made it to the top of the bluff. Somewhere on the rock face beneath her, and maybe seventy paces or so to her right, was the cave, and beneath that another ledge, the same ledge that had broken her fall when she had first come upon the shelter. But that was behind her now, and she had all of this land before her, and a big sky, and a warm sun. How cold was it? Maybe twenty degrees, but with her exertion she was ready to shed layers of clothing. She tried to speculate how far she could go in a day. Perhaps a mile, as long as the weather was hospitable. And how many miles was she from help? Without knowing the exact location of the cave, without a compass and a map, there was no way to tell. In some ways she felt she was staring out into oblivion, but instead of feeling discouraged, she was overtaken with how beautiful it all was, and she wished Farrell were with her and she could share it with him. And just as quickly as she had felt exhilarated for having made it to the top of this bluff, she felt saddened and her body began to chill from the perspiration on her skin and in her clothes, and she wanted to cry for all the times she might have had, the moments with Farrell when her mind was someplace else, afternoons when she might have been with Farrell or the children but had found a reason to be away. Errands she'd told him she had to run, or some billing she had to take care of for Aaron, and as she drove away, she would be filled with anticipation for another man, for danger and pleasure, the kind that had slipped under her skin when her body and mind were still clean, until she was no longer clean and the danger had become a craving. And yet all those hours spent in the cave, when the only thing she had to pass the time were her thoughts, it was her moments with Farrell that she relived in her mind, over and over again, as if her life with him were all that had ever been.

Amy Raye took several swallows of water, ate a few pinyon nuts. She then moved on. The sun was still at her back. Soon it would be directly above her, and then the afternoon would pass quickly. She felt certain somewhere to the west of her there was a road. Eventually she would find it.

She stopped before the shadows became too large, and smoothed out an area of snow between two large boulders. Because she wanted to save her matches, she used her fire starter instead. She cut boughs from nearby junipers to create a mattress, as well as to provide her with some insulation cover. She had divided what little meat she had left into approximately four-ounce servings. But a four-ounce serving of meat was probably no more than 150 calories. Though she'd been trying to survive on as close to a thousand calories a day as possible, to ration her supplies, she'd have to cut back more. She cooked two servings of meat that night and drank a liter of water. She would consume another serving of the elk before heading out the following morning. That would leave her with only a little more than a pound. Maybe she would be able to strike a rabbit. There should be plenty in the area now that she was off the ledge and had a greater area to cover. And maybe she would find a road or a truck within the next few days.

Shortly after she finished eating, as she lay back against her pack and warmed her feet beside the fire, the coyotes came out. She first heard a couple of yips, then a long howl, and shortly after, all kinds of high-pitched yelps and barks. She untied the fleece from around her head so that she could hear them better. She knew she was in the middle of the coyotes' courting season, and possibly still in their territorial season as well, when the pups from the previous year's litters went out on their own to find new territories and begin their own family packs. But this night, the eerie chorus, more like a maniacal laughter, sounded like that of several bands, and though she knew these jackals, or brush wolves, as they were often called, were rarely a threat to humans, and even then only in more urban areas where prey was scarce, a handful of coyotes could sound like hundreds, especially as they gathered in the evenings to hunt, and the changes in their pitch and yelps could send a chilling uneasiness over one's skin. She thought of an evening early in the fall when she'd set out with her bow and her tag for a mule deer. She had been sitting behind the deadfall of an enormous spruce, using it as a blind, when she heard the first yip and saw a young coyote trotting down the trail. Then she heard the long, high-pitched howl of the alpha. Within minutes, an entire chorus started up, and a large family of maybe eight or nine coyotes had gathered. She had never before witnessed such a sight. The pups were yipping and barking and playing, wrestling each other and turning somersaults. Within twenty minutes, the chorus was over, and each member of the pack had disappeared back into the woods.

She thought upon the families, and how after they mated, many would remain monogamous for several years. She thought of wolves, and eagles, and black vultures, and prairie moles as well, and she wondered why she couldn't have the good, decent flow of life that these animals had, as if it just wasn't in the cards for her. And yet she wanted to be like the eagles and the albatross that mated for life. She had been like the alcoholic who promises herself she won't take another drink, who wants to come clean, and then picks up cheap beer at the convenience store on a Sunday morning or a Wednesday afternoon. How much easier it would have been to tell Farrell she had a drinking problem. How much easier it would have been to ask for his help then.

Was she wrong in allowing herself the hope of seeing him again? She had been gone for over seven weeks. What might he have discovered during that time? Who of the men whom she'd encountered or been involved with may have come forward? She had been the one who managed the bills. Would Farrell have looked at old phone records or accessed her email? She had always deleted text messages and calls, but she wondered how many new messages and calls there had been.

And with the cold and fatigue and hunger and the night hours came her greatest fear. What if Farrell wouldn't take her back? There had been the time years before when she'd called Farrell from Anchorage, when he could barely understand her over the phone because she was crying and she wasn't sure Saddle was going to make it, and she needed money, she needed a way to get home. He told her he would wire her the money, he would pay Saddle's bill, but when she got home, they would need to talk.

She'd driven eight hours from McCarthy.

She'd left behind her books and the cookstove and what few belongings, including clothes, she'd brought with her. Saddle lay beside her on the bench seat of her truck, and though he was breathing, he wouldn't wake up.

When she got to Anchorage, she drove to a twenty-four-hour animal hospital she'd located from a phone book. She scooped Saddle into her arms, entered through the two glass doors, and begged someone to help her. Saddle was still unconscious. His pulse was weak. A technician led Amy Raye to an examining room. X-rays were taken; fluids were given. Saddle was bleeding internally and had a fair amount of swelling on the brain. Emergency surgery was needed. It would be expensive, and he still might not make it.

The vet was a woman in her fifties, with black hair and dark freckles and a kind face. Amy Raye did not have a credit card. She did not have enough money with her.

"Is there someone you can call?" the vet asked.

And Amy Raye thought of Farrell, and she asked to use the vet's phone. When Farrell answered, there was too much noise in the background. He was at a bar with some friends. Julia was visiting her mom. And in that second when Amy Raye first heard he was in a bar, she was angry at him that he could be drinking and having a good time while Saddle was hurt and might not make it, and she was angry that Farrell, whose love had come to her like the wind on the mountaintop and thunder in the rain, could be out drinking with friends while she was gone. She was irrational and alone, and she needed Saddle to be okay. She needed Farrell, and she needed to go home.

The vet operated on Saddle. He would be watched for twenty-four hours.

"And what about you?" the vet had asked. "You've been injured, too."

Amy Raye walked with a limp, and blood was on her jeans and on the hem of her shirt.

"I just want him to be okay."

"And if he could talk, he would say the same about you. Here, let me take a look."

The gash on Amy Raye's hip needed stitches and needed to be cleaned.

"I don't have insurance," Amy Raye told her. "And I don't have enough money."

"I can take care of that," the vet said. "Do you have a place to stay?"

"I can stay in my truck."

But the vet lived close by, and after she stitched Amy Raye's hip and bandaged the wound, she brought Amy Raye home with her, scrambled eggs and fried bacon, made coffee and poured orange juice, and Amy Raye ate as if nothing had ever tasted better. She slept a few hours on the woman's sofa, took a shower, and then went back to the hospital to be with Saddle, and she thanked God for good people, for this woman whose husband had left her, and whose heart had refused to become bitter, for Lew, and for her grandfather, and for someone as kind to her as Farrell.

As soon as the bank opened and Amy Raye picked up the money Farrell had sent her, she stopped by a grocery store to buy dog food and a sandwich and snacks for the road. After she made her purchase, she saw some hikers, a college-age group, who were replenishing their supplies. One of them had just put his cell phone away. Amy Raye asked him if she could borrow it. She would pay him ten dollars. He told her to use the phone. He didn't want her money. He told her to take her time. They were in no hurry.

She dialed the number. The phone on the other end rang too many times. She almost hung up. A familiar voice answered.

"Nan? It's Amy Raye."

The person on the other end gasped. "Oh

my God. Where are you? Where have you been?"

"I'm sorry, Nan. I don't have a lot of time. Is Grandpa there?"

The silence on the other end lasted long enough for Amy Raye to know something was wrong.

"Aims, it's been nearly six years. No one knew how to reach you."

"Where is he?" Amy Raye asked.

"Aims, he's dead. He's been dead four years now."

Nan's words were like a truck, a very large truck, hitting Amy Raye in the middle of a road, while she had been standing there looking in another direction. Her eyes filled with hot liquid. The air seemed to thicken.

Their conversation lasted a few more minutes, long enough for Amy Raye to learn that her grandfather had developed lung cancer, that it had spread to his brain, and once it was in his brain, he had gone fast. Nan had since gotten married to Danny Foster, a local boy whom Amy Raye remembered from school. Nan and Danny had moved onto the farm. They'd needed a place to stay. Grandma Tomlin needed their help on the farm.

But her grandmother wasn't there when Amy Raye called, and when Nan pressed

Amy Raye for information, she was still trying to take everything in and said she couldn't talk. She said she was borrowing the phone from someone she didn't know. She said she would call back another time.

She gave the college boy his phone. She walked out of the grocery store and got into her truck. She turned onto the highway and headed in the direction of the animal hospital, and as she drove, she screamed her lungs empty, and hit the steering wheel until her palms turned blue. And back at the hospital, she wiped the tears from her face; she got out of the truck and went in to get Saddle.

When Amy Raye returned to Farrell, Julia asked Amy Raye to promise that she would never go away again, and Farrell made Amy Raye dinner. And after they ate and were sitting on the futon on Farrell's porch, Amy Raye told him about her childhood, about her father working as a highway patrolman, about her mother working weekdays and every other weekend at the library. She told him about the horses and the barn, and she told him about Lionel and Nan. And she cried when she told him these things. He held her hands as she spoke. He kissed her face. He told her he loved her. He told her she was safe and that everything was okay now. And she had believed him because she had wanted for it to be so. “I don’t want to go back,” she’d said. “I can’t. I won’t go back there again.”

But that night Amy Raye didn’t tell Farrell about the man working next door when she was only sixteen, and the other men, until she could not remember how many men there had been. And she didn’t tell him about the night it had been raining and she was on her way home from the Sensing Farm’s Free Rein Stables where a girl from school whom she’d almost become friends with was boarding a two-year-old quarter horse mustang. The girl had wanted to show Amy Raye her new horse, and when Amy Raye said the horse reminded her of a hemlock because of the horse’s gray-brown coloring like that of the hemlock’s bark, and because she thought the horse would grow to have great stature, and a hemlock could grow to be a hundred and fifty feet tall, the girl said that was what she was going to name the horse, and Amy Raye thought the name was a fine one.

“I think his father was a free-roaming mustang,” Amy Raye said.

“I don’t know,” the girl said. “The mother came from a long line of domesticated quarter horses. I don't know much about the father."

The girl had purchased the horse with the help of her parents from a breeder in Kentucky.

"Why do you think he was free roaming?" the girl asked.

"Something in his eyes," Amy Raye said. "You ever see a wild horse?"

"No."

"There's places out west that round up the wild horses and auction them off. Maybe Hemlock's father was one of those."

"Maybe," the girl said.

"Have you ever been out west?" Amy Raye asked.

"No."

"I think I'd like to go out west," Amy Raye said. "I think I'd like to see the wild horses."

"I'll let you ride him," the girl told Amy Raye. "I'm going to start breaking him in soon."

"I'd wait another year," Amy Raye told her. "He's still awfully young, but I'd like to ride him."

The evening had grown dark and the rain was coming down hard.

"I better be getting home," Amy Raye said. "I'll see you tomorrow."

The two girls had recently graduated from

high school and were both spending the summer working at a convenience store on the edge of town. Amy Raye had plans to start college at the University of Tennessee in Chattanooga in the fall. The other girl was going to take a year off and save her money by living at home.

Amy Raye climbed into her 1991 Ford Ranger that she'd bought two years before from money she'd saved from working on her grandparents' farm. The Sensings' farm was a sixteen-mile drive from her house, down Highway 50. Amy Raye was about halfway home and was singing along to "Eighteen Wheels and a Dozen Roses" over the radio. The windshield wipers were turned on high. She might have been driving too fast, but she didn't recall. And she was so busy singing and thinking of the quarter horse mustang that by the time she saw the blue flashing lights, the highway patrolman was right up on her. She slowed down, and as soon as the shoulder was wide enough, she pulled over and came to a stop.

A lot of minutes seemed to pass before the patrolman was at her window, tapping on it with his flashlight. When she rolled down her window, the rain poured in. The patrolman asked her to step out. She rolled her window back up and did as he said. But standing outside her truck, the patrolman and she were both getting so wet, and Amy Raye wasn't wearing a rain jacket or a hat like the patrolman, but rather a pair of cutoff jean shorts and a white tank top with an Opryland decal, so the patrolman said why didn't they get in his patrol car so they could get out of the rain.

They both ran back to the patrol car and got in, and inside it was warm and dry, and because it was summer, the patrolman turned up the air-conditioning, and when the cold air blew on Amy Raye's wet skin, her legs and arms turned to gooseflesh. She scooted over close to the man, who she thought looked about forty, and other than a small belly that most of the men around his age had, he was nice enough looking. He clapped a freckled hand on her left knee, and shook it back and forth as if to warm her up a little. He asked her what she was doing out on a night like this and where she was heading to.

She said she was on her way home. She told him about the stable and the horse. "Can't you tell?" she said. She lifted her shirt out a little ways from her chest. "Don't I smell like a barn?"

"You smell good," he said, but he was looking down her shirt when he said it, so she turned toward him and pressed her hand inside his thigh.

"I'm still cold," she said.

The man looked over his shoulder, and Amy Raye could tell he was getting nervous. They were on a highway. There hadn't been any other cars, but there might be.

"You think we ought to drive somewhere and get you warm?" he said.

"I don't much care to leave my truck on the side of the road," she said. "I wouldn't want anything to happen to it." And all the while she was talking, she was rubbing her hand along the man's inner thigh, and his breathing was becoming thicker. "Oh, Jesus," he said, but he was all out of breath when he said it. He removed his gun and set it on the dashboard, and Amy Raye worked her hands up to the man's belt and lowered her head to his lap.

She left that night, without a ticket or a warning, drove herself the rest of the way home, said hello to her parents, read for a while, and went to bed. And she'd almost forgotten about the whole affair, until two weeks later. She'd just gotten home from work. Her mother had cooked a pot roast that morning in the slow cooker. Amy Raye hadn't eaten anything since lunch, a pre-made sandwich she'd bought at the store, and was looking forward to dinner. But when she walked into the house, her parents were sitting across from each other at the kitchen table. The table was bare except for her father's hands, which were clasped in front of him. The slow cooker was still on the counter, and the pot roast smelled burned.

"What's going on?" Amy Raye said.

"You have five minutes to pack your belongings and get out of this house," her father said.

"What are you talking about? What's going on?" Amy Raye was standing between the door and the kitchen table, about four feet from her parents. She had a denim purse slung over her shoulders, was wearing a pair of army fatigues and a green T-shirt from the convenience store with an advertisement for Purity Dairy products on the front and Stoker's chewing tobacco on the back.

"I won't have a whore living under my roof." Her father was staring at his hands.

Amy Raye tried to make eye contact with her mother, whose hands were in her lap. But her mother continued to stare at the surface of the table.

Amy Raye kicked the legs of the chair closest to her, knocking the chair on its side, and started to walk through the kitchen and back to her room, but her father shot up out of his chair and grabbed her arm.

"Clyde!" Amy Raye's mother said.

"Stay out of this, Sharon." He was twisting the skin on Amy Raye's arm, and his saliva had left drops on her face. "How many?" he demanded. "I know of at least one, but how many others?"

"I don't know what you're talking about."

"The hell you don't know what I'm talking about. Someone at the station says your license plate was called in the other night. Says I might want to ask David Skinner about it. Seems like there was some talk going on. So I asked Skinner, and he tells me I best keep an eye on you. Says he would have hauled your ass to jail if it wasn't for him calling in your plate and finding out you were my —" Her father let go of her arm, dropped his hand to his side. "Like I said, you got five minutes. And if you got any sense left in you, you'll get out of this town."

There was a suitcase open on her bed, and inside the suitcase, many of her clothes had already been packed. And then the tears came, burned rivers down her face. She grabbed her things from the bathroom, a couple of her books. She tried to feel anger.

She told herself he had no right. But the pain was there, in all of its shades, in her father's eyes, in her mother's voice. Maybe just for a night, or maybe a week or two. Things would settle down. Yet her heart trembled from the sheer force of what could not be undone. She closed the suitcase and carried it out to her truck. Her parents were no longer at the kitchen table. The chair she'd knocked over had been set upright. Her father was standing at the kitchen sink with his back to her. Maybe he was looking out the window at the small backyard. Maybe he was thinking the grass needed to be mowed. Perhaps he was looking at the swing set with the red, white, and blue striped poles that had rusted over the years, the one her parents had wanted to hold on to for the day when Amy Raye would have children.

The slow cooker had been unplugged and the smell of charred meat had grown stronger. She walked out the side door to the driveway, careful not to bang the door with her suitcase, and she wondered why she was being careful now. She set the suitcase in the bed of the truck. She climbed into the driver's seat, and when she turned the key, a loud announcement for Auto Rama Used Auto Fair played over the speakers. Her mother stepped out of the house and walked up to the truck. The windows were rolled down. She handed Amy Raye some money. "It's all I have."

"Is this what you want?" Amy Raye asked.

"You have to go. I can't change his mind." Her mother was crying now. She pressed the money into her daughter's hand.

"Mom, don't do this." But Amy Raye knew it was too late.

Her mother leaned in through the window and kissed Amy Raye on the cheek. "I'm sorry," her mother said. Then she turned around and walked back into the house.

The night Amy Raye left home, she drove to the Free Rein Stables. She talked to the horse named Hemlock that she was told she'd one day ride. The horse came up to her and nibbled at her T-shirt. It hadn't rained that night, and the stars were out. After she left the stables, she drove out of town a ways until she was halfway between Lynchburg and Tullahoma. She pulled her truck over on one of the dirt roads that led to Sam Burt Hill Summit. Then she climbed in the back of her truck and, using one of her sweatshirts as a pillow, lay down. She stayed awake most of the night deciding what she would do. Her mother had given her seventy dollars. Amy Raye had over seven hundred dollars in an account at the bank.

Once the sun was up she drove to the Quik Mart in Tullahoma, fueled her truck, and bought a package of donuts, an orange juice, and a United States atlas. Then she drove back to Lynchburg to the Moore County Bank. She sat in her truck in the parking lot, finished her donuts and orange juice, and studied the atlas. When the bank opened, she went in and withdrew all of her money.

On her way out of town, she stopped by her grandparents' farm. Their truck wasn't in the driveway, and she decided maybe it was better that way, because what would she tell them and how could she face them if they knew what she had done? She stepped into the barn. Van Gogh walked up to the edge of his stall like he always did when Amy Raye was around. She scooped up a handful of grain from the trough, opened his stall door, and fed him. She soaked in that warm feeling of his muzzle on her hand. "I'm going to miss you most of all," she said. Though she knew it wasn't Van Gogh she was going to miss the most.

When the pain behind her eyes and in her chest got to be too much, she kissed Van

Gogh's nose and rubbed his ears. She told him not to step on any barn cats. She told him he was her sky and that she would always love him. She closed the stall door behind her and wiped away her tears. She walked up the hill behind the barn, along the tractor road and into the woods. She sat in her blind for close to an hour, watched the birds and the dragonflies and the squirrels and the chipmunks. She wanted to tell everybody she was sorry. But she wanted them to be sorry also. She grabbed a fistful of dirt, held it to her nose. It smelled like mud and leaves and creek water. She shoved it in her pocket and stepped out of the blind.

Instead of heading back toward the barn and house, she walked a little farther through the woods until she came upon the small cemetery with the three markers, where Nan and Lionel and she used to play with their toy soldiers. They'd use the headstones, slabs of granite that stood about two feet out of the ground, as barricades. When they'd first discovered the site, there were only two headstones, but over the next couple of years, a third one had appeared. There was something peaceful about the smoothed-out clearing as they lay on their stomachs and manipulated the plastic figures, until the afternoon Amy Raye understood whose lives were buried there, and the person who had dug the small graves.

Pru

That next week, Colm brought six men in for questioning, including the husband and Aaron and Kenny, despite the men from the hunting party having already passed a polygraph test. Each night I called Colm.

"How did it go?" I'd ask him.

And each night I'd get the same answer. "Not a thing." One of the men had met Amy Raye at a convenience store. Two of the other men had met her on dating sites. Aaron said he hadn't been involved with her for six months. Kenny had broken down several times during the questioning. But every one of the men passed the lie detector test, including Farrell. And each was willing to cooperate, though Aaron was reluctant at first because of his family. He said his wife didn't know, and he had recommitted himself to her and wanted to make things right. But what got to Colm most was Farrell.

"Up until her disappearance, he didn't have a clue. Then he gets home from the search and he's trying to talk to the kids. The girl doesn't think Amy Raye is dead. She thinks her mom will be coming home, like Moab, their dog who'd run off one night, only to return the next day. So here Farrell is trying to talk to the kids, trying to hold himself together, and he goes to bed one night and turns on his wife's phone."

"I thought you were holding the phone as evidence," I said.

"Evidence of what? We didn't know about this other life she had going on. We gave the husband back all of her belongings. We'd rather spend our time pulling records than trying to break a passcode."

Colm went on to tell me that Farrell had tried different combinations of numbers, and one of them had worked. Amy Raye had at least ten new voice messages. Seven of the messages were from Kenny, telling her how much he loved her and how worried he was. Another message was from one of the men Colm had brought in. The guy had heard Amy Raye had gone missing. He'd called to hear her voice. The other two messages were from Farrell.

"And get this," Colm said. "The PIN on her cell phone was her and Farrell's anniversary."

"What about text messages?"

"There were plenty of those. And I don't have to tell you the nature of them."

"Any pictures?"

"The last pictures were from their daughter's birthday party," Colm said.

"I don't get it," I said. "No pictures from the hunt, or photos after Kenny and Aaron filled their tags?"

"I don't know what to tell you. Maybe that wasn't her thing."

"How long has the husband known?"

"A couple of weeks."

"And he didn't say anything to you? Do you find that odd?"

"You don't know men." Colm exhaled into the receiver, more like a drawn-out sigh. "Let's just say a wife's infidelities aren't something a man is proud of."

I hesitated, thinking about what Colm had said, and wondering if he had meant more. Then I asked, "How is Farrell taking all of this?"

"He's confused. He's upset. He's angry. But I'll be damned, that man loves her. If there's a trump card to this whole thing, it's that. He's got one hell of a broken heart. He really believed she'd loved him."

Colm's words made me sad, not just for

Farrell, but for the woman. I wished she could know how her husband felt.

"Have you changed your mind about Kenny?" I asked. I'd already told Colm about the photo Joseph had pulled up. I'd told Colm that we might be looking at a tree stand and that I was going to be checking it out after Christmas.

"Yeah, I guess I have."

I was sitting in the living room next to the wood stove. Joseph and I had put up a tree, a pinyon we'd cut from the woods. We'd be driving over to Boulder at the end of the week. My parents would be meeting us there, as well. "It's weird, you know. It's like we're angry with her, and we don't even know her. It's easy to forget that she's someone's mother and someone's wife, and they're having to get on without her."

The tree lights flickered. Kona was lying beside me on the sofa. I stroked his warm fur.

Colm had become quiet. After about a minute, I said, "Are you there?"

"Yeah, I'm here." And then, "When are you and Joseph heading out?"

"He's got his last final Friday morning. We'll leave after that." I had a couple of sites near the Coos shelter I still needed to check out, so I was glad we weren't leaving any sooner. Sometimes getting to those sites was prohibited by the snowy terrain, but I could at least look for any disturbances in the immediate area.

Colm had remained quiet, and in that moment, I felt a bigger sadness stirring up inside me. "Colm, are you okay? You got any plans?"

"Yeah, I'll be fine. Dean wants me to stop by their place. Wants me to swing by early so I can watch the kids open their presents." I heard Colm moving around in his kitchen, heard the sound of a skillet on the stove.

"What are you doing?" I asked.

"Just fixing some dinner."

"It's late," I said. Joseph and I had already finished and put the dishes away.

"A man's got to eat," he said.

"What are you cooking?"

Colm opened a drawer and shut it. A couple of utensils clinked. "I'm frying a steak," he said.

"It smells good."

And Colm laughed.

I heard him turn the steak over, heard a cabinet open and close.

"I better let you go," I said.

A few seconds passed. "Have a good trip, Pru. Drive safe."

"I will. Merry Christmas, Colm."

■ ■ ■ ■

I didn't know how Amy Raye's family was going to spend Christmas. But I thought about them a lot over the holiday. And while I knelt beside Joseph during the Christmas Eve service at the beautiful St. Aidan's, I prayed for Amy Raye and her family. I prayed for my family as well, and the Lidells, and I prayed for Colm. And I prayed for answers. I would be visiting the search area again. I would be checking out the possible tree stand that Joseph had identified in the photo. And I knew I would also be visiting the site where Kona had found the hat and the gun. I would be looking for some sign that Amy Raye had gotten a shot at an elk, and I hoped somewhere in the area I'd find the elk's remains, specifically his skull, which might explain the gun. I wanted Amy Raye's family to know she hadn't taken her life. And I wanted them to have the answer that her death wasn't the result of her illicit behaviors. I wanted to redeem her in some way. It would be the family's memory of Amy Raye that would get them through all of this. I wanted to do what I could to protect that memory.

Amy Raye

She awoke to a soft glow over the horizon, and a fresh layer of snow. Her body shivered against the cold, the fire no more than glowing embers now. She uncovered herself from the boughs she'd used to stay warm and brushed the snow from her clothes and hair. As the sun rose over the rocky bluffs behind her, she saw what looked like prints just to the other side of where she had built the fire. She reached for her crutch and pulled herself to a standing position, her muscles stiff, the break in her injured leg throbbing as it did every morning. She still could not will her left foot to move in any direction, and she wondered if she would ever be able to walk normally again.

Within ten feet of where she'd slept were the fresh tracks of a lion, the four teardrop-shaped toes, the heel pad with the three distinct lobes. *Leave me alone!* she'd wanted to scream, but already the air felt thin in her lungs and her stomach weak. She knelt and laid her palm over one of the prints. It came to the first bend in her middle finger, which measured about four inches from the base of her palm, same as the tracks she had seen outside the cave. Lion were supposed to be wary of people. She'd always read that they would leave an area if they perceived a threat. This lion wasn't seeing her as a threat. And then cold panic settled over her skin. A lion was a stalking predator. It would get close to its prey before ambushing it from a short distance. This cougar had been stalking her. Had she rolled over, roused from her sleep to kindle the fire, made some kind of movement or noise that had thwarted his ambush? Lion looked for vulnerable prey. Perhaps he had perceived her weakened state. But then she thought of something else. A cougar was mostly drawn by scent. He lacked the keen eyesight of other animals. The game bag that she'd used as extra insulation for her left foot had been saturated with elk blood. She knelt beside the fire pit and blew upon the embers until they reignited. Then she quickly untied the cloth and put it in the fire. She stoked the fire until the blood-stained fabric had completely disintegrated. She gathered her belongings and tried to move quickly, unable to shake the feeling that the lion was still watching her. She dropped her knife and fumbled with her bag, cursing each mishap. She would forgo any kind of breakfast. Besides, the weather seemed to be turning. There was a slight breeze that had swung around from the north. The air felt colder than it had during the night, and the wind was picking up momentum, whipping her jacket against her back. She worried about another snow-storm. She would go ahead and cover as much distance as possible while she could.

But she had underestimated the effects of the cold. After a couple of hours, she could no longer feel the toes of her left foot. With only a wool sock, she feared that frostbite would set in, especially given her foot's poor circulation and immobility. And her hunger had gotten the best of her, and she'd already had to stop more than once because of a muscle cramp in her left calf and another in her left hip that had sent such pain through the nerves of her broken leg that she'd dug her fingers into the muscles of that leg and yelled out in pain. And so she shoveled out a divot in the snow so that, despite the wind, she'd be able to get a fire going. She warmed her hands and feet but became even more worried about her left foot. Despite the heat from the fire, she still had difficulty moving her toes, and the skin was covered in patches of white.

She removed her fleece jacket and, with her knife, cut out both pockets. She then cut away the left sleeve of the jacket. She'd had plenty of blood flow in her left arm from managing the crutch and was still wearing her thermal layer. She covered her toes with the two pockets, then slipped on the sleeve and doubled it over. She could only hope this extra covering would be enough to protect her injured foot from further frostbite. She stayed by the fire another half hour to warm herself and to rest and to eat. Perhaps she should have stayed in the cave. Her body was much weaker than she'd anticipated, and she felt unusually tired. She thought about hypothermia. Her body had no doubt chilled from the sweat on her skin. She'd have to be more careful, stop more frequently, build another fire if necessary.

And so she moved on, and everywhere she listened, to the wind, to branches, to the silence as it pounded in her ears. But within a short distance, the ground began to descend more sharply and the wind speed had picked up to maybe twenty-five to thirty miles per hour. She planted her crutch downhill, and as she began to shift her weight, the crutch slipped out from beneath her. She fell onto her left side, landing on both rock and snow, and slid a good seventy feet or more until she had sunk into a drift at the bottom of the decline. All around her was snow, the drift having been more than ten feet deep, and because it lay at the base of this western-facing slope where it had received the full effect of the sun, the drift had softened to the consistency of mashed potatoes. She tried to kick-step into the sides of snow around her, but each time, her foot sank deeper, and her body became more spent from the effort. She'd been foolish to think she could find her way out of this vast place. Her calorie intake had not been enough for her to maintain her strength. Her body was malnourished. She was crippled at best. And now she was cold and stranded with no wood within reach for her to build a fire. Even if she could make it out of this drift, there would be other sink spots, more soft snow, and more ground to cover than she had the strength for, given her lack of food. She felt emptied out of anything good and hopeful. She fell back against the snow, sank to the ground. *Oh, God, what have I done?* And though it had not been the first time, she cried until there were no tears left in her. Her stomach felt small and tight like a baby's fist. She took out the remaining juniper berries from her pack, but when she bit into their bitterness, this time her body heaved. She had only a pound or a little less of meat left, and it was frozen, and there was no way to heat it. She removed one of the four-ounce cuts, held it in her gloved hand until the outer layer of frost had melted from the small portion, and then sucked on the meat, and chewed on it, like an animal from the wild. So this was it. This would be how it would all end, and she wondered if her remains would ever be found. She tried to recall the precise core temperature at which a human body would die from the cold, and thought it to be somewhere around seventy-seven degrees. She thought of her swims in Echo Lake and Evergreen Lake, where the water had been well below that temperature, sometimes only fifty degrees in June, and she wondered about that. Why had she been able to swim in those lakes? But when she swam, she had kept her arms and legs moving. She had continued to generate heat. She would have to keep moving now. But she was so weary. Perhaps if she could rest for a while she might have the strength to find a way out of here.

Meltwater trickled down her neck. Her hands and feet ached and tingled with cold. She curled up into a fetal position. Still holding on to the piece of meat, she tucked her hands beneath her head. She thought of the cave and how warm its walls had felt. She thought of the fires she had built there. Perhaps she should remove her fleece jacket and tie it over her head. Though she had kept her ears warm with the strip of fleece, she knew she was losing at least fifty percent of her body heat from her exposed head. But she was so tired, and even her thoughts felt fatiguing. The muscles in her neck and shoulders contracted, and her body shivered, and she closed her eyes, if only for a few minutes. And she dreamed of coyotes, of young pups playing and wrestling in the snow, and she heard the adult coyote bark from somewhere far off in the trees. The adult barked again, but it did not sound like a coyote. Perhaps it was a wolf and these pups weren't coyotes at all, but baby wolves. She opened her eyes. She heard the bark again, but her mind felt foggy, and she was so cold, the air like ice against the layers of her damp clothing and skin. And she wondered if she was experiencing hypothermia, if she had imagined the sounds. She pushed herself to a sitting position, her hands and feet both numb. But her body was still shivering, which she knew was a good sign. She was still getting enough oxygen to the brain. Though her mind felt dull, she knew she wasn't hallucinating. She had indeed heard the barking of an animal. She wouldn't have heard coyotes. It was the middle of the day. Coyotes did not come out until dusk. There were no wolves in the area, none that she knew of. "I'm here," she said, but her voice was weak, and a thick wall of snow surrounded her. And perhaps it was a wild dog that she had heard. But she had not seen any wild dogs in the area. She had not heard any wild dogs in all of her nights in the cave. Her legs were stiff and her muscles tight, but she forced herself to a standing position. She removed her shovel from the straps on her pack, the small shovel she had made from the elk's shoulder blade, and she began to dig, and as she dug away at the snow, the blood moved back into her fingers and into her toes and her feet. She dug faster, surprised at the adrenaline in her body. "I'm here," she cried out again, her voice raspy and weak. She was making progress, and her body was warming, and she was certain she had heard a dog, and if she had heard a dog, there was someone out there. She continued to work, packing the snow down with the shovel and her right foot as she dug a path through the drift, as she created a stretch of compacted snow at almost a forty-degree angle. Using both the crutch and the shovel as poles, she was able to plant them into the incline and pull herself forward, then step, replant the poles, and pull herself forward again until she was out of the drift and standing on frozen rock, her body drenched in perspiration and hope.

She moved in an eastward direction from where she had heard the barking sounds, returning along the same path that she had trekked earlier that day. She continued for a couple of hours, stopping only long enough to drink a few swallows of water and to call out. But the wind seemed to carry her voice back to her, as it had carried the sounds of the barking dog. Dusk was approaching. Still, she pushed on. She had maybe a half hour at best of sunlight left. She had already passed the area where she had camped the night before, and she wondered how much farther she had to go until she would be back at the cave. The adrenaline that had sped her on was quickly waning. "Please," she cried out to the barking dog and to whoever was out there. "Come back. I'm here."

She surveyed the ground, determining the course of each step, and saw a mound of snow and boughs. After a few more steps, she identified the leg of a coyote protruding from beneath the branches of the small heap. She had come upon a cache site and felt certain it belonged to the cougar whose tracks she had seen that morning. The lion had been within ten feet of her. She thought of the boughs of juniper she had covered herself with. The cougar had mistaken her for another lion's cache. Though cougars were wary of people, they had no problem scavenging another lion's kill.

This kill was fresh. Despite the fading daylight, she could make out the blood trail from where the cougar had dragged the coyote and fed off the carcass, and all the while she realized how easily this carcass could have been her. Amy Raye lifted the boughs. There was plenty of meat left. One of the hindquarters was still intact. There was meat left along the spine and on one of the shoulders. The cougar would be back, and in that instant she wondered if he was watching her, as if she could feel his stare lifting the hair on her flesh. She looked around her. But lion could be as invisible as the breeze. She removed her knife from her pack. She knelt beside the carcass. What was left of it probably weighed no more than twenty pounds. It would take less time to strap the animal to her pack than it would take to cut away the remaining meat. And yet she worried that carrying the carcass on her pack would make her more of a target for the lion. Amy Raye understood enough about lion to know that the two things a cougar would fight to protect were its kittens and a cached kill. Instead of scavenging her that morning, the lion had moved on and taken down this coyote. And then it occurred to her that perhaps there had never been a dog. Perhaps it was this coyote that she had heard. But she did not have time for these thoughts. She cut through the tendons that connected the right hindquarter. She removed a front shoulder as well. The other shoulder and the upper abdomen were already gone. Then she placed the meat in her pack and covered the remaining carcass with the boughs. She wondered if the lion would return for his kill once he'd picked up her scent. Perhaps she should have taken the entire carcass. But the decision had already been made. Each second pounded in her ears. She felt certain of the lion's imminent return.

She secured her pack onto her back and moved away from the cache site. The whole affair had taken no more than five minutes. Her heart thumped wildly. Though she remained careful with her steps, she moved quickly, glad for the rush of energy. As the rest of the daylight was extinguished, the moon rose higher. The sky had remained clear, and her eyes had adjusted to the new light. She felt amazed at the clarity of her path, the speed with which she was able to move. With the pound of elk meat she had left, and the meat from the coyote carcass, she could survive a couple of weeks, maybe more. And there was the hope that someone had found the cave where she had been staying. Perhaps the person was still somewhere close by. The barking sounds she had heard had come from that same direction. And if someone had found the cave, the person might be able to determine that all this time Amy Raye had been alive. She gave thanks for the moon and the clear sky. She thought of Christmas and Julia and Trevor and Farrell, as if all of it were in her reach. She thought of her childhood and the crèche her father would set up in their front yard, the ceramic figures arranged around bales of hay. And for a moment she imagined her father finding her. She imagined him calling to her and asking her to come home.

Another hour passed, and then another. She would walk through the entire night if she had to. She had food to eat. She still had water in her reservoir on her pack, and there was plenty of snow to melt to replenish her supply. Again she thought of the barking dog and the coyote. Once more she wondered if she had been wrong. She fought back the weariness creeping into her bones. She continued to call out. The cold air slapped her awake and squeezed the tears from her eyes. And then she recognized the bluffs ahead, the rocky ridge, and on the other side of this cliff was the cave, and she couldn't believe she had come so far. "Hello! Hello!" Every muscle in her body quivered with fatigue. She could not make it much farther. But the rest of her course would be around this butte and downhill toward the ledge that led into the cave. And then in the moonlight, in that glance of blue light over the white snow, she saw the tracks, the paw prints of a large dog, and beside those, footprints made from the treads of hiking boots.

"Hello! I'm here. Come back." And as she called out, she followed the tracks that had crossed in front of her path, that looked no different than hers and Saddle's might have years before, or hers and Moab's, the

Alsatian and husky mix that she and Farrell had adopted. The tracks led around the butte, traveled within two hundred feet of the cave, and then abruptly led away from the shelter, moved in a southwestern direction from the ledge, and disappeared into a copse of pinyon and juniper and serviceberry. "No!" Amy Raye fell to her knees. She stared up toward the entrance of the cave, the opening barely noticeable with the rocks and boughs she had used for protection from the wind and cold, her tracks from the previous day no longer visible, the wind and the snowfall from the early morning hours having removed every trace of her. Moonlight shone upon the cave. There it was. There it had been all along, a silent precipice, as if the heavens had led her to this point to see what might have been, to see every shadow that had become her life. This was her hell, her perfect understanding of how close she had come, of how everything had always existed within her reach. How many times had she bargained and resolved herself to come clean, and yet always there was something larger in her, an absence so powerful, a room so big and vacant, and she would take to the stage in that room, she would seduce the men. She would fill the big, vacant space by acting the part of someone clever or passionate, bold or interesting. And each man she would conquer, each role she would play out, would become her new narrative, and then she would reinvent herself all over again, never really knowing who she had ever been, until the only thing staring back at her was the person she had become. And now the stage had changed, and there were no more supporting cast members. This was it. This was all it had ever been. And her heart cried out in an agonizing wail of pure animal lament. "Come back!" But she didn't know whether she was crying out to the dog that had led her once more to the cave or to the phantom person whose tracks she had seen, or to herself, or to God. "Come back!" she cried again, her knees sinking deeper into the snow-covered ledge.

Pru

After Joseph and I returned from Boulder, I brought Kona out to the search site. Far too much time had passed for him to be of any use tracking Amy Raye's scent, but his canine instincts might prove beneficial in him uncovering any animal bones, and of course, in the back of my mind, I knew he might uncover Amy Raye's remains, as well. The forecast was to our advantage, with clear skies and mild temperatures, somewhere in the thirties, a welcome break after the heavy snowfall and single digits we'd experienced the past week.

It was still dark when I left the house. I made the hour-and-a-half drive to the Canyon Pintado National Historic District along Highway 139 and then turned left into State Bridge Draw. I was heading north of Cow Canyon, where we'd first found the Ford pickup. I'd decided to backtrack. I'd start at the point where Kona had found the hat and the gun, over six miles north from the tree Joseph had identified in the photo. I'd worn my Salomon snow hikers with their sawlike tread, plenty of layers, and a tall pair of gaiters that I'd tied just above my knees. And I'd brought my fifty-five-liter pack, so that in addition to food and water, crampons, and my regular supplies, I'd have plenty of room for any evidence we might come across. I stored a folding shovel inside the outer pocket of my pack, strapped my snowshoes to the pack, and slipped an ice axe into the side loop. It would be a long day, and I was prepared to work the area until sundown. I'd entered the latest PLS from the search — the location of the hat and gun — into my GPS. I'd been able to get the Tahoe within three miles of that point before what was left of the old four-by-four road became impassable. I was about a mile east of Big Ridge and was heading south. The snow would deepen the closer I got to the bluffs, but for the first mile in, I was able to get enough traction with my boots. I was moving along the southwestern slope of the ridge where the sun had created melt-off that had frozen to slick-packed snow during the evenings and on overcast days and had left the rockier ground partially covered in ice. Hiking with crampons required more exertion but also provided more traction. I stopped to hydrate and to add the crampons. Within another two hours, I approached the basin where Kona had tracked Amy Raye's hat. Here, the snow deepened significantly. Another foot of accumulation had fallen over the past few days and was mostly unconsolidated. I knew Kona and I might have to cover at least a fifty-yard radius to search for any possible elk remains, as any obvious remains close to the site would have been found during the initial search. I also knew this would mean using my shovel to remove the snow cover. I leaned against the rock where we had found the gun, removed my crampons, and strapped on my snow-shoes to allow for greater flotation over the surface area.

My goal at this point was to find some evidence that Amy Raye had indeed taken down an elk, that perhaps there had been something pure about her disappearance. We were approaching our eighth week since she had gone missing. Even the best-trained search dogs working in optimal scent conditions — cool, damp areas, with heavy vegetation and little wind — could follow a scent trail no more than three to four weeks old. And yet I had to at least try. A number of friends would stock my freezer each fall with elk meat, anything from steak to chili meat to sausage and teriyaki sticks. The night before, I'd thawed a pound of elk steak. I'd brought it with me in a plastic bag to use as a scent item. With my hand firmly wrapped around Kona's jaw so that he wouldn't take a bite out of the meat, I brought it up to his nose. He whimpered and wagged his tail. He was confused, no doubt, and salivating. "Kona, go find," I said. He pranced around a bit but mostly wagged his tail and stared at the meat. I put the steak away. Then I fed him a handful of treats that I'd packed in the zipper pocket of my fleece jacket. "Go find," I said again.

I didn't know if the meat had helped, but the way Kona moved in and out from the rock, traveling farther away each time, I could tell he knew we were there to work. I tried to think strategically, to imagine where a lion or coyote might drag an elk's remains, especially an elk's skull, which a lion could easily sever from the spine. Lion, and coyote for that matter, wanted to protect any cache they had found. They'd no doubt drag it to a grove of trees or tall shrubs. And when different animals were involved, the remains of a carcass might be spread up to a hundred yards in any direction. We'd covered at least a fifty-yard radius and come up with nothing. I'd have to cover a greater area. About sixty yards out, Kona uncovered a rib bone that could have been a couple of months old. I wasn't sure if it had belonged to a young elk or a large deer, as the bone had been broken in half, and the marrow had been cleaned out. I knew that within one to two days of Amy Raye taking down an elk, even with that early snowfall, crows, ravens, magpies, vultures, and coyotes would have been all over whatever was left of the carcass. They could have cleaned it up long before we got to this location, and before the heavy snow accumulation. The past winter I'd come upon a deer carcass, and just as I did, a whole flock of ravens lifted off it. They'd been holding back approximately twelve to fifteen magpies that then clambered over and into the carcass.

I looked at Kona. He was lying in the snow and chewing happily on the bone. He rolled onto his back as if to expose his belly to the warm sun. Even if the rib belonged to an elk, it wouldn't tell us anything without us finding the skull. And though we needed to make use of our time, I'd worked up a good sweat and wanted to replenish. I removed my pack and my fleece layer. Using my snowshoe and moving my leg in a sweeping motion, I smoothed out a space on the ground and sat with my snowshoes propped in front of me. I ate a handful of jerky and some trail mix, and drank from my hydration reservoir. And then there was quiet. Kona had stopped chewing on the bone. His eyes were closed and he was resting peacefully in a bright patch of sunlight. And in that quiet, I could hear the faint thrumming of the oil jack pumps from far off to the west of me. I thought back to the past summer's field school at the Weatherman Draw site. In addition to Glade and me, the team had consisted of six college students and Martin, the field crew supervisor. During those two weeks, we'd spent our days with trowels and line levels and dustpans and brushes excavating the cliff dwelling. In the evenings we built a fire on one of the bald cliffs and waited for nightfall, and as our voices settled into not much more than a whisper, we heard the faint rhythm of the pumps. Martin told the students they were nighthawks, but Glade said they were the drums of the Fremonts, and the students believed him. We hadn't seen any oil drills in the canyon. We hadn't seen any sign of civilization. To those six students, the drums felt spiritual. I imagined these things as I sat in the snow that day.

Imagined the ancestors of this land all around me. "Where is she?" I said.

Kona raised his head and looked at me.

"It's okay, boy," I said. But then I stood, pulled my fleece back over my head, and secured my pack onto my shoulders.

We worked the area for at least another hour and had moved close to seventy yards northeast of the rock. And then Kona was onto something in a cluster of scrub oak. He wagged his tail and blew air quickly in and out of his snout. Jutting from the ground into the branches were the tips of elk tines. I began to clear more snow from around the base of the shrublike trees. My shovel hit upon a hard surface. I cleared more snow and removed a rock. Then my shovel struck something else, and that was when we found the skull. It had been chewed on and the soft matter had already decomposed, but the skin still remained, having been freeze-dried. Overall the skull was in good condition, with the small, four-point horns still intact, and a bullet hole just below the right eye socket. We'd found it, and I knew it was hers, knew it in the way my pulse shimmied over my skin. I thought I would feel exhilarated if we found the skull, but instead I felt a soft sadness take hold, and something akin to admiration and awe for this woman whom we'd been looking for. She'd wanted to fill her tag before she and her friends headed back to Evergreen. That was all. And there was something pure and simple and courageous about that intention. She'd gone into this area alone, brought down a bull elk with a bow during the third rifle season, successfully tracked him over this complicated terrain. Amy Raye wasn't a large woman. To take down an elk, she'd have to have pulled a draw weight of at least forty-five to fifty pounds, and done so within close range of the elk, no more than twenty yards, thirty yards at most if it was a perfectly placed shot. I'd never heard of a bow hunter taking down an elk in rifle season before. The elk were too spooked by all the guns going off to get that close. In Amy Raye's tent, Dean had found a book on that, on how to hunt an elk with a bow during rifle season, and another book on the history of the Continental Divide.

I took pictures and recorded the coordinates. Then I placed the skull in a large trash bag that I had brought with me. I reorganized some of the items in my pack, placed the skull inside, and secured the pack, with the elk's tines poking out the sides of the top pocket lid. My pack now weighed at least thirty to thirty-five pounds more than when I'd set out. Though I considered myself strong, I rarely carried more than forty pounds. Now I was up to around fifty. A direct route to the location where the photo had been taken would be another six miles moving uphill, and taking me into dusk if I was lucky. I opted to hike back to my vehicle, unload the skull, and then look for a closer entry point.

After I reached the truck, I drove south on 139 until I reached Route 128. From there I took a left along Philadelphia Creek, and another left onto a switchback that led me into the southeast side of State Bridge Draw. I parked the truck. Kona and I were now no more than a mile northwest of the area where the photo had been taken, a much easier hike, even though we would still be moving uphill. It was a little after one o'clock. We had plenty of afternoon light. And so we began our hike.

I enjoyed the freedom without so much weight on my back and was eager to see if what Joseph had identified was indeed a stand. At first the ascent was steady, but the last half mile began to climb drastically. I wore my crampons for the most traction. Then one more step and my left foot slipped on some slick-packed snow. I fell face forward. I kicked my crampons out behind me as my body began to gain momentum down the hill. My ice axe was within easy reach. I wrapped my right hand over the top of the axe and covered the spike of the axe with my left. As my knees bounced against the snow and my hip grazed a rock, I locked my elbows to my sides, looked over my left shoulder, and pressed the axe into the embankment. It carved into the ice and snow, slowing me until I stopped just before reaching a thick wall of pinyon. And all I could think about was the day Amy Raye went missing, the rain and the wind and the cold, and the freezing rain and the snow. I imagined myself as her, without crampons and snowshoes and a pack full of gear. I thought of the autopsy on the lion that Breton Davies had tracked. At some point after Amy Raye had shot the elk, dressed it, and bagged it, something had gone terribly wrong.

And though this wasn't avalanche country, drifts were known to accumulate up to ten feet or more. I knew the risk I was taking in being out here alone, and for maybe a minute or more I realized how fool-headed that decision had been, and wondered at what point Amy Raye had felt the same.

Kona, who had bounded back down the

hill when I'd fallen, was now by my side and licking my face. I pulled myself to an upright position and decided on another route up the hill. Kona took off ahead of me once again. Occasionally he would stop and look over his shoulder to make sure I was still trailing behind him.

A little farther and we were in thick timber. And that was when I saw the marking tape tied to a low-hanging pinyon branch. From there, I spotted the red fletching of an arrow. I couldn't get to the arrow fast enough. She had been here, in these woods. She had released this arrow. And I felt transfixed, knowing that the memory of her lay in everything around me. I reached the arrow, photographed it, and then removed it from the branches of the tree. The elk's blood, the consistency of dried paint, was still on the shaft. The arrow must have dislodged from the elk after he'd been shot. I imagined the elk's surprise at the sudden impact of the arrow, imagined him charging through the trees. With the arrow in my hand, I checked the coordinates for the tree from the photo. I was heading in the right direction. I continued a little farther, maybe a hundred yards. I walked across a small clearing, the snow up to my knees.

And there was the stand, about fifteen feet

from the ground, tucked into the boughs of a pinyon. "Thank you, Joseph," I said. I removed my pack and set it at the base of the tree. I retrieved my phone and took pictures, then grabbed hold of the tree steps and climbed up to the small platform. Kenny had been right. The stand had been in place for some time, probably more than five years. It was weathered from moisture and sap and was showing some rust.

Unlike other platforms that used climbing sticks or ladders, this kind of stand hung from the tree. The hunter had screwed four-inch-long pegs a foot or so apart at a ninety-degree angle from one another. The platform was metal mesh, and the seat no more than twelve inches by eight inches. The apparatus was secured to the tree with ratchet straps. The climbing belt Amy Raye had no doubt used to attach to her harness was still intact, as was the green parachute cord she would have tied for hoisting her bow to the stand. I also found a gear hook slightly above the stand and to my right, where she would have hung her pack.

I'd helped Todd take down a number of stands similar to this one at the end of the final rifle season the year we had dated. Because many of the men Todd guided were from out of state, he would set six or seven of these small platform blinds before he guided folks out. Then at the end of the final season, he'd have to bring all the stands in.

After Todd and I had broken up, I saw him one other time, though I could never be sure. Joseph was three years old. We were on our way to Boulder and had stopped at a gas station in Silverthorne. After I had filled up my tank, I parked off to the side of the convenience store. I held Joseph's hand and he and I walked toward the door. Then I saw a man get out of an old Montero next to one of the pumps, and in those two seconds I could have sworn the man was Todd. The man had not seen me. I picked Joseph up in my arms as if any moment he would be taken away. We entered the store and headed straight for the restroom. And after we had washed up and I had calmed down, I knew what I had to do. We walked out of the store, but the man was gone.

I never told anyone about that day, but always it was in the back of my mind, as if I had deprived Joseph of his father. Perhaps I was depriving him now.

It was a beautiful day, really, as I sat in the tree stand, with the kind of blue sky Colorado is known for stretched vast above me. And only eight weeks before, Amy Raye had sat in this exact place. She had been right here. I tried to piece together her morning, the direction in which she had released her arrow, the distance of the shot, how the elk had appeared to her. Had she been cold? What had the air felt like? The sun would have risen from behind her, and I imagined that also. And with all these thoughts I wept quietly for the woman I didn't know. She would have died alone, as had Brody. No one would ever know her last thoughts. And I hoped she had seen something beautiful, maybe the falling snow, or the sculpted rocks that defined so much of this area. It would have been only this great wilderness that would have been witness to her passing.

I'd had similar thoughts when Brody died. No one had seen him fall. People could only speculate what had happened to him. It was those same people who would not let me see his body. When my father drove me to the scene, the field Brody's parents had leased about five miles from his house, a field I would pass on my long weekend runs, there were already many people standing around the scene of the accident. He had fallen from the combine, and I did not know why. Was he reaching for something? Had the machine struck something in the field? No one was sure, but he had fallen, and there was a lot of blood. I screamed, but I don't remember screaming. People told me they had to restrain me. They thought they were protecting me. They thought I couldn't handle what I would see. But I know if I was screaming, it was because they wouldn't let me through. Brody was mine, in the same way that I was his.

There had not been a viewing at the funeral home.

"Dad, what happened to him? Please tell me," I had asked my father.

"They think something got caught on the wheel and he had reached down, but he lost his footing."

"And then what happened?" I wanted to know.

"The machine ran over him. Pru, he was unrecognizable," my father told me.

"I would have recognized him," I said.

I climbed down from the stand and retrieved my knife from my pack. Then I walked to the tree from where I'd found the arrow and removed the orange marking tape. I cut several small boughs, some with pinecones, a few with juniper berries, and tied their ends together with the nylon tape. With the swag beneath my arm, I climbed back into the stand. Using the climbing rope, I secured the swag just above the seat of the stand. “There were people who loved you,” I said. “I hope you know that. I hope you are at rest.”

Deer

Amy Raye

Three weeks had passed since the night she had returned to the cave. She had stopped talking out loud to the cross or to the trees or to the wind. She had stopped talking to herself. But at night songs would come to her, lines from ballads Farrell had played, or music she'd listened to on the radio, or hymns that had been sung in church when she was a young girl. And without any books to read, she would repeat those lines in her head throughout the day. A song by David Gray, or Nanci Griffith, Eva Cassidy, or Johnny Cash, another by Doc Watson, or Arlo Guthrie, a hymn about walking with Jesus. She still used the crutch, and at times she was certain she would not wake up to see another morning, and then the sun would rise, and she would get up as she had done the day before, and the day before that. She would heat her water. Sometimes she would have something to eat. She had rationed the coyote meat, twelve pounds at best, for almost ten days. She'd continued to supplement her diet with the scarce pinyon nuts and juniper berries. Twice she'd killed a rabbit, and another time she'd killed a squirrel, using rocks she had thrown, and during the day when she was trying to pass the time, she would practice her aim. Once she had injured a bird, a young magpie, but she could not make herself eat it. She had carried the bird to a grove of serviceberry and left it there. She had thought about trying to nurse the bird back to health, but she had nothing with which to nurse it, and so she prayed for the bird instead, and asked for God's forgiveness. Three days later she was certain she saw the bird again. She was fifty feet from the cave and was collecting snow for water when a magpie flew above her.

The days were getting longer, and though storms had continued to blow in from the north and from the west, the accumulation was less, and each storm would be followed by days of warm sunshine. Amy Raye would climb along the ledge to the top of the cave and look out over the canyon where she was sure she could see patches of land around the rocks. But even that small attempt would fatigue her, and her weakened limbs would quiver beneath her weight as she made her way back to the cave. And the muscle cramping had become worse. She needed salt. She needed electrolytes. She thought of the Irish Republican Army strikers who had existed for over sixty days without food, consuming only water and salt. She had gone on this hunt weighing close to one hundred thirty pounds. She had always been lean. She also knew once she had lost more than eighteen percent of her body weight, all hope of surviving would be lost. She chewed on the roots of young pinyons, even sprinkled dirt into her water, hoping to absorb some of the minerals. Still, she was growing weaker by the day.

And then during the first week of February, the temperatures had felt warmer than usual, and the sun rose full-bodied in a cloudless sky. She removed her clothes and stretched her body out on one of the large boulders about forty yards to the east of the cave, so that she could reap the full benefit of the vitamins from the sun. Her hips and elbows had become prominent, and her knees knobby. For the first time she noticed just how much her muscles had atrophied, and she knew she was entering starvation mode. Her metabolism had slowed down; her fat stores had been depleted. Her body was feeding off her muscles for energy and would soon be feeding off her vital organs as well. And in that moment with the warmth of the sun and the coolness of the rock and the mountains and cedar all around her, she knew she would be okay with whatever happened to her. And with that thought, never before had she felt so free.

For a couple of hours she slept underneath the big sun, and when she awoke she found herself curled into a fetal position, shivering against the cool air. She sat up and pulled on her clothes. She hugged her right knee to her chest and massaged the aching bones and muscles of her left leg. Her thoughts turned over the lyrics to a Billy Bragg and Wilco song. And as she watched the trees, she was still hearing those lyrics in her head — *We walked down by the Buckeye Creek. To see the frog eat the google-eyed bee. To hear the west wind whistle to the east. There ain't nobody that can sing like me, ain't nobody that can sing like me.* Inside the grove of trees was an opening, and inside that opening she could swear she saw the hide of an animal. She slid down from the rock, reached for her crutch, and made her way to the small clearing. Lying in front of her, and scantily covered with snow and broken branches, was the carcass of a deer, and next to the carcass, the rakings and prints of a cougar. She had discovered another cache.

She did not have her backpack with her. She did not have her knife. And she would barely have enough strength and daylight to make it back to the cave, much less return again that evening to pilfer the cache. But where the lion's teeth had bored into the deer, Amy Raye was able to tear away at least a couple of pounds of meat. She was tempted to eat the meat raw; she was that hungry, and she thought of the minerals that the deer's blood would provide. But she didn't eat the meat raw. Instead she stretched out the tail of her thermal shirt and laid the meat against the fabric. With her left hand, she held the game close to her stomach. She would carry the meat in the same way she used to carry Matchbox cars and Legos when she was picking up after Trevor. She did not look for the lion. She thought only of getting back to the cave, and so with the crutch tucked beneath her left arm, she began making the slow ascent to her shelter. She stopped a couple of times to rest, and by the time she was inside the cave's walls, the sky was mostly dark. She cooked the meat but was only able to eat a small portion before she became full.

With her stomach satisfied and the fire now a slow flame and the cave warm, her thoughts settled around Farrell and home and the children and a second chance to find her way out. Despite her weakened state, she knew she could not postpone another attempt. She also knew that with her depleted state, it could take her days to travel even a mile. And she would need food to sustain her. She would have to return to the cache site, and this time she would bring her pack. She would prepare her things before she left: water, her metal bottle, parachute cord, fire starter, emergency matches. She would also make sure her left foot was properly insulated. Though she had not experienced complete frostbite, her toes had blistered and peeled after her last attempt. When she returned, she'd cut a V out of the right side of her boot and made slits down the other side as well. She had found that she could wear the boot this way, and that it allowed her to put some weight onto her broken foot. She would leave at sunrise and stop first at the cache site, where she would take as much meat as she could manage to carry, maybe twenty pounds, maybe only ten. Though she would be working her way down the mountain in snow cover, more and more patches of land were becoming visible in the distance. She had already thought of taking a different route than the one before. Instead of heading directly west, where she knew there were steep drop-offs and where there might be drifts, she would make her way southwest, moving in the same direction as the tracks made by the large dog and the set of boots. And she remembered having seen a road toward the southwest corner of the map. The road could be ten miles away, but without knowing her exact location, it might be closer, and she felt certain the descent would be more gradual and eventually would put her at a lower elevation, which would mean less snow.

She would need her rest, but her eyes danced with anticipation. The cougar no doubt had already returned to the cache, would have consumed more of the carcass. But the deer was a large animal, and the kill was fresh, with plenty of meat, as if the lion had barely fed on it at all. The vultures had not taken to it yet, and the carrion beetles were still underground. Amy Raye gave thanks for the deer. She gave thanks for her full stomach. Then she realized the lion would have already known she'd been at the site. Perhaps he would be waiting for her return. She'd known about making herself seem large should she come upon a lion on a trail, about throwing rocks and making noise. She would tie her jacket to her crutch and wave her crutch in the air. She would sing the songs that had played in her head. And she thought of Farrell and all the songs he had sung to her, and that clear winter night they placed their lawn chairs in the snow and Farrell had set his turntable on the stone porch, and they'd drunk from a bottle of Glenlivet and listened to Victoria Williams sing, *You are loved, you are loved, you are really loved.*

As she lay in the cave, as she waited for sleep, she dragged the index finger of her right hand along the soft sand of the cave floor, and with her eyes closed, she wrote Farrell's name beside her.

She was nineteen the first time she saw the wild horses. She'd taken a job working the night shift at the front desk of a privately owned hotel in Grand Junction. She was paid minimum wage and a room to stay in that came with a small refrigerator and cooktop stove. In the afternoons, after getting some sleep, she would climb in her truck and explore the terrain looking for the bands of mustangs in the Book Cliffs. She never found the band outside Grand Junction, but one day she headed north to Moffat County, and off Highway 318 in the Sand Wash Basin northwest of the small town of Maybell, she saw a beautiful sorrel stallion cresting the hill, and soon to follow were at least a dozen mustangs. She pulled her truck off to the side of the road and got out. The horses ignored her at first and began grazing on the hill about a hundred yards in front of her. Then another truck pulled over, shut off its engine, and a middle-aged woman joined her.

"Beautiful, isn't it?" The woman's voice was calm, almost a whisper.

"I've never seen anything like this. I can't believe I'm here."

"Where are you from?"

"Tennessee."

"You're a long way from home."

"Yes, ma'am."

The woman's face was tanned from the wind. A long black braid hung over her shoulder. She was wearing overalls and a man's white T-shirt. "He's watching us," the woman said.

The stallion was standing alert, as if paying attention to every move Amy Raye and the woman made. "See that one up there?"

The woman pointed to a gray roan. "That's the boss mare."

"How can you tell?"

"Just watch."

Despite the distance, Amy Raye was sure she could hear the stallion snorting. He lifted his head toward the roan.

"He's communicating to the head mama," the woman said.

The mare lifted her head. She moved around the other horses as if trying to get their attention and then began trotting toward the stallion. Within seconds, all of the horses were running at a strong gallop, and the stallion closed in behind them.

"He's protecting the others. That's why they band together," the woman told Amy Raye. "For companionship and protection. In a healthy band, the lead stallion and the mare will usually stay together for life, and the mare will never abandon her foals."

"Kind of like people," Amy Raye said.

But the woman didn't miss Amy Raye's sarcasm. "Don't we wish."

They watched the horses until they were gone from sight.

"Well, I best be feeding my own horses," the woman said. "You got a place to stay?"

"I'm working in Grand Junction."

"You been there long?"

"About a month. I have a job at a hotel."

"I manage a big stable operation in Steamboat Springs. I can always use an extra set of strong hands. My name's A.J. If you're ever interested, give me a call. I'm listed under equine trainers."

"I'll do that," Amy Raye said. "I really will."

"What's your name? So I'll know who you are when you call."

Amy Raye introduced herself and shook the woman's hand.

After the woman drove away, Amy Raye walked up the hill to where the horses had been. She looked out over the horizon, trying to see if she could see them, but they had moved on. Then she sat on the hill and pressed her palms against the soil where the horses had stood as if she could feel the movement of their hooves. She stayed out there till dusk, when the coyotes began to yip and she knew she needed to get back for her shift. She grabbed a fistful of the dirt and continued to hold it in her hand, even as she drove to the hotel. She thought about the soil she'd put in her pocket the last time she'd stopped by her grandparents' farm, and she wondered if losing it was some kind of omen or an act of pure carelessness. She'd stopped overnight in Oakley,

Kansas, and had washed her clothes at a Laundromat. She'd forgotten about the contents of her shorts pocket until she'd taken the shorts out of the dryer.

Back in her room in Grand Junction, she sifted the soil from the wild horses into a sandwich bag, and set the bag on the nightstand beside her bed. Just a month later, Amy Raye finished her last day at the hotel and moved to Steamboat Springs. And all those years later, she still had the dirt from where the wild horses had stood. She kept it in a jar next to her and Farrell's bed, and beside Saddle's ashes.

Pru

Just last week when I was on my way home from town, I drove by Colm's place, a small cabin he'd lived in ever since he'd moved to Rio Mesa. And in the lot across from his property, I saw a doe and a fawn feeding in that soft glow of dusk. I slowed my vehicle just to watch the whole thing, and then I realized that the *For Sale* sign was gone.

Tom Moyer had owned a number of lots around town, including the one across from Colm. One night after dinner, when Joseph and I were straightening up the kitchen, I got a call from Tom. He said a contracting company that wanted to run a pipeline through the property he owned south of town had approached him. I knew the property he was talking about, a hundred-acre parcel abutting the Grand Hogback, and full of artifacts we had yet to map and explore. When Joseph was young, Tom would let me take Joseph down to that property, and we'd spend hours splitting open shale and discovering fossils. Tom knew I had a vested interest in his parcel for all of its historical implications and wanted to know how I thought he should proceed. We talked the matter over, including him contracting a private archaeological consultant. I gave him a couple of names to follow up with. But before we got off the phone, I asked him about the lot across from Colm's property. "What about that lot you own over on Third?" I said. "I thought you had that piece on the market."

"I did have it on the market," Tom told me. "I was asking thirty thousand. Colm paid me twenty-eight thousand in cash."

"Colm bought it? I had no idea," I said.

When I got off the phone, Joseph had already put the rest of the dishes away. He was sitting at the kitchen table with the sweetest damn smile on his face.

"What?" I said.

He slouched down in his chair and leaned his shoulders against the paneled wall. "He likes you," Joseph said.

"Who likes me?" I said.

"Sheriff McCormac," Joseph said.

I leaned my backside against the kitchen counter and folded my arms. "Why would you say that?" I said.

"The way you two act with each other, like you two like each other or something."

"I wasn't on the phone with Sheriff McCormac," I said.

"I know you weren't on the phone with Sheriff McCormac," he said.

"Then what made you say that?" I asked.

"Because you were talking about him, and you wanted to know about that lot. He likes you, Mom. That's why he doesn't have anyone else."

"He just got divorced."

"That was like a year ago. You should go out with him. You're practically going out with him anyway."

I walked over to the table, pulled out a chair, and sat down. "How did I get so lucky?" I said.

"What do you mean?"

"Just look at you. All grown up and giving me advice. You're the best thing that's ever happened to me. I hope you know that," I said.

He looked bashful all of a sudden.

"I'm serious, Joseph. I'm real proud of you. I don't know what I'd do without you."

Then I said something about Joseph having homework to finish. I told him I was going to be out in the field all the next day and should probably turn in soon. He leaned over and gave me a hug. "Love you, Mom."

"Love you, too, son."

I stayed at the table a while longer after Joseph went back to his room to study. I thought about what he'd said about Colm. I was twenty-six when I had Joseph. Aside from Brody, Todd was the only other man I'd ever been in a relationship with. And yet, maybe Joseph was right.

I packed a lunch and gathered my things for my trip out in the morning. I was going to be heading into the Coos shelter area. I wanted to check on the camera that I'd placed at the site earlier that fall, and I had something else turning around in my head that I needed to sort out, as well. The camera was triggered by motions and would send digital photos to my computer. Usually those photos didn't amount to much. They could be triggered by all kinds of small animals. But early one morning a month back, I'd gotten a clear image of an adult cougar. I hadn't thought too much about it. The East Douglas area was prime territory for a lion. The rock outcroppings, canyons, and thick brush provided excellent stalking cover. And with the healthy population of deer and elk, the area provided the lion with available prey. Though deer tended to flourish where there was thicker escape cover, their diets also consisted of vegetation such as bitterbrush and Gambel oak that was abundant in these parts. Then I got to thinking about the tom we'd taken down nearly ten miles north of the Coos shelter area. Cougars were solitary predators. Recent studies of winter territories showed that a male cougar could occupy an area of up to twenty-five square miles. A female's territory was smaller, between five and twenty square miles. According to Breton Davies, the sharing of ranges typically only occurred between males and females. He'd explained that males established areas that would overlap with as many female ranges as possible for mating purposes. I could assume that the lion I'd seen at the shelter was either a transient lion, still looking to establish its territory, or a female whose range had overlapped with that of the male Breton had shot.

None of these things mattered a whole lot to me, until one night when Jeff called. He wanted to know if anything else had come of the search. I told him about the elk skull I'd come across and the bullet matching the one Amy Raye would have fired. Then he brought up something he'd been thinking about the past couple of days. Said when he was a kid, he and his brother would visit their uncle in Olathe. Olathe was a farming town in Montrose County, south of Rio Mesa. His uncle had grown corn and in October each year would open a maze where he would charge admission.

"One fall my brother and I took off in one direction of that maze while two of our cousins set out in another. But all Tucker and I seemed to be doing was going in circles. Our uncle had to come in and find us. He said the two of us had kept ending up back at the same spot on account of us both being right-handed. Said people who are right-handed tend to veer right when they are lost, whether in the woods or a big corn maze, ending up in the same area as where they had started."

After Jeff and I got off the phone, I pulled up a map of East Douglas Creek Canyon on the computer. Amy Raye's compound bow was for a left-handed person. The elk skull was southeast of the tree stand and the truck. If Amy Raye had been trying to make it back to the truck where she'd left her packing frame, and had veered left, she would have been heading in the direction of a number of some of the pipeline roads and areas of lower elevation. We'd covered that area extensively and should have found some evidence of her. But then I remembered something my dad had brought up when we were visiting over Christmas. Without the direction of the sun as a compass, a person's natural instinct is to think that if she is heading downhill, she is moving southward, and if she is climbing uphill, she's moving northward on the map. "Think about it," Dad had said. "We consider south as low and north as high."

"It's true," Greg said. "It's conditioned in our brains. We see it on every map we look at."

I told them that according to weather reports, the cloud cover had been thick that day with heavy winds and snowfall late in the afternoon. Amy Raye could very well have been in a whiteout for all we knew.

She had tracked the elk downhill, traveling northeast and moving into a gulch toward Big Ridge. With a snowstorm, she could easily have gotten turned around. I thought of the area where I'd found the elk skull and rib bones. If she'd continued east, or if she'd traveled directly south, she would have been climbing in elevation. She could have thought she was heading back to the truck. Then, if I added the dominant-handed theory, she would have been far out of our search radius and thick in the middle of Cathedral Bluffs. I'd hiked into the Bluffs just before Christmas to check out a couple of sites we planned to survey sometime that spring, but I hadn't seen any disturbance. However, I came across cougar rakings on a tree. And at one point on the hike, something had gotten Kona going. I'd thought he'd seen a deer or a coyote and was getting himself worked up for a good chase. Looking back, I wondered if maybe he'd picked up on the cougar, if maybe we were being watched.

When Breton took down the big tom, Colm and I had thought we could rule out a lion from contributing to Amy Raye's disappearance. Now I wasn't so sure. Though I knew it wasn't unlikely that a lion might have discovered Amy Raye's remains, I was cautious to think one would have attacked her. Still, I couldn't shake what Aaron and Kenny had told Colm about Amy Raye covering herself in elk estrus before a hunt, and more than once Breton had reminded us of lion relying on their scent rather than their vision.

It was a Thursday when I headed out to the Coos shelter. The weather for that day and the upcoming weekend looked mild, with daytime highs in the low forties and clear skies. We couldn't have asked for a better forecast. Soldier Creek Cattle Company was having its centennial founder's day celebration that would kick off Friday evening and last into the afternoon on Sunday. Already the one hotel in Rangely was full, as were the two hotels in Rio Mesa. Old Crow Medicine Show was scheduled to play at Rangely High School on Friday night, followed by a barbecue with a four-hundred-pound spit roast at Trip Mortenson's ranch. These kinds of events drew in crowds from several counties over, as well as folks from Wyoming and along the eastern border of Utah. The concert alone was expecting a crowd of a couple of thousand, and the barbecue would no doubt go on well into the night. Only two nights before, Colm had been called to break up a pre-celebration party that had gotten out of hand. One of the local cattle ranchers had roasted a couple of lambs, a mock commemoration of the sheep wars that used to go on about the same time the Soldier Creek Cattle Company was founded. Cattlemen didn't like their public grazing lands being taken over by the sheepherders. During those years, close to a hundred thousand sheep were killed, many having been run off the edge of steep, rocky cliffs.

Trip's property contained the original Soldier Creek homestead and was located just past Tommys Draw on the south end of Cathedral Bluffs. From the Coos rock shelter, one could look out over Bowman Canyon and spot the ranch, and in the summer recognize the irrigated pastures. On the cliff above the rock shelter was a large expanse of exposed rock, with a significant flat-surface area. I'd taken Joseph camping there the summer before to show him the shelter. He'd been impressed with the rock art, the white birds, as Glade and I called them because the pictographs looked like silhouettes of white wings against the sky, and the trapezoid figures that Joseph said looked like guardians. We talked about that as we sat around our campfire on the bluff.

"What makes you think they are guardians?" I'd asked him.

"Their bodies look like shields," he'd said. "And some of them are holding spears."

I told Joseph how the Fremonts had lived in the western Colorado Plateau and the eastern Great Basin area for almost a thousand years, flourishing as hunters and gatherers in communities of up to several hundred people. But within a hundred and fifty years, they had disappeared from Utah, and though they had begun showing up in western Colorado, their communities had dwindled down to no more than isolated farmsteads and cliff dwellings large enough to contain four or five families. Then, by 1400 A.D., they had disappeared from Colorado as well. They'd been called the vanishing people, because none of the artifacts from their culture had shown up in any other Native American cultures, meaning it wasn't likely they'd been assimilated into other groups. Joseph and I were camping in the last area where the Fremonts had lived.

And as Joseph and I sat around the campfire that night, we talked about what might have happened to the family that had lived at this particular site. The ledge that had once sheltered this group appeared as if it had been deliberately made to fall. The edges of the ledge, and the rock face it had been broken from, were sheer. There was no evidence of erosion. "There could have been disease and someone wanted to stop the disease from spreading," I told Joseph. "The Utes could have come upon the bones and decided to cover them up."

"Could the Fremonts have starved to death?" Joseph asked.

"It's possible, but it's unlikely." I told him about the middens we'd found and the evidence of a healthy diet. And we'd found granaries with corn.

"What do you think?" Joseph asked.

"I think it was disease or warfare," I said.

And then we sat quiet for a while longer.

"It's kind of unsettling," Joseph said.

"It is."

"Do you ever get scared out here?"

"No." I picked up a stick and stoked the fire. I was sitting a few feet from Joseph. "You know, when I first came out here, I really didn't know what I was going to do with my life. I didn't know what lay ahead for me. I didn't know I was going to have you. I suppose I was just trying to understand it all. When I'm out here, I feel like I'm as close as I'll ever be to finding the answers."

Joseph remained quiet.

"What are you thinking?" I asked him.

"Did you love my dad?"

Joseph had asked this question before, and I'd answered it before, as well. "I thought I loved him," I said.

"What does that mean?" Joseph's voice was subdued. He was staring straight ahead at the flames.

"I don't know," I said.

Another minute passed. The fire popped and the wood shifted.

Then I told him about something Glade had once said, how archaeology was the purest study of man. "We want to find out who we are," I said. "After Brody died, I lost my fulcrum. I guess in coming out here I was trying to find out what my new fulcrum was. Your father was a part of that."

About a half mile from the shelter, Kona and I came across cougar tracks, as well as lion scat. The tracks were fresh. Only two weeks before, the photo of what was probably the same lion had been triggered and sent to my computer. I remembered what Breton had said about lion only staying in the same area when protecting kittens or a cache, and that lion could breed anytime during the year. He'd also said that a cougar didn't wean her kittens until after the first three to four weeks, and the only time she'd leave her kittens during that time was to hunt and feed from her cache. I was probably dealing with a female cougar.

Once I'd checked the camera and made sure it was secure, I decided to explore the area further while I still had good daylight. Having accompanied Breton and Hank into the search area, I had a better idea of what to look for when exploring a lion's territory. Maybe it was instinct, or pure curiosity, but

I found myself heading in the direction I'd mapped out after talking with Jeff. I'd covered several miles and had checked out a number of potential cache sites, when I came upon about seven magpies cleaning up the remains of what looked like a fairly recent deer carcass. I flailed my arms when I approached and made a ruckus. The birds squawked at an obnoxious volume, making a louder ruckus than I, and a couple flew after me. I yelled that much louder and waved them away. As I examined the carcass, the birds continued to screech and fly directly above me. They were an aggressive breed, but given the threat to their food supply, I didn't blame them.

I knelt beside what was left of the deer. Even though most of the flesh was gone, there were still some cartilage and tendons holding the larger bones together. The smaller bones, including the ribs, had already been broken open for the marrow. Despite some strewn branches, the area hardly looked like a cache site. But when I observed the bones more closely, there was no doubt a cougar had killed the deer.

I was examining one of the ribs when the sun's rays reflected off something on the ground a couple of feet in front of me from the carcass and almost hidden beneath a branch. Within seconds I was holding a gold wedding band in the palm of my right hand and staring at that ring with all of the disbelief in the world.

Joseph had already left for the founder's day concert in Rangely. I'd just come in from taking Kona on a run when Colm called.

"He's driving over first thing in the morning," Colm said.

"Did you tell him why you wanted to see him?"

"I told him we might have some new evidence. That it would help if we could talk to him."

"How did he sound?"

"He sounded hopeful, and I hate to think of what it's going to do to him when he sees that ring."

Colm and I had met with Hank and Breton that morning. Breton talked about how lion leave scratch piles for the purpose of marking their territory, particularly around a den or a cache site. Using her hind feet, the cougar will scrape the ground, creating a small mound of dirt or snow and debris. Then the lion will defecate on the scratch pile, creating a territorial marker.

I hadn't remembered seeing scat. There was snow and a collection of branches, and scavengers had already gotten to the carcass and disturbed the area. But Breton pointed to a scratch pile in one of the photos. He believed the cougar had recently come upon Amy Raye's remains, which could have been preserved in the snow. As the layer of snow began to melt, her body would have been exposed, he'd said. The ring would have passed through the lion. Breton believed if we were to return to the site of the deer carcass and examine the scat, we'd probably find more human evidence. It was a sobering morning. Colm congratulated me on my work. So did Breton.

When Colm got in touch with me, he said he would be at the office for a couple more hours. He told me he was going to be on call that night, as well.

Then Colm said, "Pru, I don't know how you did it. I know you're not feeling real good right now, but you've done one hell of a job, and I respect you for it. If you need anything —"

"I'll be okay. Let me know how tomorrow goes?"

"I will."

■ ■ ■ ■

It was sometime after ten o'clock when Colm called me back. I was sitting by the fire reading.

"Guess who I spent the past hour talking with?" Colm said.

"Don't make me guess," I said.

"Farrell Latour stopped in to see me. He just left with Darlene to get some coffee."

Darlene was one of the dispatchers. "I thought he was driving over in the morning."

"His sister said she could watch the kids, so he decided to head over tonight."

"Except he couldn't find a room." I set the book I'd been reading aside. "How is he?"

"It's tough," Colm said. "They haven't had a service for her. Just a couple of prayer vigils. He took a soldering iron and melted his wedding band after we'd brought him in for questioning. But I got to tell you, Pru, he still loves her. Carries that bead of silver around in his pocket."

I was stretched out on the sofa with Kona at the other end by my feet. "So, tell me, Colm, what did you do with your ring?" I asked.

"It's lying in an ashtray at my house. I haven't decided what to do with it."

"I didn't think you smoked."

"I don't. She did."

Colm told me to hold on. Someone had come into his office. "Who do we have responding?" I heard Colm say. And then, "Who called it in?"

Colm got back on the phone. "A call just came in of multiple gunshots being fired near the Rangely Loop Trail."

The Rangely Loop Trail was in East Douglas Creek Canyon, near the Coos site. "Dean was the first one to respond," Colm told me. "He's got about a twenty-minute travel time. I think I'll see if Farrell's up for a ride. I'd like to have a look and make sure Dean has some backup."

Amy Raye lay beneath the stars and wept. She'd reached for her ring, as she did each night before falling asleep, and when it wasn't there, and she did not know when she had lost it, she feared she had lost Farrell, as well. When she had finished crying, she rekindled the fire and warmed her spent body. "Enough," she said. And though she did not sleep well, she slept some, and upon first light, she ate enough venison until she was full. She thanked God and the cougar and the deer for the food. She packed up her things, and with the aid of her crutch and the dry air and clear sky, she walked. And for the next four days she continued to do the same, until the fifth day about midafternoon, when the land seemed to drop off as if the earth were flat and she had reached its end. Beneath her was a rocky expanse of canyon floor, appearing to exist in another dimension, because she had no idea how she would reach it. And so she made a camp on the edge of that cliff and looked out over the land and rested her feet and thought upon what she should do. To her right and left was more of the same. She was on a table, and she needed to get down to the floor. And as she thought about her situation, and the hours passed, and the sky turned orange, her eyes recognized far below her what she was sure was one of the oil waste disposal pits she'd seen at different locations on the map. From where she sat, the pit looked like a small, dark, rectangular pond with some kind of fencing. Then she heard the scurrying of an animal behind her, and a squirrel perched itself on a rock to her left. She smiled because she had plenty to eat and she did not need to take anything from him. He squeaked and whistled and a bird squawked overhead, and she thought it was a raven. The patches of snow across the canyon floor looked like the spots on a row of dominoes, and the smattering of pinyon and juniper looked like green bristle pads.

She lay back against the rock where enough sand had deposited into a shallow crater, offering her an even layer of cushion that could fit all of her. She closed her eyes to rest for a short while. And if the answers did not come after she rested that short while, she would decide what to do in the morning. Surely the answers would come to her then. She slept longer than she thought she would. When she awoke, a breeze had blown in and extinguished her fire. The sky had turned navy blue and was full of stars and some thin clouds and a crescent moon. And though the air was cold, she still felt warm, and she thought it had something to do with her having experienced a metabolic adjustment to the climate. Hadn't she read that somewhere? Instead of rekindling the fire, she fell back to sleep, and when she was partially awake, with her face pressed against the surface of the smoothed-out rock, and her eyes staring over the southeastern edge of the ledge where an outcropping of boulders climbed upward, she saw a larger shadow and two smaller ones perched upon the highest point. And in a moment just as brief, the cougar and her kittens moved on, and the shadows disappeared. Amy Raye closed her eyes. *My mountain sister.*

I'd fallen asleep on the sofa when my cell phone rang again. "Pru, it's Colm. I hate to call you like this, but I think Joseph might be involved in something."

"Colm, what's going on?" I had already sat up and was reaching for my boots.

"Can you meet me out at Bowman Canyon? Joseph and his friend Corey may have gotten themselves into a situation."

"They were supposed to be at the concert. What kind of situation?"

Colm went on to tell me about Dean responding to the scene in East Douglas Creek. He'd found a truck parked along one of the roads that led off the Rangely Loop Trail, but no passengers. He was going to leave his vehicle and head in on foot. He called in the license plate for a red and silver GMC pickup. The truck was registered under my name.

"What's Joseph's cell phone number?" Colm asked. "I'm going to try to give him a call."

"If he's up there, he won't have a signal,"

I said. “Can you give me an exact location of the pickup?”

“BLM Route 23-Bravo off County Road Quebec-38,” Colm said. “Dispatch has the coordinates. I’m heading there now. I’m about forty minutes en route. I’ll let you know if anything changes. And, Pru, I’ve got Farrell with me.”

“I’m on my way,” I said. “I’ll have my radio and cell phone.”

The area Colm had described was close to the Coos shelter where Joseph and I had camped. They’d probably headed out there after the concert and brought their guns with them. I’d warned both of them about shooting their guns after dark, and I hoped they hadn’t been drinking.

As soon as I got off the phone with Colm, I tried calling Joseph, but there was no answer. I sent him a text: Call me.

The darkness below her looked like the sea. She could be on a bluff in Scotland or New Brunswick or Vancouver, even though she had never visited those places. She was kneeling on the ridge, imagining these things, when a burst of fireworks exploded from what must have been another ridge across the canyon floor. She scrambled to her feet. “Over here! Over here!” But as much as her body had weakened and diminished, so had her voice. As with lightning and thunder, Amy Raye tried to determine the distance by timing the seconds between the sound and light, but she could not be sure. Maybe a mile. She fumbled around for the matches in her pack. She had only two left. She placed the canister in the side pocket of her pants. Her emergency fire-starter kit would take too long. She still had her elk call. She blew into the tube, but her faint puff of breath was not strong enough to emanate a bugle or make a louder noise.

She didn't have time to question her decision. She removed her tree harness from her pack, pulled it up over her legs, and readjusted the buckles and straps to fit her smaller size. She had more than two hundred feet of parachute cord. She doubled the cord and tied two figure-eight knots that she looped through the carabiner on the front of her harness. Then she brought the rope around the trunk of the closest pinyon that grew about ten feet away from the rock face on the northwestern side of the ledge. She had not rappelled since her earliest years in Colorado when a man she had worked with had a second job on the weekends as a canyoneering guide and would sometimes ask her to come along, and they would climb up rock walls and rappel over rock ledges.

A new burst of light lit up the sky, comets and aerials, and with the next set of flares, she gleaned her surroundings. She slid her crutch through the back side of her harness. Then she set both her feet as close to the edge as possible and leaned back so that she was almost at a near perpendicular angle. She lightly pushed herself out, her right foot feeling its way for a place to land, and once it was steady, she pushed off again, using her left foot much like a stabilizer on a bow. Another push-off and step, another landing, and she had descended a couple of feet. Instead of focusing on the height and the shadows, or the muscles in her legs that had long since atrophied and now quivered beneath her weight, she focused on her feet and the rhythm of her steps and push-offs, and counted the distance by approximately two feet for each push-off and landing that she made — ten feet and then twenty-five, until she was at almost seventy-eight feet — and her right foot landed on the ground. She removed the figure eight from the carabiner and pulled the rope from the tree at the top of the ridge, until the entire length had slid down the rock face and was lying by her feet. But when she gathered the rope and went to add it to her pack, she realized that in her haste she had left the pack on the ridge next to the tree. She coiled the rope and slung it over her right arm, not knowing if she might need it again, and positioned her crutch so that it supported her left side and leg. If she remembered correctly, the oil pit should be no more than sixty yards directly in front of her. Earlier that afternoon, before falling asleep, she had memorized the different landmarks as if drawing diagrams on a map. She had been gauging the distances as she would when spotting a deer or an elk on a hunt, when she did not have a range finder and would have to rely on her natural vision. To get to the oil pit, she would cross between a rock that jutted out like a wedge of concrete and a crooked juniper, and beyond that there would be two pinyons that grew directly adjacent from each other with no other trees around. In ten more yards, she would be at the fence enclosure for the pit.

Every three to five minutes the fireworks continued, and the light shone brighter as she drew steadily closer, allowing her to focus on her markings and footpath. Relying on her adrenaline, she moved deftly around the rocks and sandstone and the eleven patches of snow between the rock wall and the fencing. A loop of wire had been wrapped around the top of two metal fence posts to keep the gate shut. She squeezed the posts together and removed the wire, then opened the flimsy gate. She tossed the coil of rope onto the ground and removed her coat. She wrapped the coat and tied it around the flat end of the crutch. She would hobble the rest of the way without her crutch if she had to, not worrying at this point about the pressure on her foot. The fireworks continued to blast through the sky. The light allowed her to see more clearly and let her know there was still someone out there. Again, she called out, emptying her lungs, and then her body felt more depleted from the effort.

Bird netting covered the opening to the pit but was loosely secured, and when Amy Raye pulled out her knife and released one of the corners to peel it back, she saw a dead swallow with a broken wing whose feet had gotten tangled. The waste level was a couple of feet from the surface and the stench so strong Amy Raye almost gagged. She reached down into the pit with the crutch, dipped her jacket into the thick sludge, and swirled it around to make sure the fuel had soaked into the cloth. If the people shooting the fireworks couldn't hear her, at least they'd be able to see her with this torch, and she'd be able to see her path and cover the distance more quickly.

I was more than halfway to Rangely and within miles of the turnoff for Highway 139 when I heard Dean over the radio: "Seventeen, Dispatch, I'm at the scene of the report. We've got a couple of boys shooting fireworks. Over."

"Dispatch, Seventeen, copy. Are there any weapons involved?"

"Seventeen, Dispatch. No firearms."

I knew Dean didn't have a cell signal. I wouldn't be able to get him on the phone. I picked up my radio receiver. "Alpha One, Seventeen."

"Go ahead, Alpha One."

"Can you describe the boys?"

"Driver of the red and silver pickup has blond hair. Blue eyes. Six feet. Over."

Dean was describing Joseph. He knew I would know that. We were on public radio. He wouldn't be able to say the boy was my son. I decided to continue on to their location. "Alpha One, Seventeen, I'm about twenty minutes en route. What is your location? Over."

"Seventeen, Alpha One —" *Static.*

I was unable to make out what Dean was saying. "I didn't copy that, Seventeen. What is your ten-twenty, come back."

Static.

"Deputy Scholtz, do you read me?" I said.

"Command, Seventeen, what is your location?" Colm was now on the radio.

Static broke over the line again, the wind blew against Dean's receiver, and from the sounds that did carry I could tell he was still on foot. There were different voices. And then Dean's. "We've got smoke coming up out of the east. Over."

"Command, Seventeen, copy."

And then, "Command, Seventeen and Dispatch, do you have a read on Seventeen's location?"

"Seventeen, Command and Dispatch, we're maybe a quarter mile northeast of last location. Smoke is coming in out of the canyon. We're heading back to our vehicles."

Static.

Joseph's voice came over the radio. He was telling Dean something.

"Come on, boys. Get out of there," I said out loud to myself. Had their fireworks started a fire?

"Seventeen" — *static* — "Jesus Christ" — *static,* and then silence.

"Command, Seventeen, do you read me?"

Colm said. "Command, Seventeen," again. "Deputy Scholtz, do you read me?"

I was certain I had heard Joseph's voice. "Joseph, can you hear me? Joseph, if you're there, pick up the radio."

She pulled out the small canister of matches, flipped off the lid, swiped the match against the thin strike pad, and lit the edge of her jacket sleeve. And the thick wick saturated with the mixture of crude oil and waste exploded into a ball of flames. She did not know how long it would burn, and she had not anticipated the sparks flying. She moved as quickly as she could from the pit and to the opening where the flimsy gate flopped over on the ground, but she had not had practice running without her crutch, and her left leg was at least two inches shorter from the break, and she had not foreseen dropping her boot, or the worn stitching of her wool sock catching on the wire and tripping her, and more sparks flying from the tied jacket as she fell to her knees and caught herself with her right hand, holding the torch six inches from the ground, but it was too close, and the jacket was melting fast, larger pieces of fabric breaking away, hot swaths of thread floating and being tossed like ashen leaves. She looked back only long enough to pull her foot out of her sock that was still snagged and to see the trail of light blossom into orange and red as the entire pit went up in flames. Before she was on her feet, intense heat pushed her forward like an explosive. She scrambled to pull herself upright and to run, and as she tried to run, she felt the bone of her left ankle cutting into tissue and tendon with each step, felt stones and brush burning against her bare skin. Smoke and ash like a parapet around her coated her eyes, making it more difficult to see. She dropped the torch when its heat had begun to melt her shirt and sear the hairs on her arm and blister her skin. And what once had been patches of snow was now mud, and twice she slipped, a sharp branch tearing down her left sleeve, warm liquid collecting in her palm. And somewhere in front of her another flare, faintly lighting her path, exposing another landmark, the large rounded boulder that only hours before she had thought looked like a meteorite that had dropped from the sky. The mile seemed shorter, her gait like that of a broken deer, her body stumbling forward, away from the direction of the flames, the direction of the wind, and toward the voices from where the fireworks had come.

A steep face of sandstone was to her left. The smoke smelled sweeter, a mixture of ash and explosives like the Fourth of July. And there were voices somewhere far above her. She called out again, the effort leaving her dizzy and weak, so that she leaned over for a moment, resting her hands on her knees. Her legs quivered. Her head still felt light. She would need to climb. She was too far below the ridge for anyone to notice her. And what if they had left? She did not see any more fireworks. "Help me," she said again, her voice not much louder than the night wind. She reached for the rock wall, lifted her right leg against the stone. But her boot was heavy and slick on the bottom and covered in mud. She bent over, unlaced and removed it, removed her sock. She raised her torso and looked up the cliff wall again, and as she did, the blood drained from her face, the ground seemed to shift beneath her, and her balance faltered. Her fingers gripped a small ledge in the rock face to steady her; the toes of her right foot dug into the only crevice she could find. She pulled and pushed herself upward and over the narrow edge, maybe six inches of sandstone that jutted out, a ringing in her ears. She reached for another handhold, tucked her right foot beneath her, pulled and pushed again, and then sweat and cold and nausea, and somewhere in the distance she might have heard voices like those from her childhood, and the night air closed in on her, the sky around her a blur as if everything were spinning, and the sensation of falling, and something as sweet as sleep.

From a distance it's difficult to see smoke in the nighttime. It can appear no different from a storm moving in. It's the air that is different, and the soot that falls on a person's windshield and clothing. And sometimes it's the great, loud popping sounds and the whoosh of heat wind.

I smelled the fire before I heard Colm call it in to dispatch. I had turned off 139 and was about ten minutes south of BLM 23, driving at high speed with my lights flashing on top of my vehicle.

"Dispatch, Command, ten-seventy-two, wildfire. Ignition spot estimated at 20-Charlie and 36-Quebec. Subjects are in the area, exact location unknown. Request full assignment, Code Three."

I picked up my radio speaker. "Alpha One, Command and Dispatch, can you give me a ten-twenty on Deputy Scholtz and the boys? Over."

"Dispatch, Alpha One and Seventeen,

evacuate the area, do you copy?"

"Alpha One, Seventeen, do you have the boys with you?"

But Dean didn't answer. I continued en route. Engines and medics were responding to the scene, working channel F3. Because Dean and the boys were on foot in the area, and because Trip Mortenson's ranch abutted the canyon to the southeast, the area had become a mandatory fire exclusion zone. Alarms went out to BLM fire dispatch offices in Rio Mesa and Rangely. Within hours the fire could be suppressed, but the winds were unpredictable. And there were the oil pits to contend with. I could only wonder if Joseph and Corey had inadvertently started the fire, but there was no way I was going to evacuate the area without those boys.

The BLM road I was driving would be the same exit route of Joseph and Corey and Dean. The smoke swept back toward the fire, as if a vault had been opened, sucking in the air. The winds were now blowing from the northwest and would be pushing the flames into the draws south of Bowman Canyon. I watched the smoke, tried to gauge the wind. Heat sources created their own currents, and an explosion in the area from one of the oil pits could change the course of the fire's path.

"Come on, Dean," I said out loud. And all the while I peeled my eyes for some sight of Joseph and Corey.

She heard the breeze. She smelled fresh burning wood, like the Douglas fir she and Farrell used to heat their home, like campfire, but her head felt dizzy, and she did not know where she was, and the ground was rocky beneath her. And then she remembered the cave. She must have awoken in the night, because above her she saw the faint etching of white birds, and she was thankful that she was warm and the fire was still burning and she could sleep longer, because all she wanted to do was rest. But she was dizzy and her head ached. Perhaps she should eat something, or drink water, but her pack was not there. She rolled onto her back, and above her was sky and stars, and a beautiful moon; had the moon ever looked so beautiful before, like a sickle of God, separating the chaff, and the night was unimagining all those things that she had become. She was the young girl counting raindrops on the window, and loving her mother who used to laugh and wanted nothing more than to bring life into the world. She was the daughter of the doting father, broken by the pain of a woman whose grief he could not comfort, whose body he could no longer hold, a wife he could not bring back, and the daughter who had betrayed him and reminded him every day of a larger betrayal of himself. She had become the mirror of each of them. And then she saw Van Gogh and Hemlock; and Saddle, who'd found her on a dark street on that windblown, snowy night in January. A stray dog, fur matted, and leg permanently crippled, who led the woman whom he had followed to the man whom she would never have found, to the only man who could love her most.

And then it came back to her, the canyon that stretched out before her, the oil pit, the flames and smoke that somehow she had outrun, or was it the wind that had kept the fire away? But she was so tired, and her body limp. Her left foot was numb. She licked her parched lips, her throat and tongue dry.

Colm and I had continued to talk to each other over the radio. Then Colm called my cell phone. We had not yet lost signal. "Pru." That was all he said.

"My son is out there," I told him.

I knew where the boys had gone. They

would have parked the truck at the base of the hill and hiked the rest of the way up to the exposed rock surface where Joseph and I had camped. They would have been setting off their fireworks from there. I knew how to get to them faster than the route Colm had taken. But Colm had started out with at least a twenty-minute advantage. A little farther in, and I lost cell signal. I radioed Colm. "Alpha One, Command. I am taking a different route. Will keep radio on."

I hit the turnoff road too hard, was thrown against the ceiling of the cab, and the smoke drifting in was making it difficult to see. I tried to anticipate the turns, avoid the washouts and boulders that jutted into the edge of the four-wheel dirt roads. Another five minutes and I saw the flashing lights on Colm's truck, then his brake lights. I pulled up beside him, saw Farrell in the passenger seat. Colm and Farrell got out of Colm's truck. I climbed out of my Tahoe.

The last word we'd had from Dean was that they were about a quarter mile on foot northeast of their vehicles.

"Stay with the truck," Colm said to Farrell.

Colm grabbed a spotlight from the cab, and we took off, making our way over rocks and deadfall and washouts. About five minutes in we heard someone yelling.

"Over here!"

"It's Joseph," I said. And so Colm and I veered to our right, through a grove of pinyon and toward the ledge I knew so well.

"Joseph!" I yelled. "Corey!"

I saw Dean's flashlight through the trees, and then they were there, right in front of us.

"There's someone out there," Joseph said. "We thought we heard a scream."

"We called out a number of times," Dean said. "We're not getting a response. I'm not seeing anything either. We'd need a rope to get down there," Dean went on. "Joseph thought he remembered a switchback. We tried it. That's when I lost my radio."

"The switchback is farther down," I said. "Another sixty yards or so."

I told Dean and the boys to stay on the ledge, to point Dean's flashlight over the canyon so I could find my way back. Colm followed me as I took off toward the east, reading the ground before me like a well-studied map. I had never navigated my way to the switchback at night. And each time I thought I had found it, each time a clearing appeared near the footpath, I discovered only another steep dropoff.

Someone whistled. I assumed it was Corey. I was familiar with how loud he could whistle with two fingers, remembered how he had tried to teach Joseph how to do it. None of us had our search-and-recovery apparatus with us. We'd left our whistles and other tools at our vehicles. Any moment the fire could turn unpredictable. Should someone be out there, we couldn't afford to waste time returning to our trucks.

"Everything okay?" Colm yelled to Dean and the boys.

"Okay," one of them called back.

And then the ground changed, turned into what looked like a small, dried-up gully that ran over the edge.

"I think this is it," I told Colm. I knelt and slid my leg over the side of the cliff. My foot reached for the rock that I knew would be about three feet below me. I landed securely and climbed down to the next rock where the switchback began. The boys thought they'd heard a scream. Dean thought he'd heard it, too. Hundreds of people had gathered for the founder's day celebration at Trip's ranch. The boys had wandered out here. Someone else might have wandered out here, as well.

"Are you sure this is a good idea?" Colm asked.

"Yeah, I'm fine. Keep holding the light. I can see better with you shining it from above me," I said.

Maneuvering my way along the first part of the path was going to require the use of both hands. Without headlamps, we were better off with Colm remaining at the top of the ridge. When Glade and I had initially explored the site, we'd lowered our gear by rope to the shelter, and had then followed the switchback until we were at the lower ledge.

Amy Raye could not move her left leg so much as an inch. Her entire body felt limp. She tried to wiggle her toes, but if they moved, she could not feel them. She did not know if she had sustained another injury or if she was simply cold, or if the large rocks pressing into her hip were cutting off her circulation. She rolled her hip slightly, moved her arms and fingers, tried to improve her circulation. Smoke swept over her like fog being blown in, and though she could no longer feel the heat from the fire, with each attempt she made to moisten her lips, she could taste the ash, like catching a snowflake on her tongue.

"Help me," she said, in a voice as anemic as she felt. "Someone please help me."

And then a whistle, muffled by the night breeze and the cliff wall, or was it a bird, and all around her the sweet waft of burning wood. And voices that sounded like thunder, but so far away. She tried to move again. If only she could stand, wave her arms, regain her voice and strength, climb the wall before her, but she could not will her body to move in the direction of the voices that sounded like thunder. And the longer she lay there, the more she shivered and her legs tingled, both feet numb now, as if her body were drifting off into a deep sleep.

There had been fireworks. She had heard voices. Yet now, the fireworks and voices seemed so long ago, like a taunting in her mind. She knew then, she was dying. This was what dying felt like. She held her arms straight out to her sides, and in that moment she began to cry. She held her shame like a heavy cross.

I love you, Farrell. She closed her eyes, imagined him fully, and beside him she saw the children, and Moab licking the children's faces, and she tried to imagine her parents feeling proud of the family Amy Raye and Farrell and the children had become.

As something close to peace moved over

her skin and thoughts, she was sure she heard voices again, only this time closer. Her right hand pushed through the edge of sage needles and loose particles of sandstone until her fingers wrapped around a stick at least two inches in diameter. She opened her mouth, strained her voice once more, tried to emit a scream. She banged a rock that lay within two feet of her. "I'm here," she cried. "Don't leave me." She gripped the stick tighter. She beat the rock as if it were a heavy drum.

And somewhere above her and to her far right, she thought she saw a light. *Please help me. I don't want to die.* A groan erupted out of her. The light disappeared. She hit the rock again. She tried to scream.

"Hello," someone shouted.

And Amy Raye cried, "Help me," and she struck the rock again and again. *Please find me. Don't leave me.*

"Keep making noise," the voice said. "I'm here. I'm going to help you."

Someone was scrambling toward her, footfall and loose rocks and snapping branches. And more voices. And the light appeared again.

At first I thought a limb had fallen, that I had loosened deadfall along my path, that the debris might have tumbled onto the boulders below. But the sound repeated itself like Morse code. "Hello," I shouted. Again the sound. My feet moved more quickly, as if body memory had set in. I had traversed this trail at least a dozen times. And by now, my eyes had adjusted to the darkness, and there was the dim light of the moon, despite the smoke that was slowly pushing in, and the occasional glow from Colm's light as I corkscrewed my way over rocks and scrub brush and dead limbs, and around the trunks of pinyon and juniper, ancient trees whose roots had found water in deep crevices along the cliff wall.

And then a voice, as plaintive as any I had ever heard.

I moved off the switchback trail and toward the voice, toward the rhythmic sound that continued to repeat itself, and as I did, I reached for my radio. "Alpha One, Command, assistance required."

The noise continued, and as I stepped through sage and edged my way around another boulder, I saw a woman lying on her back, striking a rock with a stick. A few more steps and I was kneeling beside her thin body, and her brown eyes were looking up at me. *Oh my God, could this be her?* At least three months had passed since Amy

Raye had gone missing.

"What is your name?" I asked her.

She might have said, "Amy Raye." I thought she said, "Latour."

"Does anything hurt?"

"My leg," she said.

And then I noticed her bare feet and the odd shape of her left ankle. I also noticed a gash down her left arm, her torn shirtsleeve damp with blood. And the sleeve on her right arm had been burned and was adhering to her skin.

I slid my arms beneath her. "Let me know if anything else hurts," I told her. "I'm going to get you out of here. We're going to get you help." I lifted her against me, her body like a broken bird. I thought I heard her cry, though her eyes were now closed. I carried her up to the trail and began making my way along the switchback from where I had come. I tried to move sideways, to avoid knocking her legs against any branches or rocks.

We reached a pile of boulders. I leaned my back against the smooth surface of one of the larger rocks, held the woman closer to me, used my feet for leverage as I pushed us over the impasse. Colm's light grew brighter.

"Over here," I yelled.

And then his light shone in my eyes, blinding me for a couple of seconds before he pointed the light to the ground and my eyes adjusted.

"Command, Dispatch, person down. Request immediate medical assistance."

And then, "Dispatch, Command, ambulance in the area."

Colm took the woman from me, and as he did, I grabbed the light.

"You're going to be okay," he told her. "We're almost there."

It took both Colm and me to lift the woman up the final vertical stretch, approximately six feet, to the bluff's edge. From there, Colm carried the woman in his arms like a baby while I held the light to mark his path.

And up ahead we saw Dean's light. Medics were responding. The sirens were close.

Dean told us he'd sent the boys back to the road to keep an eye out for the ambulance and direct it to the scene.

He walked alongside us, assisting us with his light. And then there were the vehicles, maybe fifty feet ahead. The ambulance was there. Two technicians were approaching Colm with a stretcher.

"Oh my God." Farrell ran toward Colm. Gently and slowly, Farrell scooped the woman into his arms, his face in her neck, and I heard him say, "I love you," and I might have heard her say it, too.

The woman was then loaded on the stretcher. I looked up to find my son. *Thank you,* I mouthed to him. I looked for Corey. I mouthed the same words to him, as well.

Colm's big warm hand reached beneath my long hair, his fingers cupped the nape of my neck, and he pulled me against him, wrapped his other arm around me, held me like a hundred million years.

Amy Raye

Amy Raye drove north on Highway 93 along the cliff band of North Table Mountain and just outside the town of Golden. The sky was blue like water without a shore, like she could swim in it forever, but she was still learning how to swim, and she knew that, too.

Farrell called. "How are you doing?" He asked her that a lot. It had become the words of an unspoken language between them.

"Today is another day," she said, also words, like stones, and each day they picked up the stones and held them in their hands.

Two fire engine crews had contained the fire and extinguished the flames from the oil waste, as well as resecured the area. Amy Raye had been taken by ambulance to St. Mary's Hospital in Grand Junction. Farrell had never left her side. She was kept in the hospital for two weeks. Her right arm had suffered second-degree burns, the three-inch gap on her left arm had been cleaned and stitched, she'd undergone surgery for her left ankle, and in another six weeks the cast would be removed and her physical therapy would begin. For a week she had remained on IV fluids, and then liquid supplements were added to her diet. And slowly the taut skin around her bones regained its elasticity. The color came back to her skin. And yet she continued to feel pain, and her doctors said this was a good thing. "You're beginning to comprehend everything that happened to you," one of them told her. "Try to focus only on the next minutes, on only one moment at a time. Work your way slowly from there."

She felt vulnerable in ways she had never felt before; the slightest gesture from someone could bring her to tears.

And when Farrell had brought the children to see her after her third day in the hospital, when she'd been afraid of their reaction to her, that her appearance might frighten them and they'd pull away, and they'd scrambled onto the bed despite the tubes and machines, and kissed her and squeezed their bodies against her, she looked up at Farrell. "I'm sorry," she said.

And she told the investigators she was sorry also, and the firefighters, and the search volunteers who came to see her. At first she did not understand why she was not charged with the fire, but she was sorry for that, too.

The sheriff told her it was the drugs. "Keep her on morphine, and everything will be all right," he'd told Farrell.

And then there was the day before she was discharged and the visitors had gone away. She was lying in the white room, with white lights, and Farrell's blue eyes, but his eyes were too blue, and she turned away. "I am so sorry," she said.

"Look at me," he said. He was holding her hand, and he tugged it gently. And when her head remained turned away from him, he said, "Why won't you look at me?"

"Because you're not safe with me," she said.

"That's not true," Farrell said.

"I don't deserve you. I can't make any promises. I don't want to lie to you anymore."

"We just need to get you well. We can talk about this later."

She turned toward him again and looked at him. "That's just it. I'm not well. I haven't been well for some time."

"I know," Farrell said.

"Do you love me?" she asked him.

"Yes," he said.

"Why?"

"I don't know."

And both of them laughed.

She'd told Farrell about the cougar and the caches. She'd told him about the deer. She told him about her last day at the cache. "The birds hadn't gotten to it yet. The lion must have been keeping them away. The eyes were still intact. And that's odd. That's not right. But I looked at those eyes, and I thought of you."

The tears mingled on Amy Raye's face. Farrell wiped them away. "It's okay," he said.

Before Amy Raye was discharged from the hospital, the female ranger came by one last time. Farrell kissed Amy Raye on the forehead and stepped out of the room.

"How is he?" Pru asked.

"He wants us to work things out."

"He loves you," Pru said.

"I don't understand," Amy Raye said.

Pru laid her hand over Amy Raye's. "You don't have to."

Amy Raye took the familiar road on her

right off Highway 93. She rolled down the windows of her truck, let the wind blow her hair, smelled the pastures and pines, the sun warm on her skin. The road veered to the left, and she followed the hard-packed gravel up to Saddleback Farm, where newly adopted mustangs and rescue horses were boarded and trained. She parked her truck to the right of the barn, took a swig of water from the bottle in her cup holder, and then climbed out.

Several weeks after Amy Raye's cast had been removed, after she'd set herself up in a small rental in the town of Golden, joined an addiction support group and continued to work with a therapist, and she and Farrell had agreed on a visitation schedule for her and the children, she completed a mustang adoption application through the Bureau of Land Management's Royal Gorge field office. Within a couple of weeks, her application was approved.

It was the second Friday in March that Amy Raye had visited the Cañon City Correction Facility, the BLM's largest wild horse and burro holding area, and one of only five facilities in the country with a Wild Horse Inmate Program. Each month, seven to ten horses from the western rangelands would be available for adoption. It was on that Friday that Amy Raye met Storm, a five-year-old roan gelding, gathered from the Salt Wells Creek herd management area in Wyoming. He stood at fifteen hands, had been in halter training for a couple of months and led around with a saddle and panniers, but had not been ridden. Amy Raye fell in love with Storm from the moment she saw him in the pen, when the trainer led him to her, and Storm let Amy Raye hold her hand to his muzzle as if it were the most natural thing in the world.

"He's friendly," she said.

"He still lunges from us in the field sometimes, but in the pen he'll walk right up to us," the trainer said.

Amy Raye kept the horse, and kept his name. She paid three hundred dollars, and the horse was delivered through an arrangement with the facility to the stables at Saddleback Farm.

When Amy Raye wasn't with the children or at work, she would be at the stables. Farrell didn't know anything about horses, but sometimes he would visit the stables with her. Easy talk would pass between them. And then they'd be standing beside each other, leaning against the fence, their shirtsleeves pressed together, forearms on top of the fence railing, the sides of their hips touching, too. They'd be watching Storm in the pasture, healthy and halterless. They'd be smoothing out a past, trying to leave its scraps behind, and each stone in their hand, each clear moment, was another stone to lay down.

ABOUT THE AUTHOR

Diane Les Becquets is a professor of English and a faculty member at Southern New Hampshire University's MFA Program in Fiction and Nonfiction. In addition to teaching creative writing, she has worked as a medical journalist, an archaeology assistant, a marketing consultant, a sand and gravel dispatcher, a copywriter, and a lifeguard, and is also an avid outdoorswoman. A native of Nashville, she spent almost fourteen years living in a small Colorado ranching town before moving to New Hampshire. Visit her online at lesbecquets.com.

The employees of Thorndike Press hope you have enjoyed this Large Print book. All our Thorndike, Wheeler, and Kennebec Large Print titles are designed for easy reading, and all our books are made to last. Other Thorndike Press Large Print books are available at your library, through selected bookstores, or directly from us.

For information about titles, please call:
(800) 223-1244

or visit our Web site at:
http://gale.cengage.com/thorndike

To share your comments, please write:
Publisher
Thorndike Press
10 Water St., Suite 310
Waterville, ME 04901